W9-ATQ-153

WITHDRAWN

THE
TAVERN IN
THE MORNING

Also by Alys Clare

Fortune Like the Moon
Ashes of the Elements

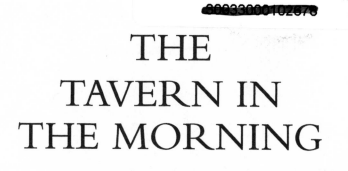

THE
TAVERN IN
THE MORNING

A Hawkenlye
Mystery

Alys Clare

St. Martin's Minotaur
New York

www.minotaurbooks.com

ISBN 0-312-26237-X

First published in Great Britain by
Hodder and Stoughton
A division of Hodder Headline

First St. Martin's Minotaur Edition: June 2002

10 9 8 7 6 5 4 3 2 1

For Richard
whom I first met in the tavern,
with all my love

Qui mane me quesierit in taberna,
post vesperam nudus egredietur
et sic denudatus veste clamabit:

Wafna! Wafna!

(Whosever seeks me out, at the tavern in the morning,
he'll be on his way, naked, after Vespers,
and thus, stripped of his garments,
he'll yell out:

Woe! Woe!)

From Carmina Burana,
'*Cantiones profane*'
(author's translation)

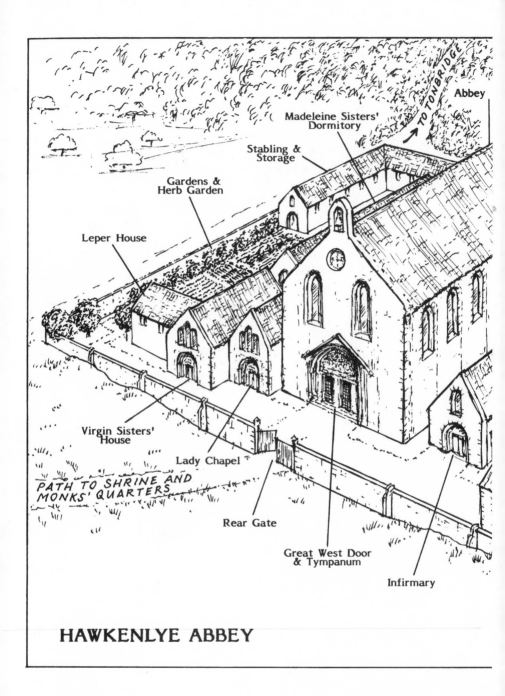

Madeleine Sisters' Dormitory

Stabling & Storage

Gardens & Herb Garden

Leper House

TO TONBRIDGE

Abbey

Virgin Sisters' House

Lady Chapel

PATH TO SHRINE AND MONKS' QUARTERS

Rear Gate

Great West Door & Tympanum

Infirmary

HAWKENLYE ABBEY

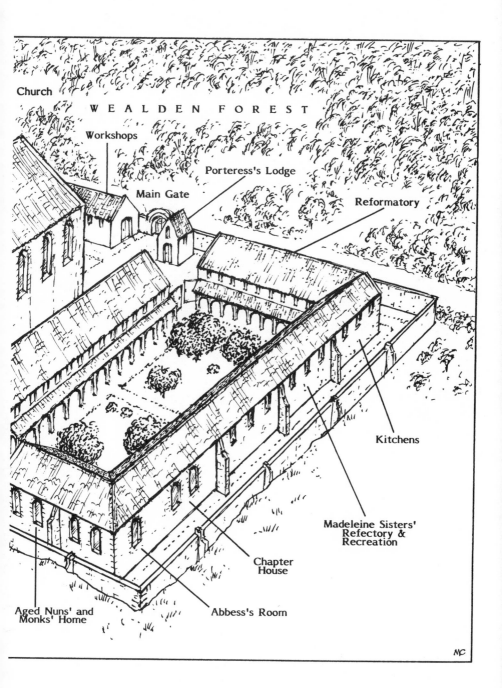

Church

WEALDEN FOREST

Workshops

Porteress's Lodge

Main Gate

Reformatory

Kitchens

Madeleine Sisters'
Refectory &
Recreation

Chapter
House

Aged Nuns' and
Monks' Home

Abbess's Room

MC

February

A night of the dark moon, the bright stars concealed behind dense, low cloud heavy with chill moisture. A night of shrieking wind, blowing out of the north east, its steady howl bringing with it a phantom hint of snow-laden steppes, unimaginably distant. Unimaginably lonely.

The inn at Tonbridge had been busy since early morning. It was market day and obvious since first light that it was going to be a poor one. In such terrible weather, merchants and stall-holders had been more than ready to forego the possibility of further dealing – increasingly unlikely as folk headed home for the comfort of their own hearths – and, turning their backs on the early-falling darkness, make their way to Goody Anne's tap room. Ah, but you could count on old Anne for a warm welcome! Nowadays, it came in the form of a tasty mug of her ale and a trencher of good fat bacon, or maybe a solid slice of hot, fragrant pie, oozing with gravy, bursting with chunks of rabbit or mutton. All the same, men had long memories, especially where their bodily comforts were concerned, and Goody Anne's tap room housed many a fellow who recalled other, more intimate services that had once been on offer.

It was getting late now. The tap room was empty of customers, its tables cleared of mugs and platters, wiped cursorily and put straight, stools and benches tidied neatly beneath. The boy and the serving maid had finished their chores for the night. Finished what they were prepared to do of them, at any rate;

they had both been on their feet since dawn, and, now that Goody Anne had turned in – if they stood still, they could hear her snores resonating from her room along the passage – neither of them saw any reason why they shouldn't, too.

In a room in another part of the inn, the bitterly cold wind drove against a flapping piece of hide stretched across the small window, easily tossing it out of the way and filling the room with air as deadly cold as the night outside. It was Goody Anne's guest chamber, fitted out with half a dozen narrow cots, all but five of which were at present stacked against one wall. The sixth was in use, fitted with a straw-filled sack to serve as a pillow and covered with two or three coarse wool blankets, much darned and none too clean.

Midnight.

As the boy and the serving maid snuggled down into their separate corners in the warm little scullery that backed on to the great kitchen hearth, gradually all sounds of life from the tavern ceased.

The wind strength grew, howling round the old building like an evil spirit, seeking access, blasting chill breaths into every gap. The rain that had finally begun to fall an hour ago turned to hail. The frozen droplets, as if they bore the stone walls a personal grudge, were being hurled against them with spiteful force, while, as a perpetual accompaniment, the wind howled its malicious song.

On the floor of the guest chamber, where he had half-fallen from the narrow cot, lay a dying man. He had come to rest on his side, the left cheek pressed hard against the thin rags that partially covered the floor. His legs and feet remained on the cot, tangled in the dirty covers.

In and around his mouth were quantities of brownish-yellow vomit, in which chunks of partially-digested meat and vege-tables stood up like islets in a stream. He had been violently sick soon after staggering away to the privacy of this room, driven to seek solitude by the rapidly increasing feelings of unease that had been overcoming him . . . burning and tingling in the mouth, and a strange sense that every object in his sight had suddenly taken on a fuzzed outline. And his tongue had gone all numb, too, so that it felt like some fat foreign object in his mouth – how they'd laughed, when he couldn't get his words out straight! To spare himself the humiliation of throwing up in Goody Anne's tap room, he had crept away, hand pressed to his lips, moaning softly under his breath, stumbling down some endless, dark passage until he came to a door. And, beyond the door, this chamber. With a cot he could thankfully lay himself down on.

He had been there some hours now. The rapid breathing that had so alarmed him had slowed, and he was slipping in and out of consciousness, only spasmodically aware of where or who he was.

In one brief moment of clarity, he thought, I shouldn't have stayed. Should have done as I planned, and turned for home soon as I'd sold my produce. Soon as the market wound up and trading finished, anyway. Shouldn't have given in to temptation, and let the lads persuade me to come to the inn with them. Spent almost every penny I made this day, an' all. Great merciful God, the ale I swigged! Greedy glutton that I was, I'm paying for it now. And that walloping great piece of pie, why, it were all I could do to finish it, me as can eat most other fellows under the table!

At the memory of his evening's consumption, his stomach heaved again. But it was practically empty now, and the agonising, dry retching brought up little but a thin stream of yellowish bile.

Dear Lord, the man thought, tears of pain and weakness trickling down his cheeks, but I'm too old for this . . .

He lapsed into unconsciousness.

The slow breathing became more laboured as paralysis increased its grip on the respiratory muscles. As the relentless fist crept inexorably towards the heart, its beat weakened.

Within the half hour, the man was dead.

Death by Poisoning

Chapter One

February, Josse d'Acquin thought miserably, was a wretched month for a journey.

He was nearly home, and he was experiencing in full the phenomenon of something unpleasant becoming far more so when one need not endure it much longer. The wind was coming steadily from the north-east quarter; into Josse's mind sprang suddenly the memory of a fellow-soldier, a man he'd known years ago, who used to refer to a north-easter as the Snowmother.

The Snowmother was making Josse about as uncomfortable as a man could be just then, he reflected grimly. His cloak was soaked through – and it was his heavyweight one, too, guaranteed to keep you dry, curse that lying merchant – and his shoulders were aching with cold. His buttocks were sore, and his thighs were badly chafed from hours of sitting in the saddle with wet hose. He was hungry and thirsty – what inns there had been on the road that were open for business had had little to offer a traveller in the depths of a harsh winter – and his feet in the sodden, mud-caked boots burned with chilblains. Burned, anyway, where they weren't frozen numb.

His horse was in little better state. 'Poor old Horace,' Josse murmured, slapping the big horse's neck, 'the things I ask of you, eh?' The horse shook his head, and small drops of ice flew from his mane, spinning through the air and catching the weak light. 'A thorough rub-down, a good feed, and tonight in your own stable, I promise,' Josse added. 'Another five miles, six at most, and we'll be safe home at New Winnowlands.'

New Winnowlands. The small but stoutly-built manor house, once forming the dower house of a larger estate, had been given to Josse by King Richard Plantagenet, in grateful thanks for services Josse had rendered. *Given*, however, had apparently been open to question, by the King at least; even when awarding Josse his prize, the words 'at a reasonable price' had crept into Richard's little speech. It had been only on the intercession of his mother, the great Eleanor of Aquitaine, wife to Henry II and beloved queen of the English people, that the gift had managed to stay a gift.

Then, damnation take it, two years on and along comes a demand for rent! *Rent!* Josse had been alarmed, horrified – the mentioned sum of rent arrears was more than sizeable, it was downright huge – and, finally, furiously angry.

'The King *gave* me my house!' he had raged, pacing up and down before his fireplace, spinning round so violently that Will, his manservant, nipped forward and rescued a tray bearing a jug of wine and a half-full goblet before Josse could send them flying. 'Two years and more ago, it was a *gift!* And now he wants me to pay for it!' He turned furious eyes to Will. 'In God's name, what can he be thinking of?'

Will, who wasn't in a temper and who therefore retained the power of logical thought, pointed out that, with King Richard still far away on crusade in Outremer, the rental demand could scarcely have come from him. 'He'll be far too busy with them devil Saracens to worry about a tiddly little manor house, sir,' Will went on, with scant diplomacy, 'you mark my words.'

Josse, amused despite himself, nodded sagely. 'How right you are, Will,' he said, in almost his normal voice. Frowning hard, he muttered, 'If not the King, then who?'

It took neither Josse nor Will more than a few seconds to come up with the probable answer. Simultaneously Will said, 'It'll be that John Lackland, I'll stake money on it,' while Josse exploded, 'That calculating, money-grabbing bastard, John! It's him!'

A demand for money, however, was a demand for money, and needed to be dealt with. Especially when it came from the King's younger brother, a man who saw himself – and was busy trying to make everyone else see him – as the next King of England. Whose coronation, if John had his way, couldn't come too soon.

The trouble was, Josse mused, as he tried to decide what to do, was that Richard, God bless his single-mindedness and his courage, seemed to have forgotten about his realm of England the moment he quit it – a matter of weeks after his coronation in September 1189 – to go off on crusade. He's playing right into John's grasping hands, Josse thought, and it's hardly surprising that people are half-inclined to believe John when he puts it around that King Richard will never come home.

And what if he's right? Crusading's no picnic, that's for sure, and our Richard isn't a man to stand at the back and order others into the fray. And, as well as the perils of fighting, there's sickness. The dear Lord alone knows what ills a man may fall foul of out there. Fevers, the flux, and who knows what others?

Supposing King Richard dies?

It was a sobering thought. The King's marriage to Berengaria of Navarre was but a few months old, and gossip was already declaring that the swift conception and birth of a son and heir was most unlikely. Well, with some justification, Josse acknowledged, since a man with fighting on his mind isn't as likely as some to bed his wife with the regularity necessary to impregnate her. As matters currently stood, the heir to the throne of England was a four-year-old boy, Arthur of Brittany, the posthumous son of Richard and John's brother, Geoffrey, and his wife, Constance.

And the word of the wise was saying that the barons of England weren't going to be happy supporting Arthur.

Would they be any happier supporting John? Surely not! No

man in his right mind would back the untrustworthy John, not all the time there remained even the slimmest chance of Richard returning home hale and hearty.

Josse slowly shook his head, his thoughts returning to that ominous demand for money. John, it was clearly apparent, was building up funds. For what? For some well-thought-out and clever plan, knowing John; whatever else you thought of him, you had to admit he was clever. Or possibly *cunning* was a better word . . .

In a flash of inspiration, Josse knew what he must do. He must put his case before Queen Eleanor. She had interceded on his behalf with her favourite son, so surely she would do the same with John.

It was worth a try.

It was, in fact, Josse's only hope.

Eleanor was lodging with the nuns of Amesbury Abbey. And Amesbury was in Wiltshire, half of the width of southern England away from Josse, whose manor was in Kent.

Still, it could have been worse. The Queen had spent Christmas in Normandy, and, had she still been there, it would have meant a dangerous sea crossing in addition to days and days on roads made all but impassable by the winter weather. It was pure good fortune that she was this side of the Channel, brought over in a rush to plead with John to abandon his scheme to ally himself with King Philip of France. Ally himself against Richard.

Nothing could have lent more speed to the Queen's feet than a threat to her beloved Richard, whose interests, both in England and on the Continent, she was doing her best to look after in his absence. With the present danger averted – for the time being – she had retired to Amesbury to catch her breath.

Which was where Josse found her.

To his amazement, she remembered him. 'Josse d'Acquin,' she said, extending a hand gloved in fine white kid fringed with some soft, dense, pale fur, 'my son's solver of puzzles.'

'My lady,' Josse replied, bending low over her hand.

'How are matters in Kent?' she enquired.

'Quiet, my lady, in this severe weather.'

'Indeed.' She nodded. 'And how fares my friend the Abbess of Hawkenlye?'

'Abbess Helewise is well, as far as I know.'

'Ah.' There was a pause. Then Eleanor said, 'Given the aforementioned weather, Sir Josse, would we be right in concluding that you have not ventured all the way from Kent purely to kiss our hand?'

Josse looked up and met her amused eyes. 'My lady, it would be worth the journey,' he began gallantly, only to be interrupted by her burst of laughter.

'In May, perhaps, but in February? What nonsense, sir knight!' she said. Smiling – really, Josse thought, she was still the most beautiful woman, despite her seventy-odd years – she said kindly, 'Now, let us waste no more time. Tell me how I may help you.'

Humbly – for it was surely a great thing, not only to be remembered fondly by the great Eleanor of Aquitaine, but also to be so unconditionally offered her help – Josse outlined his problem.

'I hesitate to put what must seem so trivial a matter before you, Lady,' he finished, 'and I only do so because . . .' He trailed off. Because your son promised that Winnowlands was to be a gift, was the honest reason. But it would sound so very blunt!

The Queen, however, was ahead of him. 'Because, as you and I both very well recall, Sir Josse, Richard gave your manor to you. Not without prompting, as I remember,' she added in a murmur. 'But a gift is a gift,' she announced grandly, 'and ever more should remain so.' With a wave of her hand she summoned a lady-in-waiting from the small group huddled around the fireplace of the Abbey's reception hall. 'Writing materials, please,' she said, and the woman hurried to fetch them.

Then, as Josse watched, Eleanor calmly wrote out three or four brief lines, decorating the thick parchment with an elegant, flowing hand. Not wanting to peer too closely, Josse made himself keep back. When she had finished, snapping her fingers at her lady-in-waiting, who proffered the royal seal, Eleanor raised her head, smiled swiftly as if she knew exactly what he was thinking, and, rolling up the parchment, handed it to him.

'Should my youngest son ever present himself in person to claim what he accuses you of owing,' she said tonelessly, 'then you may show him this. Anyone else you may dismiss out of hand.'

Thinking that such a dismissal might, depending on to whom it was addressed, be more easily said than done, Josse bowed again, thanked her, and, sensing himself dealt with, began to back out of the room.

The Queen stopped him. 'Sir Josse!'

'My Lady?'

'My compliments to the Abbess Helewise, when you see her.

She seemed, Josse thought later, in no doubt that it was *when*, not *if*.

Riding into his own courtyard, his many bodily discomforts were all but obliterated by the pleasure of being home again. And, moreover, with his mission accomplished. He patted the parchment, carefully stowed inside his tunic. Now let them come demanding rent! he thought cheerfully. I'll show them!

On reflection, it was rather a pleasant prospect. He actually hoped some agent of John *would* turn up. It would be worth the furore to see the man's face when Queen Eleanor's personal seal was waved under his nose.

Horace, who had broken into an almost eager trot over the last half mile, was urging on across the courtyard in the direction of the stables. Yelling out for Will, Josse slid off the horse's back, stumbling slightly on stiff, numb legs, and led Horace under cover.

Just inside the main door to the stables was a tinker's handcart, covered with heavy sacking. That, Josse thought, explained why Will hadn't come rushing out: no doubt he and Ella were in the kitchen, lapping up all the latest gossip. He unsaddled Horace, took off the bridle and, giving the horse a friendly slap on his broad rump, put him into a stall strewn with fresh, sweet-smelling straw, a filled water-trough on one wall.

'Wait there, old friend,' Josse said, 'and I'll send Will out to you.'

Entering the kitchen, he heard an unfamiliar voice.

'. . . sick everywhere, up the walls, all over the floor, and they do say there's a fresh mark by the window, a scorch mark, like, as if the Devil himself flew off and left a sign of his passing!'

'Ooooh!' breathed Ella, eyes wide, clutching her apron tightly.

'I don't know about devils,' Will began, 'but—'

In the doorway, Josse cleared his throat. Will and Ella spun round, and the stranger looked up and gave him a friendly grin.

'It's the master!' Will cried, leaping up and looking as guilty as if he'd been caught rifling through Josse's personal belongings. 'I'm right sorry, sir, but I didn't hear you call out.' He reached down for his sacking hood, drying beside the fire. 'I'll go and see to your horse, sir, he'll be in sore need of it on a foul day like today.'

'It's all right, Will, I—' Josse said. But Will, giving him a sheepish look, had gone.

'Sir Josse d'Acquin?' the stranger asked, getting up and making a brief bow.

'Aye.'

'I am Thomas, Sir Josse. Tinker of these parts, mender of household items, supplier of fancy goods, acquirer of rare luxuries, and bringer of tidings both good and bad.' He bowed again, more deeply; had he been wearing a hat, Josse reflected, he'd have swept it off.

'Welcome to my house, Thomas the Tinker,' Josse said. 'You have, I trust, been offered comforts?'

'That I have.' Thomas glanced at Ella, who, eyes cast down, seemed to be pretending she wasn't there; eighteen months in Josse's easy-going household had wrought little change in the diffident, nervous woman she had been when Will first brought her there to live with him. She never looked you in the face,

Josse had noticed; was it natural shyness, or was she too conscious of the slight cast in her left eye? 'She's a fine cook, your serving woman.'

'As I well know,' Josse agreed. 'Ella? May I have some of that?' He indicated the jug of mulled wine beside the fire. With a brief exclamation, she rushed to serve him, and, on Josse's nod, filled up the tinker's mug.

'You were saying something about a visitation from the devil?' Josse said, as the warm, sweet wine began to thaw him out. 'Will you repeat your tale for a fresh audience?'

'Gladly!' Thomas pulled his little stool closer to Josse. 'I was in Tonbridge day before yesterday, see, it being market day, but trade were bad. Too cold to get folks interested – it were out of the door, buy your chicken, your bunch of herbs or your tub of goose-fat, then straight home again. Nobody wanted to linger, not with that there wind howling like a hundred dead souls. Oh, no!'

'And?' Josse prompted.

'Well, like many another fellow, I made my way to the inn. A taste of Goody Anne's ale, that's what you need, Thomas my lad, I told myself. So off I went, and, to cut a long story short, sir, that's where I stayed. Afternoon turned to evening, evening to night, and there I sat in my corner, talking the hours away in good company, my mug ever-full, my platter cleared of every last crumb and every last drop.'

The disadvantage of having a professional storyteller pass on the news, Josse thought resignedly, was that they never used one word where ten would do.

'In due course we all went our several ways to bed, sir,' the tinker went on, 'and Mistress Anne were good enough to let me sleep under my barrow, in one of her outhouses, so I were cozy enough. All were quiet till morning, sir, when one of the serving folk went up to see to the guest chamber.' He paused dramatically, eyes fixed on Josse's. 'And you'll never imagine what she found, sir, not if you guessed from now till next Christmas!'

'Sick all over the floor and up the walls and a scorch mark by the window?' Josse suggested.

The tinker looked fleetingly put out, then, recovering, grinned. 'Ah, but sir, you have the advantage of having heard the end of the tale before the beginning, so as to speak,' he said. 'But, aye! That's exactly what the poor little lassie did find! Scream? I never heard the like! Woke me up, she did, and I'm no light sleeper, let me tell you, sir. I goes rushing inside, along of everyone else who heard her cry, and we all goes stumbling and tumbling along that passage.' Another pause. 'And there he is, lying there! In a pool of his own vomit, expression on his face like he'd been terrified half out of his wits, and dead as a doornail!'

'Poor man,' Josse said inadequately.

'Poor man?' Clearly Thomas had expected more of a reaction. 'I'm telling you, sir, that man died in agony! Just imagine, you're all alone, you're ill, sicker than you've ever been in your life, and you feel the despair of approaching death. Hear the steps of the grim reaper come plod-plodding up the passage, see his claw-hand open the door, watch in horror as that tall, thin, black-hooded figure creeps stealthily towards you, knowing all the while that—'

Ella gave a little scream, quickly muffling it with her apron. Josse, glancing at her white face, said, 'Quite. We see the picture. What happened next?'

'What happened *next*,' Thomas said, peeved at being interrupted in the middle of the good bit, 'was that Goody Anne came muscling into the chamber, sees all that sick all over the floor and orders everyone out. Then someone – don't ask me who, sir, as I don't know – must have gone for the Law.'

You could hear the capital letter of 'Law', Josse thought. Here, obviously, was a man who preferred to keep his distance, from both the institution and its officers. 'And so you made yourself scarce?' he suggested, grinning.

Thomas looked affronted. 'Sir! The very idea! I – well, that's to say, I didn't put myself *forward*, like, there being no point since I had nothing to offer that could possibly help.'

'Of course not,' Josse murmured.

The tinker shot him a very sharp look, then said, 'Course, I couldn't help picking up the odd titbit of information, here and there, and what I gather is that they're saying the dead man got fed a bad bit of supper. Slice of pie, portion of stew, whatever. And that whatever had got into it did for him.'

'What?' Josse was amazed. 'They're saying something served in Goody Anne's inn poisoned him?'

'Aye,' Thomas said, obviously pleased to have provoked a reaction at last. 'Threatening her with the full force of the law, they are, for feeding a man vittles that killed him.'

There were at least two things wrong with that, Josse thought. For one, his experience of Goody Anne's fare was that it was good, honest nourishment, cooked fresh each day, and that she richly deserved her reputation as a generous and skilled innkeeper. The second objection – and this was the clincher – was that, if a bad dish had indeed been served, then it was most unlikely that there would be only the one casualty.

'Poor Anne,' he said, shaking his head. 'What a misfortune! The worst thing to happen to a woman in her profession.'

From her corner, and to Josse's total surprise, Ella suddenly spoke. 'Can't you do nothing for her, sir?' she asked, face flushing at her own temerity, hands clasping at each other in anxiety. 'I'm a cook, too, sir, though I wouldn't dare to compare myself with this Goody Anne. But, sir, if someone said that food *I* had prepared had done for some poor soul, then I don't know what I'd do.' Her eyebrows descended over the mismatched eyes in a ferocious frown as she tried to imagine the unimaginable. 'Reckon I'd want to be dead, an' all.'

It was the first time Josse could recall Ella ever having ventured a remark of her own accord. Certainly, it was the first time he'd heard her say more than a few words: 'Mornin', sir' and 'Aye, a cold day it is' were normally her limit. 'Ella?' he said gently. 'You feel strongly for poor Anne?'

But her courage had run out. She had returned to her hunched position in her corner, and would not meet his eye. She grunted and managed, 'Aye.'

The tinker was standing up, draining the last of his wine with a slurp. 'I'll be on my way,' he said. 'There's an hour or two of daylight left, I'll make my next stop afore dark if I leave now.' He nodded to Ella, bowed to Josse, and headed out through the kitchen door.

Josse followed him out to the stables. Will could be heard, whistling between his teeth to Horace as, with steady, soothing strokes, he rubbed the horse down.

'Cheerio, Will,' Thomas called, bending to pick up the handles of his cart. 'Be seeing you.'

Will's head appeared over the half door of the stall. 'Cheerio, then, Thomas.' He caught sight of Josse. 'Oh! Nearly done here, sir, then I'll see about helping you with your kit.'

Josse watched the tinker set off across the yard, one wheel of the handcart accompanying the regular beat of his steps with a small squeak. 'I didn't come to hurry you along, Will,' he said, turning back to the manservant.

'No, sir?' Will looked at him expectantly.

'No.' Josse sighed. It wasn't a very happy prospect, especially when he'd been so looking forward to a few days' peace and quiet in the warmth and comfort of home. But, there you were, a friend was a friend, and one in need couldn't be ignored. Especially when, as seemed to be happening, they were being punished for something they hadn't done.

'I came to say, Will,' Josse went on, 'that I'd be grateful if you'd feed old Horace up a bit tonight.'

'Sir?'

'I'll be needing him again tomorrow, I'm afraid. It looks like I'll be going to Tonbridge.'

Chapter Two

Next day the weather had changed. Improved, almost, for, although it was actually colder, the rain had stopped and the wind had lessened. Josse set out around mid-morning under a clear blue sky, and, wrapped up in a cloak which Ella had renovated for him by lining the hood with a precious piece of fur, he felt quite cheerful.

As he and Horace trotted along, he looked round him at the winter-dead landscape. You would think, he thought, that everyone had gone, deserted their hovels and hamlets, been driven away by some dread calamity. There's nobody about, no sign of any life, human or animal.

It made him feel quite lonely. To reassure himself, he imagined the inside of a cottage such as Will and Ella lived in. Small and dark, yes, but dry, if the inhabitants took the trouble to attend regularly to their roof. Warm – the one thing everyone made sure of was to keep the fire alive, no matter how small the room, how tiny the hearth. Reasonably clean, too, provided a woman was a good manager. Sharing your home with your animals tended admittedly to make cleanliness a problem, but there were ways. Apparently.

It was, Josse realised, something about which he really hadn't a clue.

The water in the streams and ponds was frozen hard now, and, on the banks, remnants of dry grass and bracken were coated in glistening white frost. Pretty – Josse noticed a skein of geese flying in formation up ahead, alive and active in contrast to the dead hare he'd just seen beside the track, already half-eaten by anonymous predators – but such severe weather sorted the survivors from the weak, no doubt about it.

Hunching deeper into his cloak, he kicked Horace into a canter and turned his head down the long sloping road that led off the flank of the higher ground and into the valley where Tonbridge lay.

Goody Anne was in tears.

'Oh, sir, I'm that glad to see you, I can't put it into words!' she sobbed, clutching Josse's hand and wringing it between her own. She was a strong woman, and quite soon he had to disentangle himself.

'What a business, Mistress Anne,' he said, patting her plump shoulder.

'They're saying I gave him a bad plate of supper!' she said, the indignation clearly still fresh. 'Me that's been feeding folks all my life! It's an *insult*,' she went on, with quiet dignity.

'I agree,' Josse said. 'If it's any comfort, dear Anne, I don't believe for one moment that you are to blame.'

She gazed at him, eyes filled with sudden hope. 'Don't you?'

'No. If by some terrible mischance there *had* been a dish that had gone bad, where are all the other victims?'

Her lips moved in silence as she worked it out; it must be the shock, he thought charitably, she was normally a quick-witted woman. 'You mean, lots of people would have eaten the same meal, and they'd all have fallen ill?'

'Aye.'

'And they haven't.' She gave a visible shudder. 'Thank the good Lord, they haven't!'

'Amen,' Josse said. 'So, Mistress Anne, we have to look at other possibilities.'

She was looking at him keenly. 'Such as?'

'Well, perhaps the man was sick when he arrived here, and merely died in your guest chamber of something that had already written his death warrant. Perhaps he was very, very drunk. Perhaps . . .' He paused. Unable to think of anything else, he finished lamely, 'Something like that.'

Anne gave him a grateful smile. 'You've a good heart, sir knight, that you have.' Drying her eyes, she said, 'You'll be wanting to talk to a few folks, ask a few questions, I shouldn't wonder.'

Will I? Josse thought. He couldn't for the moment think what he might ask. Then, recovering, he said, 'I'd like to see the room where he died. And talk to the maid who found him.' His mind seemed to have recovered. 'And I'd better know who he was and where he came from, so that I can pay a visit to his family, whoever they are.'

'If they're sick too, it'll put me in the clear,' Anne said, accurately but with little regard, Josse thought, for the dead man's kin. Shock again, he decided. In her right mind, Goody Anne wouldn't wish a ghastly death on somebody purely to prove that her food wasn't poisonous.

'We'll start with the guest chamber,' Goody Anne announced. And led the way along the passage.

The guest chamber had, Josse was relieved to find, been cleaned. The thin rugs on the floor still showed patches of damp from their recent washing, and the cot, stripped of bedding, was covered in a haze of condensation. The leather flap over the window had been fastened back, and the cold, fresh air circulating in the room was fighting gamely with the pervasive stench of vomit. Unfortunately, it wasn't yet winning.

'We found him half on and half off the bed,' Goody Anne said, holding her nose. 'As if he'd lain down, then, feeling the sick rise up, leaned out over the floor to puke up.' She muttered something else, something about folks that hadn't the decency to find a bowl to be sick in and save other folk from the mopping up.

'Had he been drinking hard?' Josse asked.

Anne gave him a look. 'They'd *all* been drinking hard. Always do, market day. It's my best day.'

'Do you think a surfeit of alcohol killed him?'

She considered. 'I've heard tell of such things,' she admitted. 'Young feller I knew when I was – er, when I was younger, it happened to him. He got drunk, then fell heavily asleep on his back, and choked on his own vomit.' She shook her head. 'But that can't be what happened to this poor soul.'

'It can't?'

She sighed. 'No. Like I said, he was leaning out over the edge of the bed. The vomit ran out of his mouth, not back down his windpipe.'

The talk was becoming rather too graphic, for Josse. Especially standing in a room that reeked all too strongly of its last occupant's demise.

'I'll talk to the girl who found him,' he announced, striding for the door. 'Come on, Mistress Anne.'

The serving maid who had discovered the corpse was a small, thin, pale-faced girl of about fourteen or fifteen. She had light brown hair tied in a knot on the nape of her neck, pale bulging eyes with light-coloured lashes, spots on her chin and lumpy hands reddened from constant contact with cold water. She had a permanent sniff, a habit of wiping the dewdrop off the end of her nose with the back of her hand, and she answered to the name of Tilly.

For some reason, Josse detected instantly, she was very disturbed by his gentle questions.

'I can't tell you *nothing*!' she kept crying. 'I went in and there he was, and that's all there is to it!'

'You knew who he was?' Josse asked.

'Eh? How d'you mean?' She looked cagey.

Josse tried another tack. 'Were you serving in the tap room the previous evening?'

Tilly hesitated. 'Might have been.' Josse waited. Eventually, as if even Tilly's limited intelligence realised there wasn't much future in evading the truth on a point that could instantly be decided by others' testimony, she said, 'Yes.'

'And you served the dead man?'

'No,' she said instantly. Then: 'Yes, maybe. It's hard to tell, when we were so busy.'

'I'm sure,' Josse said soothingly. 'What I'm asking is, when you saw the dead man in the morning, did you recognise him as one of the previous evening's customers?'

She looked at him as if he were daft. 'Course I did! He'd stopped the night, hadn't he?'

This was getting nowhere. Realising that he still didn't know the dead man's identity, Josse thanked Tilly for her help – she wouldn't have noticed the mild irony – and sent her back to the kitchen.

He spoke to half a dozen men who had been in the tavern the night the man died before anyone could tell him the dead man's name.

It was Peter Ely. He had been in his mid-thirties, it was guessed, and he farmed a few meagre acres in the Vale of Tonbridge, some five or six miles out of town. He was in the habit of coming to the market, where he would sell whatever produce he'd brought with him before repairing to the tavern for a drink and a bite before setting off for home.

Nobody knew whether he had family. Nobody, it become clear, knew very much about him at all.

If he was already ill, Josse mused, taking a break from questioning the clientele of the tap room and strolling around the yard, then that's an easy answer, and I almost hope it's the right one. Because if he wasn't, and if, as I strongly believe, we can rule out a dish of bad food, then somebody must have killed him. Slipped poison into his food while he wasn't looking, and murdered him.

And if that's what happened, I'm left with the question, who? Who on earth, and for what purpose, could have wished to kill a poor, humble peasant who doesn't seem to have had anything remarkable or memorable about him whatsoever?

He shook his head, stumped.

A thought occurred to him, prompted by a sudden rumble from his hungry stomach.

Food. The dish of food.

Was there any chance . . . ?

Hurrying back inside the tavern, he raced to find Tilly.

'It's a-cause of all the pother,' she said, indicating with a hopeless gesture the piles of food-encrusted trenchers, platters and dishes stacked in a lean-to abutting the kitchen. 'There's always a lot, see, after market day, and, what with getting the body out, and the clearing-up, and all the comings and goings and what-not . . .' The words ended on a weary sigh, as if she didn't have the heart to finish.

Three days after market day, and washing-up not yet done. No, Josse thought, he could quite see that wouldn't accord with Goody Anne's orders under normal circumstances.

'Never mind, Tilly,' he said encouragingly. 'I'm quite sure nobody's going to be cross with you.' She turned mournful eyes on him, as if she didn't share his confidence. 'Anyway, as it happens, it may prove to be very helpful that the platters are still soiled.' He ran his eyes over the mess, wondering where to begin. 'Er, Tilly, could you try to think back and tell me what the dead man ate for his supper?'

She didn't answer. Turning, he noticed her expression. Pale eyes wide, face even whiter and glossed with a fine sheen of sweat, she looked terrified.

'Tilly?' he repeated, trying to sound gentle. 'What's the matter?'

She shook her head, and emitted a strangled sound. He waited. Then, whispering the word as if admitting to some dread crime, she said, 'Pie. He had chicken and vegetable pie.'

Wondering as he did so why she should make such a scene about a question which surely could not have been unexpected, Josse attacked the stack waiting for Tilly's attention. He didn't bother to look at any of the rough wooden trenchers from which the tavern's customers ate their meals; there was absolutely no way he could have told which one had been used by

Peter Ely. What he wanted to inspect was the considerable number of larger serving platters, on which, presumably, each dish had been cooked, and from which individual portions would have been cut.

There seemed to be dozens. Oh, Lord, he thought, overcome by the task, this is hopeless! Even given that I can detect which serving platters held pie, then what? I'm . . .

At the bottom of the second stack, where it had been supporting a tottering column of trenchers which Josse had one by one removed and discarded, was a big pie dish. Scraps of pastry adhered to its rim, and in its base was a congealing mass of meat, gravy and vegetables. He picked it up, looked questioningly at Tilly and, after a moment, she nodded.

He gazed into the pie dish, suddenly reluctant to take his testing to the next logical step. A roomful of vomit, a man's dying face contorted in agony . . .

Firmly he took hold of a piece of onion between finger and thumb. He brought it up close to his face and stared at it. He sniffed it. Then, finally, he touched it very lightly against the inside of his lower lip.

Nothing.

He waited. Tilly's watching eyes seemed to burn into him. Nothing.

He put the piece of onion carefully back in the pie dish, and then replaced the dish on the floor of the lean-to.

Still nothing.

I was wrong, he thought. Wrong about that dish, anyway, which means I'll now have to go through the remaining three stacks to see if I can discover another pie-dish.

Which was not a pleasant prospect.

'Tilly, I'm going to continue the search,' he said. 'Can you remember how many pies you got through on market day? Because—'

A tiny tingle in his lower lip.

He stopped what he was doing, straightened up. Waited.

No.

Ah well, it was—

Yes! From an all-but-undetectable tingle, now the spot inside his lip, where he had touched the onion to the gum, was burning as if he'd put a live coal on to it. Elbowing Tilly out of the way, he ran for the pump in the corner of the yard, working the handle feverishly, holding his open mouth beneath the stream of icy-cold water. It was only self-preservation, not deliberate action, that made him hold his head so that the water ran into his mouth and then straight out again, rather than going down his throat.

The burning sensation soon began to diminish. He went on rinsing out his mouth for some time after it had ceased altogether. By then, not only his lower lip but his whole face was so cold that a burning coal might actually have been quite welcome.

He rinsed his hands as well, rubbing the finger and thumb of his right hand over and over again.

Then, when at last he was satisfied, he asked Tilly for an old sack, and, careful not to touch the pie dish again, enveloped it in the sack and went in search of Goody Anne.

She was sitting in the tap room with her feet up, drinking a mug of her own ale. She looked up apprehensively as Josse entered.

He held up the sack. 'I've found the culprit,' he said quietly. 'Not your pie, Goody Anne, or, at least, not your pie as it left your capable hands.'

She looked doubtfully at him, obviously not prepared to be relieved until he'd told her everything.

'And?' she asked.

'I suggest we destroy this,' he said, swinging the sack. 'Smash the platter, bury it somewhere no creature will dig it up.'

She whispered, 'Why?'

'Someone put poison in it,' he said. 'Unless I'm mistaken, which I don't believe I am, someone put a large dose of wolf's bane in a portion of the chicken pie. Then they fed it to Peter Ely.'

*   *   *

25

Now that he knew about the poison, the chief reason for visiting Peter Ely's home – to see if anyone else in his family had fallen sick – seemed to have been removed. But Josse decided to go, anyway: it didn't seem right that nobody went, and, with the forces of law and order stirred up like a henhouse circled by a fox over the discovery of the wolf's bane, it seemed that, if Josse didn't make the effort, nobody else would.

Sheriff Pelham and Josse had met before. Josse wasn't keen to renew the acquaintance, and nor, it seemed, was the sheriff.

'You again!' he greeted Josse when, preparing to set out for the Ely acreage, Josse approached him to ask to be given Peter Ely's meagre personal effects.

'Me again,' Josse agreed. He explained his mission, and the sheriff, having scratched his head to see if he could come up with some objection, discovered he couldn't and grudgingly handed over a small bag made of coarse linen.

'I'll have that back when you're done,' he said, pointing a dirty-nailed forefinger at the bag. 'That's official property, that is.'

'I wouldn't dream of depriving you of it,' Josse said. He didn't wait to hear Sheriff Pelham's reply.

The Ely home was a small and ramshackled cottage, a lean-to, in fact, tacked on to the end of a row of three other cottages which, on first sight, seemed better maintained. Peter Ely, Josse observed, hadn't been a man to turn his hand to a repair; the roof was holed, the door was off one of its hinges and the whole place had an air of squalor and neglect.

He dismounted and, tethering Horace, walked up to the door and put his head inside the cottage's single room.

'Hello?'

Two figures materialised from the gloom, followed by another, smaller one; as his eyes adjusted, Josse thought they might be Peter Ely's father, wife and adolescent child. Whether the latter was male or female was not immediately apparent.

'Eh?' said the old man.

'I have ridden out from town,' Josse began, not really sure where to start – did these wretched people even know Peter was dead? – 'to seek out the kin of Peter Ely.'

The woman, gazing at Josse dully, said, ' 'E be dead.'

'I know,' Josse said. 'I'm very sorry.'

There was a silence. The three Elys went on staring. Finally, Josse remembered the bag. 'These belongings were his,' he said, holding out the bag. The woman shot out a hand and grasped it, swiftly tucking it away inside some fold of whatever garment she was wearing in what looked like an automatic gesture. 'They are Peter's effects,' he added. 'Found on his – found on him.'

'Aah,' said the old man.

'I'm 'aving 'em!' the woman hissed, giving the old man a vicious dig in the ribs as if fending off an attempt to wrest her late husband's possessions from her. 'Anything 'e 'ad, it's mine!'

Nobody seemed to wish to dispute that.

The four of them went on standing there for some time. Eventually Josse said, 'Er – it appears Peter was poisoned. More than that I'm afraid I can't tell you.'

'Poisoned,' echoed the old man.

It was the only response any of the three made. And even then, it seemed more an observation than a grief-stricken moan.

Despairing of them, Josse said curtly, 'I'll wish you farewell,' mounted Horace, spurred him and hastened away.

It was clear he would have to put up at the inn overnight. For one thing, it was getting dark and, for another, he still had so much to find out.

He hoped Goody Anne could offer an alternative guest chamber. Fortunately, after making a few hasty rearrangements, she could.

After supper (mutton stew washed down with ale, and quite delicious), he was lingering by the fire in the tap room, reluctant to go up to a cold bed, when Goody Anne came hurrying in.

He could tell from her face that she had something to tell

him; giving her a quick grin, he said, 'Well? What have you found out?'

She smiled back. 'T'isn't me, it's that wretch of a girl.'

'Tilly?'

'That's the one. She's – oh, you'd better come and see for yourself, no doubt it'll be quicker in the long run.' She took his mug from his hand, thumped it down and, grabbing his sleeve, hurried him out of the tap room, down the passage and into the kitchen. Tilly, face in her hands, seemed to be sobbing.

'Come on, then, my girl!' Anne said angrily. 'You can tell the gentleman here what you just told me!'

'Oh, *no!*' Tilly wailed.

Anne folded her stout arms across her deep bosom. 'Either you do or I shall,' she said relentlessly.

'Come, Tilly,' Josse said, moving forward and crouching down beside the girl. 'What can be so terrible?' He tried a small laugh. 'After all, *you* didn't poison the old man, did you?' He chuckled again. Very soon, he realised he was laughing alone; Anne was staring at him with a face like thunder and Tilly had broken into renewed wails.

'Dear merciful God,' Anne muttered. Then: 'Tilly, you didn't poison him, not really, and no one's going to say you did, not while I've got life in my body. You mayn't be much,' she added, half under her breath, 'but you're better than nothing, and I won't see you dragged off and accused of sommat you didn't do.'

Tilly, who seemed to find that slightly reassuring, had raised her head and was now looking at Josse out of pink-rimmed eyes. Her distress, he noticed, hadn't done anything for her looks.

'Tilly?' he said gently.

She took a deep, gulping breath, then said: 'It were the last bit of pie, see. There was this man – handsome, he were, lovely black hair all glossy like an 'orse, he gave me such a nice smile and he said, what did I recommend? What was really tasty? And, what with it being the last bit, and him being so nice, I, well, I—' She started weeping again.

'You were serving a nice, friendly man,' Josse said, trying to pick up the narrative, 'and you were going to serve him the last slice of pie. Is that right?'

Tilly nodded. 'Aye. I was just putting the trencher together – bit of pie, gravy, stack of vegetables, slice of bread, when Tobe yells—'

'Tobe?'

'Tobias,' Goody Anne said. 'The boy.'

'Ah. Go on, Tilly.'

'Tobe, he yells out, another chicken pie! and I thinks to myself, that'll mean starting a new one. Then, like I says because 'e were so nice, I thinks, why not give *'im* the first slice from the nice fresh pie, and the last bit of the old pie to whoever else wanted pie? 'Specially when I had a look and saw it was some silly fool of a man, half-drunk at that, who'd been going to get the new bit.' She glanced at Josse. 'See?'

It was a rambling explanation, but Josse thought he did see. 'You had two orders for the pie,' he said slowly, 'one from your nice handsome man, and one from the man who we now know was Peter Ely. Yes?' Tilly nodded, wiping a long trail of greenish snot on to the back of her wrist. Josse stepped back a pace. 'There was only one serving left in the pie you'd been dishing out and, naturally, you'd have served it to the handsome man rather than cut into a fresh pie. Yes?'

'Aye,' Tilly agreed. 'She – the mistress – is very strict about that. We always have to finish one dish before we start on the next.'

'Quite,' Josse said. 'But then, just as you were about to take the handsome man's meal out to him, Tobias calls through *another* order for the pie, which means you can give the last of the *old* pie—'

'I don't know as I care for all this talk of *old* pie,' Anne interrupted plaintively. 'It wasn't old, it were made fresh that morning, same as all the day's food!'

'Yes, Anne,' Josse said, trying not to let his irritation show. 'I'm only saying *old* pie to distinguish it from the uncut one. All right?'

Anne sniffed. 'Suppose so.'

'Now, Tilly.' He turned back to the girl. 'You decide to give the last slice of the *cut* pie to Peter Ely, and you prepare a pretty trencher of the pie you've just cut into for your handsome man. Yes?'

'Aye!' Tilly risked a thin smile.

'There!' Josse exclaimed. 'That wasn't so bad, now, was it?'

But the girl had slumped into despondency again. 'I gave 'im the pie what killed 'im,' she moaned.

'Yes, child, but it wasn't your fault!' Josse said, exasperated. 'You didn't poison the remaining slice in the cut pie, did you?'

'Course not!'

'Well, then. And—' He had been on the point of saying, and if you *hadn't* swapped the portions, your handsome man would have died instead of Peter Ely. But it wasn't a comment which stood any chance of cheering Tilly up, so he didn't.

Later, lying on a narrow cot under covers so thin that he was glad of his thick cloak – Goody Anne had explained that he could normally have had more blankets, only the ones Peter Ely had sicked up on still weren't dry – Josse reviewed the day's progress.

It didn't take long.

Someone had wanted to kill someone. They'd tracked him to the inn at Tonbridge, spied for long enough to hear him order his supper, then somehow they'd sneaked into a busy kitchen and slipped a fatal dose of wolf's bane into the portion of pie destined for the victim.

Wolf's bane, Josse thought, momentarily distracted. Also known as monk's hood, because of the hood-shaped blue flowers, it had leaves like parsley and a root like a little brown turnip. Used by healers to rub on the skin for pain relief, but to be handled with care as all parts of the plant were poisonous. One of the oldest of mankind's poisons, well-known to – probably well-used by – the Greeks and the Romans.

Easy to get hold of, here in south-east England? Josse didn't know. But, easy or not, someone had managed it.

The poisoned pie was virtually on its way to the victim – he picked up his thread – when young Tilly swaps the trenchers so as to reward her friend the handsome man with the newly-cut pie. Poor lass, he thought, distracted again, I don't think such a small philanthropic gesture would have got her very far with her glossy-haired fellow, not given the child's meagre appearance, dull wits and habit of wiping her nose on her hand.

Where was I? He was becoming sleepy. Ah, yes, the swapped pies.

No wonder he'd had difficulty imaging the innocuous Peter Ely as a murder victim. He hadn't been. The poisoned pie hadn't been destined for him, but for Tilly's handsome man.

And now the handsome man had gone on his way. He'd left more than three days ago, probably innocent of the fact that someone had just tried to kill him. With nobody knowing who he was, where he'd come from or where he was going, it looked as if Josse's next step in unravelling the murder had already been laid down for him.

Chapter Three

————◦◦◦————

Helewise, Abbess of Hawkenlye Abbey, was recovering from a
severe bout of fever.

She said she was recovering. Her infirmarer, Sister Euphemia,
said she was still very sick. The debate had reached an uneasy
stalemate; Helewise had won the battle of whether or not she
must remain in the infirmary, but Euphemia had triumphed over
the question of putting a truckle bed and a small brazier in
Helewise's room.

Now the Abbess could stay at her duties for as long as she
could manage, then, when she had to give in and have a sleep, all
she needed to do was walk acoss the room and lie down.

Helewise was uneasy. It was not right for a nun to have the
unheard of luxury of a fire in her room! Why, none of the other
sisters enjoyed such comforts! Even in the infirmary, only the
very sick had heat! What of my vows? Helewise demanded
angrily of herself. What of poverty, when here I lie, snuggled
under covers of soft wool, hot coals pulsing orange warmth not
three paces from my bed!

Back to work, she ordered herself. I have been sleeping since
the midday meal, and it's high time I did something construc-
tive.

She swung her feet to the floor and sat up. Instantly her head
began to spin and she thought she was going to be sick. Black
spots floated before her eyes, quickly growing and massing
together till they were one big black hole.

Sinking back on to the bed, she reflected that perhaps Euphemia was right after all . . .

She dozed for some time, drifting in and out of a restless, guilt-ridden sleep. So much to see to! So much she ought to be attending to! Her anxiety permeated her dreams; she saw Brother Saul, the most capable of the lay brothers and her secret favourite, kneeling by her bed, whispering, 'I know you're sick, Abbess, but others are more sick, and need you to mend their hoods because the rain is getting in,' whereupon he took a plump wood pigeon from his sleeve and stroked its throat until it began to sing like a blackbird. Then Brother Saul turned into fussy old Brother Firmin, who stood over her with a huge Bible in his gnarled hands, holding it above her face and bumping it none too gently against her forehead . . .

. . . which, as she awoke with a start, changed into the regular pulsation of pain searing just above her eyebrows.

All right, Helewise thought wearily as she sat up again – more slowly this time. All right. Back to work.

She moved over to the high-backed wooden chair that stood behind the broad table at the end of her room. Both items were well-made and costly, relics from her former life as the wife of a knight. Dear old Ivo had given her the table, which, in those earlier times, used to be stacked with items representing the many aspects of Helewise's duties: mending for the two boys – her sons had always been harsh on their garments; bundles of herbs or bunches of flowers, to be turned into some useful cream or potion for the benefit of some member of the household, human or animal; and, always, the accounts. Ivo, who himself hadn't been able to write much more than his own name, had treasured his literate wife, her head for figures and her fine hand.

Helewise brought herself back from her reverie – really, what was wrong with her today? She just couldn't keep her mind on her work! – and sat down, pulling towards her the great leather-bound ledger into which were inscribed details of

·everything and everybody coming into Hawkenlye Abbey, and everything and everybody going out again.

She was totting up for the fourth time the amounts given away by Brother Firmin to itinerants calling at the Holy Shrine down in the Vale – she had arrived at a slightly different amount on each of the first three attempts – when there was a very soft knock on her door.

Resisting the temptation to fling her quill across the room, instead Helewise laid it carefully down, folded her hands in her lap and said calmly, 'Come in.'

The door opened a fraction and the earnest face of Sister Ursel appeared in the gap. 'You're not asleep, then, Abbess?' she whispered.

'As you see, Sister Ursel, I am not.' Helewise forced her features into an expression approximating welcome. 'So there's no need to whisper.'

'Ah. No, no indeed.'

'And do come in and close the door, Sister.' Helewise's smile was feeling increasingly like a rictus.

'Oh. Ah. Yes.' Sister Ursel did as she was told, closing the heavy door behind her with exaggerated care. Stepping forward, leaning towards Helewise, she said, 'Now, how are you feeling, Abbess? Sister Euphemia said I wasn't to tire you out by chatting, and not to come in at all if you were resting, only you're not, so I can tell her it was all right to go in. Come in, I mean.' She frowned. 'Or is it go in? I—'

'Sister Ursel?' Helewise prompted gently. 'You wanted to see me?' Oh, dear, she thought, as well as a wandering mind, I'm presently cursed with a very short temper. Here's poor old Ursel, doing her best to be kind and considerate, and here I sit wanting desperately to fling this wretched ledger at her . . . She made a mental note to make humble and contrite penance for being so uncharitable to a fellow sister, then gave Ursel an encouraging smile.

Which, unfortunately, cannot have looked to Ursel as Helewise had wanted it to, since the porteress gave a muffled gasp and took a step back. 'Abbess! Have you taken a turn for the worse? Should I fetch Sister Euphemia?'

'No,' Helewise said rather too firmly. 'I am quite all right, Sister Ursel. Now, will you *please* tell me what you want of me before I— Well, just tell me.'

Sister Ursel gave an injured sniff. 'That Sir Josse's outside,' she said shortly. 'Wants to know if he can come in to see you.'

She muttered something that sounded like, wouldn't bother if *I* was him, but Helewise, her spirits lightened immeasurably at the prospect of seeing her old friend, scarcely heard. 'I'd *love* to see him!' she said happily. 'Send him straight in, please, Sister!'

Josse, stomping into the room a few moments later, wore a cheerful, expectant grin. Which, on seeing Helewise, rapidly changed to an alarmed frown. 'God's boots, what have you done to yourself?' he enquired, hurrying towards her, ignoring her outstretched hands and instead taking a firm grasp on her elbow and ushering her back to her chair. 'Sit down, sit down! Before you fall down,' he added with a grunt.

'I am *quite* all right,' Helewise said, for the second time in a very few minutes.

Josse was staring down at her, still frowning. 'You're not,' he stated. 'I dare say your sisters allow you to tell them that you are, but I'm not going to join them in flattering your vanity.' He came to lean on her table, bending down and putting his face close to hers. 'You've had the fever, I would say, and you've got yourself up and gone back to work long before you should.'

'But I—' Helewise began.

With a wave of his hand, Josse shut her up. 'But nothing!' He curled the hand into a first and thumped it down on the table. Helewise's abandoned quill bounced up and fell on the floor. 'You may think you're indispensable, Abbess, but you're not. Nobody is. What's this you were doing?' Before she could stop him, he had turned the large ledger round and was studying it. 'You're doing the accounts!' He stared at her, his expression as amazed as if he'd found her painting pictures of naked men.

'Somebody has to,' she said primly. 'And it's my job.'

He gave an exasperated sigh. 'When you're well, yes. But surely you can delegate?'

'Not many of the others can read and write,' she said,

registering in passing that she seemed to be taking his proposal seriously, 'and of those who can, I don't know who would have a sufficiently fair hand.'

He was nodding infuriatingly, as if she had proved a point he was trying to make. 'Just as I said! Indispensable, aren't you? The only nun among – how many is it? Nigh on a hundred? – who can write neatly enough for the account book. It's not an illuminated manuscript!' he cried. 'Not holy writ! Would it really matter if, just for a week or so, the records were kept in a less than perfect hand?'

'Yes!' she protested, automatically. Then – her headache was getting worse by the minute – she said in a whisper, 'No. Of course not. As long as we do our very best, there can be no grounds for complaint.'

She dropped her hot face into her cold hands, momentarily luxuriating in the comfort afforded by the contrast.

She sensed him coming to stand beside her. A moment later, there was a tentative touch on her arm. 'Abbess?' His tone was kindly now. 'Would it be against all protocol for you to talk to me while lying in your little bed there?'

She looked up. His strong-featured, humorous face was creased into anxious lines, as if he really was afraid his suggestion would have mortally offended her. Wanting to laugh, valiantly she suppressed it, said meekly, 'Not in the least, Sir Josse,' and allowed him to lead her the few steps to her truckle bed. He propped the pillow behind her head, covered her with the blankets and then stood back.

It was, she had to admit, a huge relief to be lying down.

He watched her for some moments without speaking. In case he was waiting for her signal to speak – what *had* he come to see her about? she wondered – she said, 'Sir Josse? You are, naturally, a welcome visitor, but was there something particular you wanted to discuss?'

He had, she observed, backed away until he was standing against the door. Assuming this was how he imagined a man should behave when in the same room as a nun lying on her bed, again she wanted to laugh.

'I don't think I should be bothering you with my worries,' he said. 'Not when you're meant to be convalescing.'

'Well, you're here now,' she replied. 'Why not tell me anyway?'

'Very well.' He gave her an intent look. 'But only on condition that you kick me out when you've had enough.'

'I promise.' Smiling, she closed her eyes. 'Now, proceed.'

She listened as he told her what had happened in the inn at Tonbridge. Of the dead man, Peter Ely, of Josse's own discovery of the pie poisoned with wolf's bane, of Tilly and the swapped plates. Despite the gruesome details, she found she enjoyed listening to him; he told a tale well, in an orderly manner and with sufficient details for her to imagine the scenes he was describing. Reflecting on how pleasant it was to have a visitor bringing tidings of the great world beyond the walls of Hawkenlye, it was a few moments before she realised he had stopped speaking.

She opened her eyes, to find him bending over her. 'Sorry,' he said, instantly backing away. 'I thought you might have nodded off.'

'In the midst of such a narrative?' She smiled up at him. 'Heaven forbid!' He grinned back, apparently relieved by her response. 'So, what now?' she wondered aloud. 'If I were in your position, I should return to Peter Ely's family and question them as to whether or not the dead man had any dealings with a man of the handsome stranger's description. At first sight, that is the obvious solution, that the two were somehow in league and the stranger wanted to silence his accomplice.'

Josse said, 'Exactly what I did do, Abbess! But to no avail, I'm afraid.'

'Why? What happened?'

He gave a brief snort of laughter. 'I got them all out of that hovel of theirs, standing in a line blinking in the sunshine, and I said, did Peter know anybody from noble circles? Well, that was silly, to start with, since none of them had a clue what I meant, so I narrowed it down a bit and said, did he know a handsome man with shiny dark hair, well-dressed in expensive clothes? I managed to get a detailed description from little Tilly, who, I conclude, has more than a crush on the man, so I was able to add that he wore tan leather boots, a dark-red tunic and a heavy cloak bordered with braid.'

'And what did they say?'

This time Josse laughed aloud. 'Nothing. They stood before me staring at me with their mouths open and their eyes popping, like a row of sheep hearing angels sing. I tell you, Abbess, I was in some doubt that they'd taken in a word I said.'

'Did they say *anything*?'

'After what seemed an age, the woman – Peter Ely's wife – announced, " 'E din' mix with gentry." Then the three of them turned round and shuffled back inside. I did call out to let me know if any strangers came calling, and that I could be reached at the inn. But I doubt if they took any notice.' He sighed.

'Hm.' She was thinking. 'I don't believe I can offer you any suggestions, Sir Josse. Although one thing does strike me.'

'What?' he said eagerly.

'Oh, don't set any store by it,' she replied, 'it's only a very small point.'

'Let me have it anyway,' he encouraged. 'I'm at my wits' end!'

'I doubt that very much,' she said. 'Very well. What occurred to me was that this stranger did nothing to disguise himself. Quite the opposite, it appears, since he wore good clothes, which he must have known would stand out in the tap room of the inn, and, by your account, he flirted quite openly with the little maid.'

'We don't *know* he did that,' Josse said. 'We only have Tilly's side of the story. And, Abbess, she's not a girl *I* would flirt with.'

'Nevertheless, he spent the evening in the tap room, with the evening's company, appearing as himself. Yes?'

'Ye-es,' Josse said cautiously.

'So I conclude that he wasn't there for any nefarious purpose. His visit to Tonbridge was innocent, and therefore he didn't care who saw him.'

'Because, if he *had* come on secret business, the last place he'd have gone would be the inn! Yes, Abbess, you're quite right!'

'Might he have been a guest of the Clare family?' she suggested. 'His sort of people, wouldn't you say?'

'I would.' Josse frowned again. 'But if he were, then why eat his supper at the inn?'

'Did he put up there for the night?'

Josse shook his head. 'I don't think so. Mistress Anne says that the dead man was her only guest that night.' He smiled briefly. 'Although guest is hardly the word, under the circumstances.'

'Does anybody know where the stranger went, on leaving the inn?'

'No.'

'Might he have returned to Tonbridge Castle?'

Josse folded his arms across his broad chest, tapping the fingers of one hand against the opposite upper arm. 'Yes, I suppose so. But it doesn't sound very likely, does it? A nobleman – if we may surmise that from descriptions of his dress and his manner – comes to visit friends, leaves them to take his supper at the local inn, which, for all that it's a decent one, is still an inn, then, having tucked away his meal, goes back to beg a bed from his hosts.' He shook his head. 'Doesn't accord with anything *I've* ever heard.'

'Nor I, I have to agree.' Helewise struggled to sit up.

'Where do you think *you're* going?' Josse demanded instantly.

'Nowhere!' she protested. 'I merely need a change of position.'

'Hmm.' He eyed her suspiciously, as if half expecting her to filch the ledger off the table and return to her accounts. Then: 'We *are* right, aren't we, Abbess, in assuming the handsome stranger must have been the intended victim?'

'Yes,' she said firmly. 'I'm sure we are.' It was pleasant, she thought, to be *we* again. A satisfying challenge, once more to unite her wits with his over this new conundrum. 'And I do think that there is only one logical next step, Sir Josse. To find out the identity of the stranger, and what he was doing in Tonbridge that someone else didn't want him to do.'

'Aye,' Josse said heavily. 'I agree. For all that I don't relish the task, I agree.'

'Can there have been so many handsome strangers in town recently?' she asked. 'You do, after all, have a good description.'

He grinned at her. 'Abbess, do you ever visit Tonbridge?' She shook her head. 'Well, I fear you have a somewhat inaccurate picture of the place.'

'It used to be a quiet little town,' she mused, 'the castle guarding the river crossing, and—'

'Aye. The river crossing,' he interrupted. 'And what crosses the river?'

'The road, of course.'

'Aye. The road from London to the coast. Abbess, traffic has increased, I imagine, since last you were there. To our present disadvantage, since that traffic includes, in with the merchants, the pilgrims and the local travellers, any number of richly-dressed strangers, handsome or otherwise.'

'Oh.'

'Don't sound so woebegone!' He seemed to rally, unfolding his arms and straightening up. 'It's a starting point, at least. Better than nothing. And I shall set off immediately and begin making enquiries.'

'Such fervour,' she murmured.

He was looking at her, his expression softening. 'May I report progress to you in a day or two?'

'I should be most upset if you didn't.'

'And you'll promise to rest? Get someone else to see to those accounts?'

'I will.' Someone, she thought tiredly, who could add up a column of figures better than she could at the moment.

He opened the door. 'Do you wish me to send anyone in to see to you? Fetch you a drink, or something to eat?'

The thought of food made her feel slightly sick. 'No, nothing, thank you.'

'Then I'll tell Sister Euphemia you're resting,' he said, easing his way out. 'Sleep well!'

'Farewell, Sir Josse, and good luck.'

She listened to his heavy footsteps marching away along the cloister. Then, giving in to her fatigue, she turned on her side and was very soon asleep.

Chapter Four

As he rode away from the Abbey, Josse wondered if his last action before leaving would be deemed by Helewise to be uncalled-for interference. If, when she learned of it, she would be angry with him.

He hoped not. But if she were, it was a price he'd have to pay.

He'd been to see Sister Euphemia, and told her he'd been horrified at the Abbess's appearance.

'You've no need to tell *me*!' Euphemia had protested angrily. 'I've got eyes in my head! And you should have seen her last week! Dear merciful Lord, I feared for her life one night, her fever rose that high!'

'What ails her?'

Euphemia shrugged. 'There's any number of fevers about, folks say. It's a harsh winter we're having. This particular sickness was brought by pilgrims to the shrine. There was four of them, two old people, two young 'uns. The old folk died – there wasn't anything we could do for them, and the holy water doesn't always work its miracle if a body's too far gone.'

'Did many of your nuns and monks fall sick?'

Euphemia gave a 'huh!' of indignation. 'Most of our nuns and monks kept their distance, I'm ashamed to say. The Abbess herself took a turn at nursing, with me and Sister Caliste, and Brother Saul relieved us all when we went to our devotions. I reckon we escape most infections, Caliste and Saul and me, because the good Lord above gives us His protection, us being in permanent contact with the sick. But the Abbess, now, she's different. She was worn out even when she came to help us, Sir Josse, and it does seem to be the way of it, that fevers more readily strike at those whose energies are running low.' Euphemia shook her head sadly. 'She takes on too much, I'm always telling her. Fat lot of good it does, though, I might as well save my breath to cool my porridge.'

'Sister Euphemia, she must do less,' Josse said. 'She was busy writing in her ledger when I went to see her just now. Can you send some capable nun in to relieve her of that, at least? Just till she's better? There must be someone suitable.'

'Course there is,' Euphemia agreed. 'Leave it with me, Sir Josse.'

'Could it be arranged for all her duties to be taken over by others? And it might be wise to have someone sitting with her,' he said, aware as he did so that he was robbing Helewise of her precious and, as well he knew, limited solitude. 'To make sure she rests.'

Euphemia shot him a look, as if she knew exactly what he was thinking. 'Aye,' she said. 'As I say, leave it with me.'

He was, he reflected as he kicked Horace to a canter, quite fortunate to be making his escape. At least it wouldn't be he who had to endure Helewise's reaction when she learned what Josse and Euphemia had arranged for her . . .

He reached Tonbridge in the early evening, glad to be within its outskirts. It was now fully dark, and the temperature had dropped again. Despite his fur-lined hood, Josse's ears were aching with cold.

He ordered a generous supper. Not, he thought, that he had earned it; his day's labours had got him virtually nowhere. And now there was the Abbess to worry about, in addition to everything else.

Ah, well. At last she was in good hands.

Not wanting to face either Mistress Anne's questions or

Tilly's anxious eyes when he had nothing to tell them, Josse finished his supper, drained his mug of ale and retired early to bed.

Mid-morning the next day, he set out for the castle.

It became clear, even as he approached up the steep track that led from the ford, that there were few, if any, members of the family about. The frosted ground bore little evidence of having recently been trodden, and the drawbridge had been raised halfway up. Only a thin trickle of smoke rose up from within the stout walls, and looked, Josse thought, more likely to be from an outdoor brazier than from the huge fire in some great hall's hearth.

In answer to Josse's call, a man appeared at the opposite end of the drawbridge. Making no move to lower it and allow Josse to cross, he shouted out, 'Yes?'

'Is the family in residence?' Josse shouted back.

'No.'

The man went to return inside, but Josse stopped him. 'A moment!'

Reluctantly the man turned round again. 'What do you want?'

'I am looking for a stranger, a nobleman, possibly a friend of the family,' he said. 'I believe he may be lodging with them, or at least come to visit.'

'We've had no visitors,' the man replied. 'Like I says, the family's away.'

Where were they? Josse wondered. And what on earth had persuaded them to leave the comforts of home, in this freezing weather?

'You'd be best advised to get away an' all,' the man was saying. 'If you value your health, that is.'

'Why?' Josse felt a shiver of alarm run up his spine.

'Sickness,' the man said, with the self-satisfied air of one imparting news of some danger from which he feels himself immune. 'There's fever, down in the new Priory. Never should have built it, they shouldn't, not down there beyond the ford, so close to where all them streams flow together. Marshy, it is, down there. There's bad air, spreads all manner of pestilence. Family's gone away to Suffolk, and I have my orders to keep this here drawbridge up.' He gave the stout planks a reassuring slap with the flat of one hand. 'You can't come in, whoever you are, and I ain't coming out.'

You could, Josse thought, see his point.

'And you've had no callers? No visiting nobleman?'

The man gave a chuckle. 'He'd have had to swim across,' he said, pointing down into the sludgy waters of the moat, dark with unimaginably foul detritus and half-frozen over. 'And *that* I wouldn't recommend.'

Josse raised an arm. 'I thank you for your time,' he called, wheeling Horace and preparing to leave.

'Time I have,' the man replied, turning back into the deep shadow of the gatehouse. 'Good day to you!'

Looking back over his shoulder to give an answering good day, Josse thought he saw a movement. Up high, on the battlements . . . a head, peeping over the sturdy wall, quickly withdrawn . . .?

He stared, holding Horace still. But there was nothing to see.

Probably a bird, he told himself. Nothing more sinister than that. After all, as that fellow said, any uninvited guest would have had to swim across.

Inattentive, he didn't notice that his horse had picked a different track for the descent. About to pull him up and return to the track they'd gone up by, suddenly Josse noticed something.

Hoof prints.

Someone had gone up that smaller, half-concealed track. Quite recently, too.

The man, whoever he was, returning from having gone out for supplies?

No. He'd made it quite plain he intended to stay shut away safely inside the castle until the danger was past.

Then who?

Telling himself he shouldn't jump to conclusions didn't seem

45

to be working. Resigning himself to the prospect of several hours in the cold, Josse dismounted, led Horace into a grove of hazel trees which, full in the weak rays of the February sun and protected from the wind, provided at least a small amount of shelter, and prepared to endure a long wait.

He should, he thought late in the afternoon, have brought food with him. And he'd have to give up soon, if nothing happened, for Horace's sake if not for his own. The sun was low on the horizon, its light and its paltry warmth even weaker now. It wouldn't be long till darkness.

He made himself wait a little longer.

As the light faded, there was a noise from above, from the direction of the castle. A mutter of voices, quickly cut off, and a long, low rumbling sound, terminating in a heavy thud. After the briefest of pauses, the rumbling noise was repeated.

And there was the faint sound of a horse's hooves – unnaturally faint, surely? Could they have been muffled some-how? – coming down the narrower of the two tracks.

The one that passed right by Josse's hiding place.

Pulling back deeper into the hazel grove, he put a quieting hand on Horace's nose. The horse from the castle came closer, closer . . . Josse could hear a tiny jingle of harness.

He held his breath.

The horseman rode straight past.

It *was* a man, Josse was certain, even from the brief glimpse he'd had through the hazel trees. Heavily muffled in a volu-minous cloak.

Waiting until the man was out of earshot, Josse then led Horace out from beneath the hazel trees, mounted, and rode off in pursuit.

It was difficult to judge a safe distance, where Josse would be able to keep his quarry in view yet not be detected. The poor light was both help and hindrance.

Josse followed the rider for a few miles, then, as he suddenly drew his horse to a halt, quickly pulled Horace into the shadow of an oak tree. The rider had dismounted and, as Josse watched, he bent down to remove covers of some sort – they looked like pieces of sacking – from his horse's feet.

A departure at twilight, Josse thought, and one whose very sound is minimised.

Now who was going about – what had the Abbess's word been? – nefarious business?

The rider entered a thick band of woodland, a part, Josse thought, of the great Wealden Forest, although, in this cloudy and starless night, he had lost his bearings. Riding on, he realised quite soon that he had also lost sight of the horseman.

Hellfire and damnation!

He urged Horace on, peering through the trees, trying to make out any movement among the winter-bare branches.

Impossible! He just couldn't see anything.

Pulling Horace up, he sat and listened.

Not a sound.

After a while, he dismounted. The hard ground might yield a hoof print, you never knew. Crouching down, he took off one of his gloves and, fingers spread, felt around the forest floor for any sharp indentations indicative of recent passage.

It was hopeless. He couldn't see anything now, and any vague thoughts he'd had of following the track, it being the most likely route taken by the horseman, faded. He couldn't make out the track anymore.

He took a desultory pace or two forward, bending down to have one last try at seeking out a hoof print. Then suddenly Horace gave a whinny of alarm and, jerking his head back, pulled the rein out of Josse's free hand. Just as Josse began to straighten up, he heard a thin whistling sound by his right ear.

In the same instant as alarm began to surge through him, the blow fell.

Intense pain, concentrated on a point in the middle of the back of his head. A vague awareness of the cold smell of the forest floor, and shards of ice from some small puddle pressing against his cheek.

Then nothing.

He woke to feel something tickling his nose. Something soft, but which smelt very strongly. What was that smell? Goat? No, sheep.

A piece of sheepskin.

Smelly it might be, but it was beautifully warm. Josse wriggled his toes. They were warm, too. Bliss! From somewhere nearby, he could hear the soft hiss and crackle of a fire. Fire. Sheepskin. Warmth. Ah! This was *good*. Better than standing in the cold below Tonbridge Castle, trying to keep Horace from pacing in circles and giving them away . . .

Horace!

Josse sat up.

His head seemed to explode and, all thoughts of Horace flying from his brain, he groaned aloud.

A voice said urgently, 'Lie back!'

For a moment, Josse thought he was back with Helewise and that, by some strange mirror-imagery, she was now nursing him, persuading him to rest. Had he taken on her head pain? Not that he'd mind, not really, only it did seem weird . . .

No. He couldn't be in Helewise's little bed. Helewise would not lie beneath a cover that smelt like this one did.

Gathering himself for a huge effort, Josse opened his eyes.

By the greyish light of morning, he could see that he was lying in a shack, crudely made of wooden posts tied together with woven willow withies. Cold air was coming in through the many gaps in the walls. He seemed to be in a bed of bracken, and the stinking cover was indeed a sheepskin, not very well cured.

A movement caught his attention. Turning his head – very carefully – he saw a figure standing in the low doorway.

A small figure, this one. By his dress, a boy. Eight? Nine? Josse, despite being uncle to several young nephews, was not very good with children's ages. As he watched, the boy came into the shack and knelt beside Josse. He held a cup and, raising Josse's head with a gentle hand that was careful to avoid the wound, he held the rim of the cup to Josse's lips.

Some sort of warm liquid, flavoured with something reminiscent of onions, trickled into Josse's mouth.

Mmm. Not bad.

'Mmm. Not bad,' Josse said aloud.

'It's onion broth,' the light voice said. 'Anyway, it's meant to be. I don't do very much cooking. Still, it tasted all right to me.'

'Possibly a tad more salt,' Josse remarked.

'Yes! But, actually, I haven't got any salt.'

'Oh.'

There was a silence. The lad settled himself on the floor of the shack, close by Josse, and then said, 'I'm Ninian. Ninian de Lehon. I'm not supposed to tell people, but you won't say I did, will you?'

Josse twisted round so that he could look up into the boy's innocent eyes. They were bright blue. Rare, he thought, to see such an intensity of colour. Recalling the trusting question, he said, 'Of course I won't.'

'I'm seven years and five months old,' Ninian went on, 'I like riding and I like making camps – this is my camp. It's my latest one and my best one. I like hounds – I'm going to have a hound of my own when I'm ten – and I don't like lessons.'

'Nor do I,' Josse agreed.

The boy giggled. 'You're too old for lessons.'

'Aye. But I remember well enough I didn't like them.'

'My pony's called Minstrel,' the boy said, 'and—'

Pony. Horse. Horace! The memory came back again. 'Where's Horace?' Josse demanded.

'Is he your horse? He's fine,' Ninian said. 'I've put him in the shelter with Minstrel. I took off his saddle and put Minstrel's spare cover on him, only it's a bit small. I would have taken off his bridle, but I didn't know how to tether him if I did, the shelter's not very strong and he might have pushed his way out. So I didn't.'

'Thank you for looking after him,' Josse said gravely.

'That's all right.'

Silence fell again. With the fingernail of one forefinger – a filthy nail, Josse observed, on an equally filthy hand – Ninian picked at a scab on the back of his opposite wrist. The scab came away, leaving behind a drop of blood, which the boy sucked up. Then he ate the scab.

'Nice?' enquired Josse.

Ninian put his head on one side. 'It could do with a tad more salt.' He laughed. 'You didn't go, eugh!' he said. 'My mother always does. She—'

Suddenly his expression changed. Leaping up, he said, 'Got to go. I'll come back, I promise.' He bent down over Josse, and, spitting into his right hand, held it out. 'But *you've* got to promise not to follow me,' he said, anxiety in his voice.

Josse pulled his own right hand out from the sheepskin, spat in the palm and smacked it into Ninian's in a firm clasp. 'You have my word.'

Ninian nodded. Then he rushed out through the doorway and was gone.

Some time later – early afternoon, to judge from the light; Josse, who had been asleep, hadn't been aware of the progression of the hours – Ninian came back.

He was carrying a cloth bag, out of which he took bread, a piece of hard yellow cheese, a flask of water ('I wanted to get you some wine, but they would've seen me so I didn't'), a somewhat overripe apple and a small cake with a nut on the top. Josse, who hadn't been aware he was hungry, ate the lot and instantly began to feel better.

'I brought this, too.' The boy undid a length of rope from around his waist. 'I thought we could make Horace a head collar, then we could take his bridle off.'

'How very considerate,' Josse said. He took the rope from the boy and quickly knotted it. 'There. This length over his ears, then tighten this loop a little, and the loose end to tie him up by.'

Ninian stared down at the improvised halter. 'Oh.'

Oh indeed, Josse thought. Horace was a very big horse and Ninian a rather small boy. 'Would you like me to see to it?' he offered.

Ninian's blue eyes shot to Josse's. 'No, you must go on lying down, you've had a severe blow to the head.' He sounded, Josse thought, amused, as if he were quoting some overheard remark. 'I'll manage.'

He was on his feet before his courage failed. In the doorway, he turned round and said 'Er – he doesn't *bite*, does he?'

'Never.'

Josse waited. Horace was, despite his size, a well-mannered horse, especially towards those trying to help him.

In a very short time, he heard Ninian's racing footsteps returning.

'I did it! I did it!' the boy yelled, doing a little dance, no easy feat in the limited space of the hut. 'He almost said thank you when I took off his bridle! The halter went on fine, I didn't make it too tight, and now good old Horace can have a rest, too!'

'That was bravely done,' Josse said. 'Thank you, Ninian de Lehon.'

Ninian grinned. 'That's all right – I don't know your name, so I can't be formal back.'

'Josse d'Acquin,' Josse said.

'Acquin,' the boy repeated. 'Is that in France too?'

'Aye.' In France *too*. Yes, he'd have laid money on Lehon being a French name.

'You remember you promised not to tell, don't you?' Ninian said warily. 'About my name, I mean.'

'Of course.'

'I won't tell anyone yours either, if you like,' he offered. 'That'll make it fair. Won't it?'

'Aye, it would.'

Josse, who had drunk most of the flask of water, was beginning to feel an urgent need to relieve himself. But he wasn't sure if he could stand unaided. Staring up at Ninian, he said, 'I believe I need your help over something else. As well as the food, I mean, and taking care of Horace.'

'Anything!' the boy said generously.

Josse grinned, feeling awkward. 'I need to –' what phrase would a child use? He had no idea – 'I need to make water,' he finished lamely. 'Is that how you'd say it?'

'*I'd* say, I need to do *pipi*,' Ninian said. *Pipi*, Josse thought, transported back to the nursery at Acquin, *faire pipi*. Well, the lad does have a French name, even if he speaks fairly accentless English. 'But that doesn't matter,' Ninian went on. 'Because I don't, anyway, and you do, so I'd better help you up . . .'

It took quite a long time to get Josse outside, relieved – he made Ninian go away while he urinated, leaning against a tree – and back on his bracken bed again. The effort made Josse feel terrible. Ninian, with the tact of a much older person, made no comment but tucked him up under the sheepskin, put a full water flask beside him together with the last crust of the bread, then made himself scarce.

Daylight faded and Josse's second night in the shack loomed. Ninian managed another visit before full darkness fell, thoughtfully bringing a lantern with him, and then Josse was left alone.

In the morning, Josse woke early. He felt better and the improvement increased as he drank from the flask and consumed the bread. He managed to crawl outside to his tree by himself this time.

He was back in bed, running a thumbnail over two days' growth of beard, when he heard footsteps outside.

'Good morning, Ninian!' he called out. 'I hope you've brought me some more bread, I'm ravenous! And I'm—'

The footsteps had reached the door of the shack, and Josse broke off.

Because the figure standing in the doorway wasn't Ninian. It was a woman.

Chapter Five

A very beautiful woman.

In her early twenties, at a guess, of medium height, with a generous, womanly figure which yet, possibly because of her air of tension, gave an impression of strength. She was wearing a plain costume of some brown fabric, over it a man's cloak. At her waist hung a small satchel made of soft leather.

She had a woollen shawl over her head, beneath which was a plain white headdress, loosely worn. Quite a lot of smooth, brown hair emerged from underneath it, braided in a long plait which came forward over her right shoulder. Her face had high cheekbones, a straight nose and a wide mouth, the lips well shaped.

Her eyes, large under the high forehead, were dark.

Whoever Ninian had inherited his blue eyes from, Josse thought absently, it wasn't his mother.

For that she must surely be: nobody else could have had that same combination of curiosity, indignation and protective fierceness as this woman when, with no preliminaries whatsoever, she demanded, 'What do you want with Ninian?'

'He has been looking after me,' Josse said quietly. 'I was attacked, in the forest. He must have found me and dragged me here.' A strong boy, he reflected. Strong and determined. 'I want nothing of him, lady. That I promise you.'

She took a step closer, the dark eyes intent on Josse. He met her stare.

'Looking after you,' she repeated, half under her breath. 'You are injured?'

He sat up carefully, leaned forward and pointed to the back of his head.

She looked. 'Ouch!' she said sympathetically. Then, as if remembering her defensive attitude, 'What were you doing in the forest? Who attacked you? You must have been up to no good!'

He smiled faintly. 'I was in the forest because I was following someone, a man whom I want to speak to concerning a matter in the tavern, at Tonbridge. I thought I was a skilful pursuer, but clearly not – I surmise that it was he who doubled back behind me and struck me, presumably because he didn't want to be followed. As to my being up to no good, well, lady, you must judge that for yourself.'

He lay back. For some reason, he was feeling exhausted suddenly. It was probably, he reflected, not without small amusement, having to endure the intensity of that dark-eyed glare.

She was still staring fixedly at him, as if she feared that taking her eyes off him for an instant would enable him to leap up, attack her and make off. Probably with Ninian over his saddle bow.

'Truly, I mean you no harm, you or your son,' he said quietly.

The dark eyes widened. 'He's not my son! He's . . . he's . . .'

'Madam, I have had more practise than you in the art of deception.' He smiled at her, hoping to remove any offence from his words. 'A piece of advice: if you're going to tell a lie, prepare it thoroughly beforehand.'

'But he's not my son!' she insisted. 'He's – a boy in my household!'

'Very well. It remains as true, however, that I intend no harm to either of you.'

She went 'Huh!', but he thought he detected a slight softening in her ferocious expression. 'Let me look at your wound,' she said, kneeling down beside him. 'Turn round – no, not that way! Yes, that's better. Hmm. A deal of swelling –' her fingers gently probed the bump, and he winced – 'and the skin has been broken in a couple of places.' She lowered his head down again and sat back on her heels. 'I'll warm some water and apply a poultice. It will sting, but it will draw out any dirt and allow the cuts to heal. Ninian!'

From somewhere outside, the boy called back, 'Here!'

'Put some water on to boil!'

'There already is some.'

'Good, good,' she muttered, getting up and sweeping out of the shack in one swift movement.

Presently she came back, bearing in her hands what looked like a lump of green mud. A strong smell accompanied her into the shack; a pleasant smell, which, as he breathed it deeply into his lungs, gave him the impression of being slightly light-headed . . .

'Don't breathe it in too deeply,' she warned belatedly.

'Why?' He leaned forward and she bent over his head. 'What's in it?'

'Primarily comfrey and lavender.' He felt a sudden heat as she put the poultice to his wounds. 'Plus one or two secret ingredients of my own.'

'Where did you find comfrey and lavender in February?'

'I brought them with me. In my satchel. They're dried, of course, not fresh, but even dried, they retain some of their goodness. There.' She had secured the poultice with a strip of linen, which she was tying off. 'How does that feel?'

He thought about it. 'Better,' he said eventually. 'The whole of the back of my head feels warm, the stinging sensation has eased off and in fact . . . yes. It's going nicely numb.'

For the first time she smiled. The effect was considerable; he couldn't resist smiling back. 'Excellent!' she said. She held out a small mug. 'Drink this. You ought to drink plenty, it's bad if you get thirsty.'

He thought at first that it was plain water. But there was some sort of aftertaste to it, a slight bitterness. He wondered why he wasn't instantly on his guard. Why he appeared to have put his trust in her so unreservedly.

He watched her as she packed up her leather satchel. She was humming quietly; a soothing, soporific sound. He gave a great yawn. 'Sorry.'

'You're drowsy,' she observed. 'Have a sleep. It'll help your body heal itself.'

'Very well.' He could feel his eyelids drooping. Closing.

'I'll be back later,' she said softly. 'I've filled your water flask, and left you some bread and dried meat. I'll bring you more food when I return.'

He opened one eye. She was still there. He closed it. When, an instant later, he opened it again, she had gone.

He wondered afterwards what she had put in the cup. Some strong sedative, that was for sure. Well, he had to conclude that she knew what she was doing; waking up late in the day, when the long shadows cast by a low sun in a clear sky told him it was almost dusk, he discovered he felt much better.

He lay staring out at the sunset. The sky was clear, not a cloud to be seen. As he watched, the orange glow began to fade and, in the deep navy of twilight, the first stars came out. There was the Great Bear – idly his eyes followed the line of the constellation – there were the Pointers, there the North Star, and, over there . . . ah, yes! There was Cassiopeia.

She had said she would come back, and he knew she would. Eventually, she did.

She was breathless, and had obviously been running. 'It's going to be a very cold night,' she said without pausing to greet him. 'There's no fire out there this evening, so you'd better come with me. Can you manage to mount your horse, if I help you?'

He sat up. So far, so good. 'Aye,' he said. He had been

outside several more times to answer calls of nature, and getting on to Horace shouldn't present any problem. He rolled over on to his knees, then very slowly got to his feet. Not too bad.

She held his arm and they went outside. Somebody – the woman? – had put on Horace's saddle and bridle, and beside him stood a stout bay pony, also tacked up.

Josse pointed. 'Minstrel?'

'Minstrel.'

The woman bent down and held her joined hands beneath Horace's left stirrup. Josse put his knee into her hands, and, holding on to the saddle, heaved himself up while she pushed from beneath.

Lord, but she *was* strong! He hardly needed to pull, she was doing most of the work.

He settled himself – his head was spinning wildly – while she mounted the pony. 'You're no weakling,' he remarked.

She shot him a glance. 'Four months of taking care of us has developed muscles I didn't know I had,' she said. 'I can split logs and carry loads as well as a man.' Then, as if regretting her words, her expression closed down. Face severe, she nudged the pony closer to Josse. 'Look, I'm sorry but I'm going to have to blindfold you.'

'*What?*'

'I'm sorry,' she repeated, 'but it's necessary. You have to agree,' she went on, earnest now as if it mattered that she convince him, 'there's no point in discovering a perfect hiding-place and then letting a total stranger know where it is. Is there?'

'No.' She was right, he did have to agree.

He leaned down to her level while she tied a soft cloth round his eyes, over the top of the band holding on the poultice. She tied it tightly and efficiently: he couldn't see a thing.

'And I'll have to tie your wrists to the pommel of your saddle,' she added, doing so before he could protest.

'I won't take the blindfold off, I promise,' he said quietly.

'I believe you.' He sensed from the warmth in her voice that she did. 'But suppose your horse were to trip? Natural instinct would be to uncover your eyes, despite your promise.' He made no reply. 'I won't let that happen,' she said. 'Won't let your horse trip, I mean. I know the way, and he'll probably follow on quite happily behind me. If he gets uneasy, I'll dismount and lead him. All right?'

'All right.'

They travelled for some time. Josse, in the blackness of his blindfold, disorientated and dizzy, concentrated on clinging on to the saddle, and on coping with the sickness that kept coming in vertiginous waves.

After a while, he sensed they were no longer beneath the trees. The ground seemed a little firmer and once or twice one of the horses struck a shoe against a stone. The air felt colder and colder. Josse was shivering almost constantly now.

They climbed a slight rise – instinctively, feeling Horace's effort, he put his weight forward slightly – and then they were there. He sensed walls around them, a building of some sort, and then the woman was beside him, untying his hands, removing the blindfold.

'Thank you.'

She stared up at him. 'No. It is I who must thank you. Not a journey for a sick man, I'm afraid, especially when he has been deprived of his sight.'

'Only temporarily,' he murmured.

She helped him down, and, as she led Horace and the pony on into the building – it appeared to be a barn, which had been fitted with internal partitions to make two or three rough stalls – he leaned against the door frame, trying to stop the spinning in his head. He noticed absently that one of the stalls was already occupied, but the light inside the barn was too dim for him to make out details of the horse. Perhaps – probably – it was the woman's mount.

Soon she came back. '*They're* all right,' she said. 'Noses in the manger, happy as jesters. Now, let's see about you.'

Now he needed her support. She shoved her left shoulder under his right arm, bracing his back with her left hand, and, slowly and steadily, got him out of the barn – pausing to secure the doors – and across what seemed to be a paved courtyard. In front of them loomed the bulk of a house. Quite small, square in shape, enclosed at the back by tall trees.

She helped him up a flight of steps to the entrance to the main room, situated over an undercroft. She opened the heavy wooden door and warmth and candlelight flooded out to embrace them. She ushered him quickly inside and Ninian, who had sprung up from where he had been sprawling beside the fire, rushed to close and bar the door behind them.

'Hello.' Josse gave the boy a grin, which the boy returned.

'Hello, Sir Josse d'Acquin.' The boy glanced at the woman. 'You can tell *her* you know what my name is,' he added, 'it's the others that—'

'Ninian!' the woman said warningly.

The boy gave a strangely adult shrug.

The woman was putting cushions on to a thin palliasse placed in front of the wide hearth. 'Come, lie down,' she ordered Josse, 'it's not much, but it's better than my son's camp. Oh!' She straightened up, looking aghast at Josse.

'I already knew,' he said gently, 'despite your protestations to the contrary. Or, rather, I guessed.' He longed to ask why it was so important to pretend Ninian wasn't her son, but everything about her spoke of someone who was fiercely resisting others' curiosity. Others' attentions.

She would have much preferred to leave me out in the woods, he thought as he lay down. Only her good Christian heart made her bring me here, out of the cold.

As if she knew what he was thinking, she said, 'I think you would have suffered sorely out there tonight. I did not want Ninian to be out at his camp, where he might have tended you and kept the fire in. He cannot play there anymore, not now that I know—'

That you know someone is looking for you? he wondered. No – more than that. You'd have been aware of that all along. But now you have to accept that he's closing in.

He. Who is *he?*

Is it – can it be – who I think it is?

The woman brought him food – a hot, thick soup with some pieces of chicken in it and some sort of mushy pulses, accompanied by bread – and gave him a very welcome mug of mulled wine. Then she presented him with another little cupful of water.

He pushed it firmly away. 'No, lady.'

She met his eyes. She didn't try to deny that the water was drugged; she merely said, 'You need to sleep.'

'I shall sleep,' he assured her. 'Ex-soldiers have the knack of sleeping to order. Didn't you know?' She answered his smile with a faint quirk of her lips. 'I need to wake up to order as well,' he added, his voice too low for Ninian to hear. 'Don't I?'

Her eyes widened as she understood. 'Oh, *no!* Don't even *think* that!'

'Face the truth!' he hissed. 'He's close. Isn't he?'

He had half hoped that if he pretended to know more than he did, she would lower her guard and tell him everything.

She didn't.

Instead she raised her chin, stared him out and said haughtily, 'You have not the least idea what you are talking about, and you won't trick me into telling you. I'm no fool, Sir Josse.'

'I didn't think you were,' he said. Then, for she was angry now and he knew the moment for confidences was past, he added, 'I intend to sleep until first light. Then I shall leave. I suggest you escort me to some place where I can find my bearings. I will allow you to blindfold me again, if you wish it.'

'I do,' she said frostily. Turning away, she said, 'Until first light. Come, Ninian.'

The boy gave Josse a wistful look – you're here, and I'm so glad, but you've got to be going again! it seemed to say – and then meekly fell into step behind his mother. They disappeared up a narrow staircase which had been concealed behind a hanging in one corner of the room, and for a short time he heard their footsteps overhead.

Soon, the whole house was quiet.

As he had promised, Josse lay down his head and went to sleep.

In the morning, he was awake before her.

He made his way outside, where he found a water butt. The top couple of inches of water were frozen solid, and he had to break the ice with a stone. He filled a bowl, and took it in to heat it over the fire, which he had fed on waking, tickling it into a good blaze.

He had brought his small saddlebag in from the barn, and now, for the first time in three days, he enjoyed the luxury of a wash and a shave. Before dressing again, he brushed down his tunic as best he could. He gave his boots a shine, and tried to get some of the forest floor vegetation out of his hair. But it was difficult to do so without disturbing the poultice and its linen tie, and he soon gave up.

By the time the woman came down, he felt almost presentable.

'You look better,' she said, looking him over.

'I feel better.'

'You should keep the poultice in place for another day or two. But it has probably done its work already.'

'I'm grateful.'

'No need to be.'

They shared a light breakfast, then she stood up, raising her eyebrows at him.

'Ready?'

'Ready.'

They went out to the barn, and he tacked up Horace while she saw to the pony. Why not her own horse? he wondered, if that was what the other animal was. Too conspicuous? Better to ride her son's sturdy pony? There was no way of knowing for sure. He stood before her for the blindfold, and, once he had mounted, she secured his wrists as she had done before.

'I'll go ahead,' she said. 'I've attached a leading rein.'

He didn't answer. There didn't seem anything to say.

It was a far longer ride this time. Trying to work out their direction from the way the sun's rays were falling on his shoulders – not easy, with a weak winter sun – he had the distinct impression she was taking them round in circles.

Finally, she drew rein. 'This will do,' she said.

He heard her dismount and approach. His wrists untied, he reached up and took off the blindfold, wordlessly handing it to her.

Then he looked around to see where they were.

He didn't recognise the spot.

She said, 'The road down to Tonbridge is half a mile along the track, in that direction.' She waved an arm. 'You can get your bearings there?'

'Aye.'

He looked at her, then looked away. He wanted very much to say something – something about being there to help her, whatever her trouble was, if she'd only swallow her pride and let him. Something about the importance to her of a true friend. The friend that he could be.

But her chin was in the air again, and instead of offering his loyalty he almost said, do it your way, then! But don't come crying to me if it all goes to the bad!

He knew she wouldn't go until he was out of sight, in case he was watching to see which direction she took. So, with the briefest of nods, he kicked Horace and set off down the track.

She called, 'Sir Josse!'

He stopped, turning round in the saddle to look at her. 'What is it?'

For a moment, her despair and her need were naked in her

face. 'I—' she began. Then, with a visible effort, violently she shook her head. 'Nothing. Farewell.'

'Farewell, lady.'

He turned back to face out along the track once more. This time, he encouraged Horace into a canter and, when once more he looked round, he had left her behind and out of sight.

Chapter Six

Helewise was feeling well again.

Three days' total bed rest had done the trick. She was a robust woman, and, as Sister Euphemia remarked, it had only been necessary for her to act sensibly and take to her bed, which had allowed Mother Nature to do the rest.

Sitting at her table once more, the truckle bed and the brazier – such signs of weakness! – removed, out of sight and out of mind, she was eagerly going through Sister Emanuel's entries in the accounts ledger.

She was, although she didn't admit it to herself, looking for mistakes.

There weren't any.

Sister Emanuel, whose usual duties revolved around the care of the elderly folk in the retired nuns' and monks' house, was an educated woman. She was – and this was another thing Helewise didn't care to admit – probably more learned than her Abbess.

Helewise came to the end of Sister Emanuel's entries. Closing the heavy ledger, she folded her hands on top of it and tried to empty her mind of the many other items clamouring for her attention.

I resent the fact that another nun has just proved herself as capable as I over this matter of keeping the accounts in a neat, legible hand, she thought, spelling it out relentlessly to herself. My pride is bruised, because she can do a task I liked to think only I could do.

This I must confess, and I must do penance. Pride is one of the Seven Deadly Sins, and particularly ill-housed in a nun.

Then I shall humbly ask Sister Emanuel if, amid her busy life, she can find the time to help me out by taking on the task of keeping the accounts ledger up to date.

That, Helewise was well aware, was going to *hurt*.

All the more reason, said her conscience firmly, to do it. When it hurts, it means it is important.

What, then, shall I do with the spare time I shall have bought for myself? she wondered. Then, as she sat there, still trying to empty her mind so as to make it receptive, she remembered a scheme she had dreamed up long ago, in the heady days when she had just been appointed Abbess of Hawkenlye and believed she could change the entire religious world single-handedly.

I shall teach my nuns to read and write.

Oh, not all of them! That would be impossible! For a start, there are too many, and secondly, many are not . . . She tried to find a way of expressing the fact that many were not bright enough for such skills without it seeming patronising or condescending (which would have added to her present weight of pride). Many are possessed of talents that do not suit them to the acquiring of literacy, such as skill with plants or animals, the ability to sew beautiful embroidery, a tender and patient hand with the sick.

Was that all right? she asked the Lord timidly.

She found herself suddenly feeling much happier. As if she had been . . . lifted. Taking this as a sign of the Almighty's approval, she got up and went in search of Sister Emanuel.

When the company of Hawkenlye Abbey was leaving the Abbey church after Nones, there was a sudden commotion at the gate. Helewise hurried across to join Brother Saul, Sister Martha and Sister Ursel: Sister Martha was holding the reins of a large, heavy horse, soothing him and gently stroking his nose; Brother Saul and Sister Ursel were bending over the figure who had just slid off the horse's back.

'It's Sir Josse!' Sister Ursel said, which Helewise had just seen for herself. 'He reached out to push at the gate, fell off his horse, and had landed on the ground before I could rush out to aid him!'

'He's barely conscious,' Saul said. He was sitting on the hard earth, with Josse's head cradled in his lap. 'He's been hurt – there's a bandage round his head.'

'Sister Martha, would you please take Sir Josse's horse into the stables and see to him?'

'Of course, Abbess.' Sister Martha led Horace away.

'Brother Saul, can we, do you think, help Sir Josse between us to the infirmary, or should I summon help?'

'I can walk!' Josse said from the ground.

'Come, then, Sir Josse,' Saul said, helping him up, 'the Abbess here and I will support you.'

Helewise went round to Josse's other side, and they half dragged him the short distance across to the infirmary, where Sister Euphemia, assessing her latest patient with a practised eye, put a hand to his forehead, nodded and said, 'No fever. Put him in the little cubicle at the end, please. No need to make him lie with my fever patients.'

Helewise and Saul did as they were ordered. Then Sister Euphemia shooed them out. 'My nuns and I can manage now, thank you,' she said firmly.

And Helewise, longing to ask Josse a dozen questions, had to nod meekly and leave.

Sister Euphemia came to report to her soon afterwards.

'A bad blow on the head,' she said, 'which, according to Sir Josse, happened three nights ago. He's confused, though, and he may not really know for sure. Says he was following someone through the woods, and was struck from behind. That he was, indeed. He was cared for, so he says, by some woman.' Euphemia gave a sniff. 'Put a poultice on his head, she did.' Another sniff, as if Euphemia had trouble with the concept of anyone but herself having sufficient wits and knowledge to apply a poultice properly.

'And did her nursing have any effect?' Helewise made sure to keep her tone neutral.

'Aye,' Euphemia admitted grudgingly. 'He's on the mend. Leastways, his wounds are. But I reckon he's still suffering from concussion. He's complaining of dizziness – which was how come he fell off his horse, and that wasn't the first time, either, when he came a cropper outside our gates. He says he's been on the road since first light, only he fell off earlier, and must have lain senseless for some time before he came to again.'

'Oh, dear,' Helewise said, frowning in anxiety. 'This sounds serious.'

'Don't you fret now, Abbess dear,' Euphemia reassured her. 'He's a tough one, is Sir Josse. It'll take more than a bash on the head and a couple of tumbles off his horse to keep *that* one down!'

'I pray you are right.' Helewise hesitated. 'May I visit him, Sister? I must admit, I'm longing to talk to him. Or would it be better to let him rest?'

'I think he'd rest better if he talked to you first,' Euphemia said. 'He's fretting, see.' She gave Helewise a speculative look. 'Seems there's something he wants to tell you.'

Josse looked, Helewise thought, stepping into the curtained-off cubicle where Euphemia had put him, pretty dreadful. She opened her mouth to say something bracing, but he got in first.

'Don't even try,' he said wearily. 'I'm quite sure I look as bad as I feel.'

She folded her hands in her sleeves and said, 'Sister Euphemia says you wanted to speak to me.'

'Aye.' His voice dropping, he said, 'Can we be overheard?'

She glanced out through the hangings. 'No.'

He beckoned her closer. 'Only it's a secret. I gave my word I wouldn't tell, but I've stumbled into a right clutch of adders,' he said softly. 'On the trail of little Tilly's handsome stranger, I saw a man in Tonbridge Castle who wasn't there, and, when I tried to trail him, he ended up following *me*. Then, when he surprised me, he hit me hard enough to half kill me.' Leaning forward so that he spoke almost into Helewise's ear, he whispered, 'I was saved by a child with incredibly blue eyes, whose mother is plainly so desperate to keep her whereabouts a secret that I felt obliged to leave her before I should have done.' Sinking back, he said, 'And here I am.'

Helewise, trying and failing to make sense of what he had just told her, wondered if he were still fuddled. 'A man who wasn't there?' she asked softly. 'What does that mean?'

'I was *told* nobody was at home,' Josse said irritably. 'In the castle. At Tonbridge. The Clares have gone to some other residence of theirs, to escape the sickness down in the valley. Their man told me nobody was at home, but I saw him. The man. Then I waited, and, when he sneaked out at dusk, I followed him.'

'Ah, I see.' Helewise nodded. 'Was he the man from the inn?'

'I don't know.' Josse frowned, the movement of his brows bringing his fresh white bandage down low over his eyes. 'Every instinct tells me he was, but I have no grounds whatsoever for saying so.'

'Assuming he was,' Helewise said tentatively, 'why should he attack you? Because he knows you're investigating the death at the inn, and he's afraid you'll find out something he doesn't want you to?'

Josse said tiredly, 'Abbess, we don't even know that the man at the inn is involved in the death! In fact, since he himself seems to have been the intended victim, then he's surely the last person we should suspect. A man's hardly going to poison himself, now, is he?'

'No, no.' It was her turn to frown. After a moment's thought, she said, 'Sir Josse, what about this? Somebody else knew why he had come to Tonbridge. They tried to stop him – with the poisoned pie – but the wrong man died. Now this stranger is pursuing whatever brought him here, and *that's* why he attacked you. Because he must keep his purpose here a secret. Which surely points to its being something suspicious? Something, can we propose, to do with your mysterious woman hiding in the woods?'

'You reason well, Abbess.' He gave her a weak grin. 'As ever. But no!' he said suddenly. 'What of our earlier conclusion, that he can't have been here for any evil purpose because, if he had been, why advertise his presence by spending the evening at the inn?'

'Oh.' Helewise felt deflated. But then she said, 'Unless he *had* to go to the inn!'

'Why?'

'I don't know . . . to meet someone? To seek information?'

'Hm.' Josse closed his eyes, and, in repose, Helewise saw the lines of pain and fatigue in his face.

'You need to sleep,' she said, moving away from his bed. 'Let me worry over this puzzle for a while, Sir Josse.'

He opened his eyes again. 'I wish you joy of it,' he murmured. Then, making a visible effort, he added gallantly, 'I can think of nobody more likely to come up with an answer.'

His faith in her was, she had to admit as she prepared for bed that night, generous but ill-founded.

The trouble was, there was so much that they had to assume.

That Tilly's stranger and the man who attacked Josse were one and the same, for one thing. That the man had been searching for the mysterious woman, for another. Oh, dear, this was getting them nowhere!

She lay down, wondering if there were any chance at all of quieting her mind to enable her to sleep.

Poisoned pie. An attack in the woods, a child with blue eyes, a poultice that managed to win Sister Euphemia's vote of approval.

Something was stirring on the very edge of Helewise's mind. Mentally, she ran towards it, only to have it recede.

Go to sleep, she ordered herself. There's nothing more to be done tonight.

*   *   *

She went to see Josse in the morning, after Tierce. He looked better, but was very drowsy. Helewise was quite relieved when Sister Euphemia asked her not to stay with him long. She had nothing to tell him, and didn't want to admit it.

Back in her room, she was surprised a little later by Sister Ursel announcing a visitor.

'A man, Abbess, well-dressed, well-set up, like.'

'I see, Sister. And his name?'

'He says he's Denys de Courtenay, Abbess. Means not a jot to me.'

Nor to me, Helewise thought. 'Did he say what he wanted?'

'He did not. A private matter, for your Abbot, he said. Course, I put him right on *that*, soon as you like!'

'You'd better show him in, Sister Ursel.'

A stranger, Helewise thought as Sister Ursel went to fetch the visitor. Anybody familiar with the area would know that Hawkenlye Abbey was headed by an Abbess . . .

Sister Ursel opened the door, announced, 'Denys de Courtenay,' then, with a brief nod to the Abbess, departed.

The man stood just inside the door. Helewise looked at him, briefly taking in his details. Quite tall, with dark, shiny hair, worn a little longer than was the fashion. Dark eyes, with a particularly watchful look. Handsome face, wearing a wide smile. Clothes well-made, the colours chosen carefully to blend together pleasingly; dark red hose, tunic of a slightly lighter shade.

A man, Helewise thought, who was aware of his impact on others and who enhanced it to the utmost of his ability.

A man whom she mistrusted on sight.

'Come in and be seated,' she said, indicating the wooden stool she kept for guests.

'So kind, Abbess – er – Helewise.' The smile stretched still wider, revealing white, even teeth. 'Good of you to see me. I am most grateful.'

'Is there any reason why I shouldn't?' she asked, making herself return his smile.

He laughed. 'No, no, of course not!' He lowered himself on

to the stool. 'I meant only that you must be busy and I am intruding on your time.'

'We are here to help those who ask it of us,' she said.

'I *do* ask your help,' he said, his voice urgent suddenly. 'For your prayers and your help. In a delicate matter, indeed, a family matter, one which has brought me here in wretched anxiety, eager to offer my support and my comfort, only—' He smiled at her again. 'But, no. I must begin at the beginning.'

'It would be best,' she agreed. I must keep an open mind! she told herself firmly. But, fighting as she was with the instinct that told her she was witnessing a very clever, calculated piece of play-acting, she knew it wasn't going to be easy. 'Pray, begin.'

He sat in silence for a moment, eyes raised towards the ceiling, hands pressed together, for all the world as if he sought heavenly guidance. Then, bringing his gaze to rest on Helewise, he said, 'Abbess, I have a niece, by name Joanna. She is lost, and I fear for her very life.' He leaned forward, as if increased closeness could convince her of his sincerity. 'Both her parents are dead and her elder brother died in infancy, the year after she was born. She is alone, Abbess, and this is not a fit world for a girl alone!'

'How old is she?'

He gave a short, indulgent laugh. 'I say a girl, for indeed that is how I think of her, the dear child. But, let me see . . .' He made a pretence of calculating, counting on his fingers. 'She would be twenty-four years old now! In faith, I can scarce believe it!' He laughed again. 'How they do grow, Abbess!'

'Quite,' Helewise said. 'How does she come to be lost, sir?'

'Ah, Abbess, a terrible tale! She was wed, to an older man, yes, but a fine one. He cared for her, cherished her, showered gifts and trinkets on her, and made her lady of his estates. But tragedy struck, for he was out hunting when he was thrown from his horse and killed! Dead before they got him back to his own hall, God rest his soul.'

'Amen,' said the Abbess. 'How shocking it must have been for your niece, to lose a husband in such circumstances. When did this happen?'

'A much-loved husband,' Denys said, ignoring her question.

'*Much* loved, despite the difference in their ages.' He seemed, Helewise noticed, strangely insistent on the point. 'Yes, a shock indeed. And, Abbess, I hate to say this, but the horror of it unhinged my niece.'

'Unhinged her?'

'Yes.' He gave a dramatic sigh. 'Before his family could step in and take care of her, she had run away! Can you believe it, Abbess Helewise? She packed up a few belongings, crept out at dead of night and was gone! Lost!'

'A worrying business,' Helewise said. 'And presumably you have reason to believe she may have come here? To Tonbridge, you think?'

He edged the stool even closer. 'I believe it may be a possibility, yes. I – she—' For the first time he hesitated. Then, as if he realised he had no option but to respond to what was, after all, a perfectly reasonable question, he confided, 'She has a friend hereabouts. A woman. I'm not sure where she lives, but I do recall hearing Joanna speak of her.'

'And you think this woman may be caring for your niece?'

'It's the only thing I can think of!' Denys de Courtenay flung his hands up in an expansive gesture. 'No family of her own, as I said, save myself! And, for reasons which I cannot even begin to guess, she wished to distance herself from her late husband's kin.'

She also wished to distance herself from you, Helewise thought. Or so it appears. 'She did not try to contact you?' she asked.

'She –' The smile spread out across the handsome face, white teeth gleaming in the smooth, olive skin. 'Abbess, she had no way of knowing I was at present in England.' Leaning confidingly towards her again, he whispered, 'She knows me to be a King's man.' He nodded as if in confirmation of his words. 'Joanna, I am certain, would have believed me to be in Outremer. With the King.'

He obviously expected her to be impressed, so she said, 'Indeed! With King Richard!'

He looked smug. 'I have enjoyed the great privilege of being permitted to be of use to His Majesty in the past, I have to own.

He knows he can depend on me, when he needs a good man in a fight.' He examined the long fingernails of one hand.

'But not this particular fight,' Helewise said softly. 'This supreme fight in which King Richard is now engaged, to regain the Holy Places.'

Denys de Courtenay raised his head and glared at her. The unctuous charm had quite vanished, and, for a split second, she saw something feral, something infinitely sinister and cunning, in his dark eyes.

He recovered as swiftly. So swiftly that she could almost have thought she had been mistaken.

Almost.

'Abbess, Abbess,' he smiled, 'what can you know of the world of fighting men?' Quite a lot, she could have answered. 'I see I must enlighten you!'

'Please, don't trouble yourself,' she said quickly. 'My ignorance must remain, for there are weightier matters for our attention. You were speaking of your niece's friend, the woman with whom she may be lodging.'

'Yes, yes, so I was.'

'What is the woman's name?'

Again, there was that strange reluctance to divulge details. Instead of answering Helewise's question, Denys said, 'I suppose it is too vain a hope to ask if she has been here? Joanna, that is?'

'Here?' After her initial surprise, suddenly Helewise was quite sure this was what de Courtenay had been leading up to. The simple question: have you seen her? Then why all the rigmarole? Why all the acting? 'Has she been to the Abbey, do you mean? Or to the Holy Shrine down in the Vale?'

She thought it was the first he had heard of any Holy Shrine. 'Oh – here, I meant. Seeking food or shelter, perhaps . . .?'

'I recall nobody named Joanna among our recent visitors,' Helewise said. 'More importantly, for she could easily have used a different name, I recall no young noblewoman. Our visitors, sir, tend more usually to be the poor and the sick.'

'Of course, of course,' he said smoothly.

'What name does she go by?' Helewise asked. 'I ask in order

that I may enquire of my nuns, monks and lay brothers, those, that is, who have dealings with the outside world.'

He had got to his feet, and she thought for a moment he wasn't going to answer. His expression was stern, distracted, almost . . .

Then, replacing the seriousness with another smile, he said, 'Her name? Did I not tell you?'

'No,' Helewise said. 'You only said she was called Joanna.'

'She was born Joanna de Courtenay,' he said, 'the daughter of one Robert de Courtenay.'

'Your brother.' So must the woman's father have been, for Denys de Courtenay to be her uncle.

'No, Robert de Courtenay's father and my father were brothers.' Denys laughed lightly, as if indulging a perfectly natural mistake.

'Then,' Helewise persevered pedantically 'I believe that makes you and Joanna second cousins, or in fact first cousins with one degree of removal. But not uncle and niece.'

'Does it indeed?' He laughed again. 'I never was very good at the complicated network of kin relationships. Not that it matters the smallest bit!'

'Only if you wished to marry her,' Helewise observed. 'Second cousins have been known to be wed, given the proper dispensation, whereas uncle and niece cannot, such unions being commonly regarded as incestuous.'

There was an instant's icy silence in the room. Then Denys de Courtenay swept his cloak across his shoulder, bowed to Helewise and said, 'Ah, well. There it is. Now, I fear, Abbess Helewise, that I have wasted your time.'

'But what of your niece's friend?' Helewise said. 'Her woman friend? Surely—'

But he acted as if he hadn't heard. Bowing low, he said, 'I would ask, Abbess, that you and your nuns keep Joanna in your prayers. If it please God, I pray that she and I may soon be reunited.' His eyes on Helewise's, he went on, 'You *will* tell me if you hear word of her, won't you? Or if, by God's grace, she comes here?'

Helewise didn't want to undertake that she would. Adopting her guest's evasive tactics, she said instead, 'And how will we find you to tell you, if we do have news?'

He said, 'No need for that. *I* will find *you*.'

And just why, Helewise wondered, does that sound so ominously like a threat?

'Now,' de Courtenay was saying, 'I have, as I said, taken up far too much of your precious time, so I will take my leave.'

Bowing again, he had let himself out and closed the door behind him before Helewise could say another word.

It did not occur to her for some time that, if Joanna de Courtenay had been married, then her name must now be something other than de Courtenay.

Something else which her uncle – in fact, her cousin – had chosen not to divulge.

She went straight over to tell Josse.

He was awake, in the middle of eating what appeared to be quite a substantial meal. He was, as she had hoped, riveted by what she had to say.

'He *has* to be Tilly's handsome stranger!' he said, his mouth full of boiled hare. 'Your description and hers tally far too closely for him not to be.'

'It does seem likely,' she agreed. 'Denys de Courtenay. A King's man. Have you ever heard of him, Sir Josse?'

Josse shook his head. 'No, but that alone doesn't mean he's lying. About his royal connections, anyway. And, if he was the man I saw at Tonbridge Castle, that implies a link with the Clares and *they* certainly have court connections.'

'If, if, if,' Helewise said dismally.

'One less *if* now!' Josse reminded her.

'Probably,' she said.

'Oh, Abbess, let's be rash! It *is* the same man!'

'Very well. Which leads to the next question: is your mysterious woman in the woods the missing Joanna de Courtenay?'

'She could well be,' Josse said. 'Although her name is not de Courtenay, or, at least, her son's name isn't. It's de Lehon, and it's a French name.' He fixed Helewise with an intent look. 'Did this Denys say she'd lived in France?'

Helewise thought back. 'No. But, there again, he didn't say she *hadn't*. He was, as I said, very reluctant to tell me anything definite.'

'Strange,' Josse mused. 'And, Abbess, I'll tell you what else is strange. Your friend Denys didn't seem to know that Joanna had a son. Did he?'

'He didn't mention any child,' Helewise agreed.

There was a reflective silence. Josse finished his meal, wiped his hands, and, taking a long drink, lay back on his pillows. 'I'll tell you one thing,' he offered. 'Well, I'll tell you two.'

'Yes?'

'First, if he's the man responsible for my sore head, then it's just as well we didn't come face to face just now. I should not want blood spilled in the sacred confines of Hawkenlye Abbey.' He smiled at her, but she wasn't at all sure that he wasn't deadly serious.

'And the second thing?'

'If we're right in our guessing and it *is* Joanna whom de Courtenay is searching for, then, believe me, she doesn't want him to find her.'

Helewise saw the man again in her mind's eye. Tall, strong, oozing a charm that was far too obviously false. And, worst of all, that frightening moment when he had lowered his guard and allowed her to see him for what he really was.

She shivered. 'No,' she said. 'I believe you readily enough.' She raised her eyes to meet Josse's. 'And, having met him, truly, I can't say that I blame her.'

Death by Drowning

Chapter Seven

Josse discharged himself from Sister Euphemia's care the next morning.

'*I* don't know!' she complained, giving the wounds on the back of his head a final inspection. 'You and the Abbess Helewise, you're a right pair! You both believe the world'll come to an end if you're not around to make sure it doesn't.'

'How true,' Josse agreed. 'Of myself, in any case. I always was an arrogant fellow, Sister Euphemia.' He gave her a wink, and she blushed faintly.

'Go on with you!'

'I'm going.'

'You hurry *straight* back, now,' she said, trotting along the long, open space between the infirmary's many beds to keep up with his strides, 'the moment you start to get head pains, or dizziness, or—'

But, with an acknowledging wave of his hand, he had gone.

In the crisp morning air, the heavy frost sparkled pure, dazzling white. Horace's breath hung in clouds, like the smoke of some idling dragon.

Josse met nobody on the road down into Tonbridge. Which was no surprise: it was too cold a day to venture out of doors and go off journeying unless you really had to.

He rode straight for the castle.

He hadn't really hoped he would find his stranger there, which was just as well since he didn't. The drawbridge was now fully up and the castle looked, if it were possible, even more abandoned than it had on Josse's last visit.

A woman passed by, a bundle of kindling under one arm.

'You'll get no welcome from *them*,' she remarked, nodding in the direction of the castle. 'They're away. Gone, they have, and gone they'll stay, s'long as there's sickness in the valley.' She sniffed. 'Don't have no truck with the idea of *helping* the sick and needy, they don't.'

'Ah.' Trying to sound casual – a passer-by venturing a conversational remark – he said, 'I'm surprised they don't leave at least a small staff, though. After all, there must be caretaking duties and there's security to think of . . .' He trailed off, hoping she would take up the opportunity of a bit of a gossip.

She did. Putting down her kindling and folding her arms, she said, 'Security? I don't imagine *that* bothers them, not with that ruddy great drawbridge pulled up. I mean, who's going to try to climb up *there*?' She jerked her head towards the castle's formidable walls. 'And why bother, that's what I say! If them grand folks don't want to associate with the likes of us, then there's no call for us to go bothering *them*.'

An independently-minded woman, Josse reflected. 'Is there truly nobody within?'

'Oh, there's your caretakers, all right.' She sniffed again, then suddenly her face lightened into a smile of genuine humour. 'You're not thinking, mate,' she said. 'Course there's got to be *someone* inside, else how'd they raise the drawbridge?'

He grinned in response. 'Aye. You're right there.'

'There's any number of them,' she continued. 'Caretakers, like. But they ain't going to come out all the while there's food and water within. They'll see the advantages of keeping themselves apart from the sickness, same as their precious lords and masters. You mark my word, there'll be no comings and goings over that drawbridge till spring.'

'I did have a faint hope of finding an acquaintance of mine here. I heard tell he lodged with the family . . .?'

The woman shook her head. 'Unlikely. As I've already told you –' she was eyeing Josse suspiciously now, as if trying to decide if he had evil intentions or was just plain stupid – 'the family's away. If your *acquaintance* is in there, he must be a guest of the caretakers, not the Clares.' Another assessing look. 'And you'll be a better judge than me, sir, as to the likelihood of that.'

'No, no, as you say, he can't be. I must have been mistaken.' Keen to allay her curiosity – he didn't like the idea of her passing on details of her meeting with a man nosing around outside the castle and asking daft questions – he said, 'I'm for the tavern. A mug of ale and a spell of warming my toes by Goody Anne's fire sounds just the thing for me. I wish you good day.' He bowed, swung up on to Horace, and set off down the track towards the river.

When he risked a glance behind him, the woman had picked up her bundle and was striding away.

The inn was bustling. There seemed to be as many people milling around in the yard as within, Josse thought as he pushed his way inside. And there was a deal of animated chattering going on, too.

Goody Anne was in the tap room, sleeves rolled up to display her well-muscled forearms, handing out jugs of ale to a band of men.

'How goes it, Mistress Anne?' Josse asked when, catching sight of him, she nodded a greeting.

'Rushed off my feet, as ever.' She gave him a friendly grin. 'Thanks to you, sir, people haven't been scared off.' She winked. 'If you get my meaning.'

He did. Standing beside her now, he said softly, 'Glad to have been of service.'

'Any news as to who did for poor old Peter Ely?'

'No.'

'And now there's this new business. I really don't—' A voice demanded service, followed by a chorus of others, and, interrupting herself, Anne said, 'You'll have to excuse me, sir, I'm that busy.'

'Of course.'

He took his ale and went to lean against the wall. What new business? Tuning in to conversations around him, he tried to find out.

It didn't take long.

'. . . seems she'd been there for days!' a man beside him said in an awed voice. 'Well, ain't no surprise, right out there in the wilds.'

'Aye, you're right there,' agreed another, and his two companions nodded sagely. 'Reckon she'd her own reasons for keeping herself apart, an' all.'

A cold hand took hold of Josse's heart. He said to the man nearest to him, 'What's happened? Who are you talking about?'

The man, fortunately, was too fascinated by the tale to worry about why a stranger should be so eager to know. 'Why, they've found a body, in the woods. Dead, she is, found with her head in a foot of water.'

'Who was she? Does anybody know?' Josse looked wildly from face to face. 'Come on, one of you must know *something*!'

'Steady on, there, sir!' one of the men protested. 'No need to get agitated, like!'

'It were that old biddy as does the spells,' another man said, putting a hand up to his mouth and whispering from behind it. 'Can't say as I know her name.'

'Nor I,' said another.

But Josse wasn't listening. Grasping the shoulder of the man who had first volunteered information, he said urgently, 'Old. You said she was old. Can you be sure?'

'Aye, aye, sir!' The man gave an uneasy laugh. 'She were old, all right. Not only my mam but my grand-mam an' all used to speak of her and her potions.'

A huge relief was sweeping through Josse, so that, inappropriate though it was, he felt like cheering. Instead, he offered to fill each of the men's mugs, then, having been given directions for how he might find the scene of the drowning – the information was pretty vague, but better than nothing – he was on his way.

He would not have found the pond so readily had it not been surrounded by a large group of the Sheriff's men. Might not, even, have found it at all, for it was in a secluded spot deep in the forest, and it was the sound of loud voices that had drawn him to it.

He stood on the edge of the small clearing, surveying the scene.

The pond was about five paces by ten and along its far bank was a row of willows, now quite bare of leaves. On the near bank was a vegetable patch, showing evidence of regular and diligent care. Behind the vegetable patch was a little hut made of a sturdy framework of posts filled in with wattle and daub. The roof – made of reed thatch – looked well-maintained.

On the far side of the hut, in a place where, Josse judged, it had been put so as to catch what sunshine made its way into the clearing, was a herb garden.

The body lay half on its side, with its legs and lower torso on the bank. Its head, shoulders, arms and chest were in the pond.

Josse moved forward and approached Sheriff Pelham, whom he assumed to be in charge.

'Good day to you, Sheriff,' he called, still sitting astride his horse. 'I heard tell of this death while I was at the inn, and came to—'

'Came to poke your nose in, as usual. *King's* man,' the Sheriff finished. 'Well, I don't reckon there's much to interest you here. She slipped, it seems, fell with her head under the water and she drowned.'

Josse dismounted, tethered Horace to a stout branch, and went to the pond's edge. Crouching down, he realised straight away why nobody had yet removed the dead woman from the pond.

The water had frozen hard around her.

He said to the Sheriff, 'Does anything strike you about her, Sheriff Pelham?'

The Sheriff glanced around at a few of his men to make sure they were listening. 'She's dead,' he said, with an unpleasant laugh. 'Or didn't you notice?' He was rewarded with a few guffaws. 'People do die, with their heads stuck in ponds. They drown, like.'

Josse said, 'People drown in water. This pond is covered in a thick layer of ice, and has been, I would guess, for –' he paused, calculating, 'for the last three days, I'd say.' Yes. That was right. It had been milder, the night he'd slept in Ninian's camp. Then, the next night, the temperature had gone down sharply and Joanna's pity had led her to take that great risk of bringing a strange man into the shelter of her secret hiding-place.

The Sheriff said aggressively, 'So? What of it?'

Josse suppressed a sigh. 'Then this woman must have been lying here for three days. At least.'

'How can you be sure?' demanded the Sheriff.

'Because she must have gone in when the pond was water,' Josse said patiently. 'Which was either three days ago, when the weather relented a little, or some time before that.' He glanced down at the body. 'I would doubt, however, that she has been here long.'

'Got a scrying glass, have you?' the Sheriff asked nastily, raising a few more guffaws, although Josse doubted very much if many of the men knew what a scrying glass was; he was quite surprised that the Sheriff did.

'No. I don't need one,' he replied. He pointed to the corpse's abdomen, touching it gently. 'There's no bloating, whereas, if she'd been here much longer than three days, she would have begun to swell up.' He had observed such things in battlefield corpses. It was one reason for burying your dead quickly; corpses became progressively more unpleasant to deal with if you delayed.

'Got any bright ideas as to how we're going to get her out, have you?' Sheriff Pelham asked caustically; he was, Josse noticed, getting more irascible the more his weaknesses were exposed. But it was so difficult *not* to expose them . . .

Josse had drawn his sword and, using the point of the hilt as a mallet, was gently cracking the ice around the corpse's head and shoulders, making attractive star patterns on the smooth surface. 'I think,' he said, 'we might be able to release her fairly easily. The pond's not frozen solid, it's only the first few inches.'

Observing what he was doing, one or two of the brighter men came to help. Soon, the ice around the upper part of the corpse was shattered into a hundred fragments and Josse and his two assistants were able to extract the old woman from her frozen tomb.

Her face, Josse noticed as he turned her over on to her back, was badly bruised . . .

'She must have banged her face on the ice,' Sheriff Pelham observed, leaning over Josse's shoulder and breathing open-mouthed into his ear.

'Think again,' Josse said. 'If she fell when the pond was iced over, she wouldn't have been down there beneath the surface, frozen into it.'

Momentarily, the Sheriff was silenced.

Rapidly Josse inspected the rest of the corpse. As well as the bruised face – the nose had taken a direct hit, and, as he gently probed inside the mouth, he saw what looked like a recently-broken tooth – she had damage to both hands.

Josse held the dead hands in his.

Pity surging through him, he realised that someone had deliberately broken two fingers on each of the dead woman's hands.

He laid her head down again and, on the sloping bank, she rolled over until she was lying face-down.

And Josse saw, on the back of the carefully-laundered white cap, a clear boot print.

Someone had savagely beaten her, then dragged her to the pond and held her head under the water with a foot until she died.

Why the beating? To what purpose had somebody tortured her like that?

Why, he answered himself, were people usually tortured in this wicked world? To make them tell you something that they knew and you didn't. Something that you badly wanted to know.

Oh, God, Josse thought.

'When you've quite finished,' the Sheriff said from just behind him, 'we'd better see about taking this here into town for disposal.'

Disposal.

'You've got a murder on your hands,' Josse said softly. 'Didn't you realise?'

'Murder my arse!' The Sheriff spat on to the frosty grass. 'She went to get water, slipped, bashed her head and fell in the water.' He put his face up close to Josse's and added with quiet intensity, 'That's what I say. And what I say goes.'

Unfortunately, as Josse well knew, it did.

He said, 'Aren't you even going to determine who she was?'

The Sheriff, grinning, raised his eyebrows at one of his men. 'No need for that. Hugh?'

The man, stepping forward, said, 'She were Mag Hobson. She were my mam's aunt.'

With nothing further to add, Josse watched as a hurdle was brought up, and, with a scant amount of respect which he felt was only employed because he happened to be watching, the men got the body on to it and began the long walk back to Tonbridge.

Leading Horace, Josse fell into step beside the man called Hugh.

'Did you know her yourself?' he said quietly; no need for the Sheriff to know he was asking questions.

'Old Mag? No, can't say as I did.'

'But your mother did, presumably.' The man didn't answer. 'Did she visit her aunt? Your mother, I mean.'

'Might have done.'

Josse wondered why the man was being so wary. Then, thinking back to what he had already been told – and to that neat herb garden – he said, 'She was a wise woman. Wasn't she?'

Hugh shot him a swift look. He muttered, 'Aye.'

'That's why she lived out here all alone,' Josse went on, thinking out loud. 'Why people preferred to keep her at arm's length.'

'She were good,' Hugh supplied, as if belatedly prompted to defend his dead relative's reputation. 'Fixed things for lots of folk, though they didn't like to say so. Me, I preferred to keep right out of it.'

Superstition, Josse thought. No, folks wouldn't want it widely known that they had consulted a wise woman. You never knew, and it was best to be on the safe side where meddling in that sort of thing was concerned.

'I understand,' Josse said. 'And many people wouldn't want it known that their mother's aunt was a wise woman.'

Hugh seemed to be battling with some inner conflict. 'Makes me angry,' he finally admitted. 'They jeer at her and say she's an old witch, but who is it they go running to after nightfall when they want a love potion or a wart charm? Ain't right.'

'It's not,' Josse agreed. 'But it's human nature, I'm afraid, Hugh.'

'She learned her craft young, they do say,' Hugh volunteered. As if, having admitted to the fact of his mother's aunt's oddness, there was no further barrier to discussing her, he went on, 'When she were still at the big house, she were trained by an older woman, her what did the heavy washing. That's the way of it, that an older one passes on the secrets to a young 'un. Or so they do say.'

'Aye, so I've heard,' Josse agreed. 'At the big house, you say? What, she lived in a house of her own?' It didn't seem very likely.

'No, bless you!' Hugh gave a faint laugh. 'She were housekeeper. Well, that's a deal too grand, it were only a small household. But she were their main indoor servant, that's for sure.'

'Whose?'

Hugh's face creased into a frown of concentration. 'I don't know as I ever knew their name,' he admitted. 'They was old, an

87

old man and an old woman. They lived alone, mostly, only they sometimes had folks visiting. Kin, I reckon. I know that for a fact because she – Mag – would get my mam in to help her with the cooking and that, when the visitors came.'

'I see.' Barely daring to ask the question, Josse said, 'And you don't know if they're still there? The old couple?'

'Lord, no, they'm dead.' A reflective pause. 'House'd be empty now, I reckon. Mag, she used to keep an eye on the place. Never could fathom why – maybe in case some long-lost relation came back to claim it one day. Or maybe because Mag weren't a woman to let any place go to rack and ruin, not if she could help it.' He sighed.

They walked in silence for some time. Josse, digesting what he had just been told and thinking furiously, was beginning to draw some tentative conclusions when Hugh said, 'Do you reckon it were how the Sheriff says? An accident, like?'

And Josse said, 'No, Hugh. I'm quite certain it wasn't.'

'Will you see her right?' It was a whisper that Josse barely heard.

But he recognised the question for what it was. It was a man's conscience speaking, a man who, stirred to pity by the brutal death of a relative – admittedly a distant one whom he usually preferred to forget about – wanted justice to be done.

'Yes, Hugh,' Josse whispered back. 'I promise that, if it's in my power, I will.'

Chapter Eight

'. . . and I can't help but think that it was Mag Hobson whom Joanna de Courtenay – Joanna de Lehon – came here to find,' Josse concluded, having detailed his theory to Abbess Helewise for the last half hour.

'She being the woman friend of whom Denys de Courtenay spoke? But –' Helewise had her doubts, although, at first, she could not put a finger on them.

'But?'

She thought back to that interview with de Courtenay. What had he said about the woman Joanna might be seeking? Precious little, now she came to think about it. *She has a friend hereabouts. A woman. I'm not sure where she lives.*

Was there anything in those few words to imply the woman must be a noblewoman, someone from the same station of life as Joanna de Courtenay? No. There wasn't. The description could equally well apply to a wise woman living out in the forest, although quite how Joanna would have come to know such a person was less easy to fathom . . .

Josse, she realised, was waiting. 'There isn't a but. You are right, Sir Josse. Poor Mag Hobson could well be Joanna's friend.'

'The Sheriff's man, Hugh, told me Mag used to work for an elderly couple in some modest manor house,' Josse said eagerly, 'so it seems to me that—'

'That they – the old people – were kin to Joanna, and that she met Mag, who was their servant, while staying with them.

Yes, yes, it does appear to fit. Yet why did de Courtenay not mention the old couple?'

'Hm.' Josse's heavy brows descended into a scowl. 'Her mother's kin, do you think? Distantly related, so that de Courtenay has never come to hear of their existence?'

'No, no,' Helewise protested, 'he knows – or so we presume – of her connection with Mag Hobson. Surely he must also be aware of how she came to know her.' A thought occurred to her. 'Sir Josse, what do you think of this?' She paused, putting her thoughts in order.

Yes.

'It is significant,' she said carefully, 'that, during my interview with Denys de Courtenay, he did his best not to reveal anything he could avoid telling me. For instance, he made only the briefest mention of Joanna's woman friend, revealing neither her name and her whereabouts, nor her occupation. Looking back, it seems to me that he only mentioned a friend in the area at all as a reason for his looking for Joanna around here.'

'Ye-es,' Josse said slowly.

Helewise leaned forward eagerly. 'Don't you see? He didn't mention the elderly couple because he didn't need to! Having told me about the woman friend, that was enough! So the fact that he didn't mention the old people doesn't for one moment mean he didn't know *about* them, even though his knowledge did not extend to the details of where they lived!' She sat back, elated.

'You reason well, Abbess Helewise,' Josse said.

'Ah, but I do have the advantage of having spoken to Denys de Courtenay face to face,' Helewise said modestly. 'Not that it is an experience I would commend to you.'

'No, indeed.' The deep frown had descended again. 'Especially now that we know what he's capable of.'

Helewise felt a chill creeping over her flesh. 'You really believe it was he who attacked and murdered that poor old woman?'

'I do.'

'But, Sir Josse, should we be accusing him, even in the privacy of this room, before he has had a chance to speak up for himself? For us to accuse, judge and condemn is surely going too far!'

'Abbess, think it through!' Josse protested. 'De Courtenay learns that his niece has fled her marital home, has come over the Channel to England, where, instead of seeking out her sole male relative and putting herself under his protection, she heads off into the wilderness of the great forest to try to find some old wise woman she once knew, when she used to stay with her mother's family. In a house whose whereabouts de Courtnay doesn't know. Now doesn't that alone make you suspect that de Courtenay had something planned for Joanna that she knew she wouldn't like?'

'Not necessarily!' Helewise protested.

'Well, at least would you agree that it suggests Joanna had very good reason to dislike her uncle?'

'He's not her uncle, he's her second cousin. Well, actually, she is his cousin's child.'

'He's *what?*'

'Her second cousin. De Courtenay explained that he and her father were cousins, so she and Denys are cousins distanced by a degree.'

'Don't you see the relevance of that?' Josse demanded. 'Abbess, I do wish you'd told me this before!'

'I thought I had,' she said feebly. 'And, yes, of course I see the relevance. It means—'

'It surely means that, having acquired his dispensation, he can marry her!' Josse exploded. 'Great God above, Abbess, isn't that motive enough for a man to torture an old woman for information, and kill her when she won't oblige?'

'You mean, if Joanna were an heiress, or something?'

Josse muttered something under his breath; he seemed to be appealing for divine patience. '*Yes*, Abbess dear, I do mean if she were an heiress or something.' He shook his head, grinning at her. 'I suppose I must make allowances,' he said kindly, 'you have, after all, recently been sick.'

'I am perfectly well now, thank you very much!' she said, stung. 'And there is nothing whatsoever wrong with my reasoning powers. It is only your own imagination that makes Joanna a rich heiress. There is nothing to prove it!'

Josse looked downcast. 'Aye, I hate to admit it but you're right.' He sighed. 'The woman I met certainly shows no evidence of wealth. The house was pretty comfortless and Joanna herself was dressed more like a peasant than a noblewoman. But that could be to disguise herself!'

Helewise laughed. 'You never give up, do you?'

'No,' he said, getting to his feet.

'Where are you going?'

He stared down at her. 'Abbess, we're forgetting about the first murder. Somebody put poison in the pie meant for Denys de Courtenay and that somebody must have been inconspicuous enough to slip into Goody Anne's tap room, hear de Courtenay give his order, then somehow get to the pie before the serving girl did and lace it with poison.'

'Inconspicuous,' Helewise repeated. 'Which appears to rule out Joanna, since, even disguised as a peasant, her cousin would recognise her. Yes?'

'Aye,' Josse confirmed. Helewise noticed a slight softening of his expression as he added, 'She's a striking woman.'

'Ah.' Putting that aside to consider later, Helewise said, 'So you're thinking it must have been Mag Hobson who was the poisoner?'

'She was a wise woman,' Josse said, making for the door. 'We know that she was skilled, that people spoke highly of her.' He gave Helewise a courteous bow. 'There's an hour or two of daylight left – I'm going back to have a look in her herb garden. I know it's February and nothing much is growing above ground, and I'll probably fail miserably, but I'm going to see if I can find any sign of wolf's bane.'

Instinctively she called out, 'Be careful!'

But he had already gone.

* * *

92

He found the way back to the pond and Mag Hobson's little hut quite easily; the track had been well marked by the boots of the Sheriff's men, and here and there he saw snapped-off twigs and leafless branches where the hurdle-bearers had caught their burden against the trees.

The clearing was deserted now. Tying Horace's rein to a tree trunk, Josse looked around him. The hole in the ice which he had made to extract the corpse had already frozen over again, but now the ice stood up in sharp little peaks, like a miniature mountain range. The many muddy footprints at the pond's edge had also frozen hard.

With the body gone, the clearing felt different. Josse stood still, letting his senses absorb information. After a while, he thought: yes. That's it. It feels – *good* now. Earlier, the horror of that brutal death had overlaid the normal atmosphere of this place, but now she's been taken away, the positive mood is returning.

It felt, he thought, a nice place. The very air seemed to have a quality that promised to make a man feel well . . .

But he was not, he reminded himself firmly, there to take the air.

He strode over to the shack. The door was neatly tied shut by means of a length of twine passed through two iron eyes, one on the door, one on the door post. The Sheriff, Josse concluded, couldn't have bothered to look inside Mag's home; Sheriff Pelham wouldn't have wasted his time tying the twine into that intricate and attractive knot.

Untying it, saying a silent apology to the dead woman for his violation of her handiwork, Josse unthreaded the twine and opened the door.

The interior was as neat, tidy and clean as he had expected. There was a small hearth in the centre of the beaten earth floor, stones laid in a circle, with kindling and small logs laid ready. Over the hearth, hanging from a simple tripod, was an ancient blackened pot. Empty.

On the far wall were several wooden planks serving as shelves, each bearing a load of containers of various sizes. There were also some implements: a knife, a mortar and pestle, some small pottery bowls, a row of flasks. All appeared scrupulously clean.

There was a three-legged stool beside the hearth, and, hanging on the wall behind it, a heavy cloak.

A short ladder led to an upper platform; standing on the second rung, Josse found his eyes came level with the platform. On it were a straw-stuffed palliasse and some covers.

Making a mental note to come back and inspect the shelves if he had no luck in the herb garden, Josse went outside again, looping the twine back through its eyes and re-tying it to secure the door. His knot, he noticed, was nowhere near as elegant as Mag's.

He ignored the vegetable patch, on the grounds that even the most junior wise woman would know better than to grow her wolf's bane in with her cabbages. Squaring his shoulders – he was feeling distinctly uneasy about his quest – he walked over to the carefully-tended rectangle where Mag Hobson had culti-vated her herbs.

Some plants he recognised straight away. Evergreen ivy, juniper and the tough, spineless stems of broom. Others he was less sure about: some tiny green shoots poking out from the ground could be saffron and these woody stems, sharp-edged where the dead growth of last year's flowering had been cut back, might they be dill? He grinned to himself. They might. But, given the paucity of his herbal knowledge, they might be virtually anything.

Divisions had been made in the garden by means of low hedges of box. There was a small bed, roughly square, which was entirely hedged in; wondering if this were a method which Meg had employed to keep the most deadly plants separate, Josse went to have a closer look.

Hunching into his cloak, putting up the hood – he was rapidly becoming colder and colder – he crouched down over the sleeping ground.

The earth had recently been disturbed, that he could see. But it looked more as if someone had been planting things than digging them up. Would that be right? Would a herbalist be planting, in the middle of an icy February? He had no idea. This, he realised, was hopeless; unless he dug over the entire bed and just happened to find the radish-shaped tubers of wolf's bane – and was he going to be able to distinguish them from similar tubers, without the grave risk to himself of putting them to the tasting test? – then he might as well give up.

Wearily, he rubbed his hands over his face. It had seemed such a good idea, but—

'Don't move,' a voice said softly right in his ear. He gave a great instinctive start – he had heard nothing! no footfall, no sinuous approach – which wasn't very sensible since someone was holding a blade to his throat.

He said, equally softly, 'I won't. Not until you move that knife.'

As soon as he spoke, he felt his assailant relax.

And Joanna said, 'Sir Josse! I thought you were—' She stopped.

'Denys de Courtenay?'

She stood a pace off, eyeing him. In the dim light of the clearing, it was difficult to read her face, shaded as it was by a fold of her woollen shawl. To her credit, she didn't even try saying innocently, 'Denys who?' Instead, sheathing her knife, she remarked, 'You've met him, then.'

'Not I. But while I was being cared for by the sisters at Hawkenlye Abbey – for the after-effects of my concussion – he paid a visit to its Abbess.'

'Abbess Helewise.' She nodded. 'I have heard tell of her.'

'Do I sense approval?'

'You do. They – my informant held her in high regard. She – they only knew of the Abbess by repute, but that was enough for the formation of a good opinion.'

'Rightly founded. Abbess Helewise is a fine woman. Who, I might add, shares your opinion of Denys de Courtenay.'

'I was not aware of having ventured an opinion,' Joanna said frostily.

'You don't deny that you know him?'

She hesitated. 'No. There seems little point. He and my late father were cousins.'

'And he is searching for you,' Josse said. 'According to him, you are half out of your wits with grief, unhinged from the pain of losing your husband in a hunting accident and you—'

'I'm *what?*' She burst out laughing, a musical peal that rang through the silent glade. 'Is that the best he could do? Anxious cousin, sole strong, protective male relation, searching for grief-stricken and feeble young widow? Great heavens, I'd have thought Denys could have come up with something a little more original.'

'Neither Abbess Helewise nor I believed him,' Josse said.

'Why not?' she demanded instantly.

'Me, because I had met you. Seen your fear, observed your desperate need to hide from someone, whom I guessed to be Denys. The Abbess because, as I said, she has met *him.*'

'And she didn't take to him.' It was a statement, not a question.

Josse laughed briefly. 'You could say that.' His knees were beginning to ache from contact with the cold ground. 'May I get up?'

'Oh, yes, yes. Of course.'

They faced each other from two paces apart. He could see her face more clearly now; the dark eyes were watchful, and the slight frown suggested she was thinking hard.

Thinking that it might not be such a bad idea after all to confide in him?

He said tentatively, 'I have a great will to help you, Joanna. I believe I know more about you than you think and, if you will accept my word, I swear to you that I will protect you from—'

'I don't need protection!' she cried.

He took a step closer to her. 'No?' he shouted. 'Perhaps not, although I wouldn't back your small blade against the man who damned nearly smashed my head in, for no greater provocation than that he didn't want me following him!'

'You let him take you unawares,' she shouted back, 'as you did just now with me! I know him better, sir knight, and I take more care!'

'He will find you, Joanna!' Josse insisted. 'You know now what methods he uses – you *must* agree!'

She had gone very still. 'Methods?' she repeated, her voice a whisper.

Good God, didn't she know? 'Mag Hobson is dead,' he said gently.

'Yes, so I heard.'

'You have contact with the world, then? You speak to people, now and again?'

She shrugged that off. 'I go in for provisions sometimes. My face well covered, you'll be relieved to hear. News of Mag's death was still fresh, the last time I visited Tonbridge.'

'So fresh, I would judge, that they didn't know how she died.'

'She drowned! Slipped on the icy bank and fell into the pond!' He made no answer. 'Didn't she?'

He was reluctant to tell her. But perhaps, if he did, it would serve to persuade her of her vulnerability.

No woman, he was sure, not even Joanna, was a match for Denys de Courtenay.

'Mag was attacked,' he said neutrally. 'She was beaten, some of her fingers were broken, then her head was held down under the water till she was dead.'

Joanna's hands flew to her mouth, half muffling her cry. 'Oh, *no*! Oh, Mag, no!'

Pursuing the advantage of having breached her defences, he said, 'To make her tell him where you were, do you think? To make her reveal the whereabouts of that old manor house she took you to? Where she hid you away, so that he couldn't find you? Where she—'

'*Stop!*' she shouted. Then, her shoulders beginning to heave as her sobs took hold, she said shakily, 'Please, please, stop!'

And the gloved hands now entirely covered her face as Joanna gave herself to her grief.

It was more than he could stand. He stepped forward and took her in his arms, cradling her face against his chest, stroking the back of her head. The rough shawl fell back, and he felt her smooth hair, slipping easily beneath the leather of his gloved palm. 'I'm sorry,' he murmured, 'so sorry, Joanna. But you have to know the truth, you must be aware of the lengths he will go to in order to find you.'

She went on sobbing. He closed his arms around her, bending to kiss the top of her head. His gestures were instinctive, intended to comfort her, as he might comfort a child or a frightened animal. To let her know she wasn't entirely alone, that someone . . .

Whatever he intended, it was not what she understood. Leaning back in his arms, face turned up to his, suddenly she put her hands behind his head and, pulling him down towards her, kissed him hard full on the mouth.

With her strong, lithe body pressed against him, he began instantly to respond. His mouth opening, he eased her lips further apart with his tongue, caressing hers, feeling the violent sexual excitement flood through him. He could feel her breasts pushed up against his chest, feel her muscular legs firm against his thighs. Feel his erection, hard and full.

Breaking away, she stepped back a pace. Wiping the tears from her cheeks, she said, 'I'm sorry. I shouldn't have done that.'

Lost for words, he said the first thing that entered his head. 'Isn't that what I'm supposed to say?'

Amazingly, she chuckled. 'Not when it was so plainly I who started it.' Then, remembering, she said, 'Oh, sweet Lord. What am I to do?'

'Let me help!' he said quickly. 'Let me come with you!' She shot him a quick glance. 'Oh, Joanna, not for *that*!' He grinned. 'Remember, I offered my aid before you flung yourself into my arms.'

'You did,' she agreed.

'Well, then! Can you not trust me?'

She went on staring at him, as if her very life depended on her decision.

Which, Josse thought, perhaps it did.

'I——' she began. Then, more firmly, 'Let me think about it.'

'What is there to think about?'

'*You don't know!*' she shouted, angry suddenly. 'It's not as simple as you seem to think, sir knight! There are many things to weigh up and only I can do so.'

'Can't I help?'

'No, you can't.' Anger gone, she gave him a sudden sweet smile. 'Yes, I dare say you could in fact be *very* helpful and I can't say I'm not tempted. But I need some time on my own. To think it all through, without you going and confusing me by kissing me again.' Now the smile was wide and free, and he could see just how beautiful a woman she was.

'*Me* kissing *you?*' he murmured.

'I'm going now,' she announced, tightening the cord around her waist. 'You mustn't follow me. If you do, you'll never see me again.'

It sounded overdramatic, but he had a good idea she spoke the truth. Just how *would* he set about finding that ancient manor deep in the forest, unless she gave him a clue? 'Very well. You have my word.'

She nodded. 'Thank you. Stay here by Mag's house for a slow count of a hundred, then you may go.'

Mag's house. Belatedly he remembered why he had come. 'Joanna!'

She had turned away, but now spun round to face him again. 'Yes?'

'Who dug up the wolf's bane and smuggled it into the pie? It *was* Mag, wasn't it?'

But, her face shadowed suddenly, she didn't answer except to remark, 'You *have* been busy.' Then, running out of the clearing, she shouted, 'Start counting!'

He counted to a hundred extremely slowly. She might be counting, too – in fact, undoubtedly she would be – and he didn't want her to think he was cheating. It mattered terribly that she trust him.

When the hundred had long been reached, he untied Horace and, leading him along in the deepening gloom of approaching night, headed back towards the Abbey.

Chapter Nine

Josse spent an uneasy night. His visit to the Abbess the previous evening had been brief; he had wanted to reassure her that he was safely back, but it had been too late for long discussions.

And, somehow – he was not quite sure why – he had been reluctant to talk to Abbess Helewise while his blood still sang from the after-effects of kissing Joanna de Courtenay.

When he finally got to sleep, it was to dream that the Abbess held Joanna's knife in her strong hand and was using it to cut great branches of holly which she insisted were wolf's bane. 'It's for my wedding garland,' she kept saying . . .

It was quite a relief to wake up.

She sent for him in the morning. Now, with the residual unease from his dream to add to his disturbing memories of Joanna, he was even less comfortable in the Abbess's presence.

'What ails you, Sir Josse?' she asked, noticing his fidgeting within moments of his entering her room.

'I – er, nothing, Abbess.' He managed a smile. 'I'm just impatient to be doing something, I suppose.'

She nodded sagely. 'I quite understand,' she said. 'Having offered Joanna de Courtenay your help, and feeling that she is so close to accepting it, you must itch to be with her again.'

Oh, how I do, Josse agreed silently. And not only in the way that you, dear lady, imagine. 'Well, I do feel strongly that she is in danger all the while she is alone,' he said.

The Abbess nodded again. 'Off you go, then,' she said, with an encouraging smile.

'Where am I going?'

'To find her, of course!'

'But I undertook to give her time to think it over! Only then would she . . .' He trailed off. Only then would she come to find him? But she had no idea where he was!

Half out of the door, he heard the Abbess say, 'Good hunting, Sir Josse.'

He retraced his footsteps to the place where the track up from Tonbridge entered the forest. Then, riding very slowly, he tried to recall how far into the woods he had been when Denys de Courtenay attacked him.

It was difficult to judge. Everything looked different in the daylight. And, besides, the last time he went that way he had been concentrating on trailing his quarry without being seen — something at which he had failed abysmally — and had taken scant notice of his surroundings.

But he must find the spot. Because he had reasoned that the child Ninian could only have moved a semi-conscious, well-built adult a very short way, which meant Ninian's camp must be close to where Josse was assailed by de Courtenay.

And Ninian's camp — if he ever managed to find it — was the one slim contact he had with Joanna. Ninian might be allowed to play there again, she herself might think to look for Josse there . . .

Riding on, realising with dismay how hopeless his search was, Josse's spirits slowly sank.

What else could he do, though? Go back to Mag Hobson's house? Would *that* be where Joanna would go looking for him?

Cursing himself for not having made a more reliable plan, Josse dismounted and, leading Horace, pushed on into the woods.

Presently he found himself walking along the top of a slight rise. Something about the place seemed familiar . . . Stopping, he stood still, listening, sensing the air.

And heard, from somewhere close at hand, the sound of running water.

Yes!

The boy had clearly had a source of fresh water near at hand; he had brought Josse onion broth which he had made himself. And later, Joanna had requested hot water with which to prepare Josse's poultice.

Josse had been listening to the sound of the small bubbling stream, now he came to think of it, all the time he had lain in Ninian's camp.

He looked down into the little vale that ran along below the track. Nothing to be seen there.

Pressing on, he rounded a bend and found that the track entered a sort of passage, formed by overhanging branches. It had been difficult to negotiate it in the darkness, he remembered, and . . .

. . . And it had been just after emerging from it, he recalled in a flash of memory, that he had dismounted to feel for hoof prints!

Moving forward eagerly now, he repeated what he had done before. I bent down about *here*, he thought, and again *here*. And over *there*, unless I'm much mistaken, is where I fell. With my cheek in that very puddle, now frozen over.

So far, so good.

He stood in the place where he had lain, staring all around him. There was a gentle slope in front of him, leading down into the valley where the stream ran. The track ran on fairly straight ahead, and, behind him, the ground rose quite steeply.

The only direction in which a seven-year-old boy could possibly have dragged a large adult was down into the valley.

Tethering Horace beside the track, Josse made his way cautiously down the slope.

He had to search for some time before he found Ninian's camp, and then it was only some pieces of charred wood that gave the location away. Assuming them to be the remains of the boy's last small fire, Josse began to search the immediate area, working outwards in concentric rings.

And, finally, he found what he was looking for.

Whoever had taught the lad about woodcraft had done a good job, Josse reflected; Ninian had located his secret hiding-place half under a ledge of sandstone, and concealed the opening behind a thorn bush. Josse recalled the thorn bush, once he had seen it again, from his awkward trips outside to relieve himself. But, had you not known there *was* a camp thereabouts, and consequently persevered with the search, you would never have found it.

As the euphoria of success quickly faded, he thought, so, what now? There was nobody here – had he really thought Ninian and Joanna would be sitting there beside a cheery campfire, huddled together in the boy's smelly old sheepskin, just waiting for Josse to happen by? – and the camp gave no sign that anybody had been there recently.

I'll wait, Josse thought. If she wants to find me, surely she'll come here looking. Won't she? I'll give her until the light begins to fail. If she doesn't come today, I'll come back tomorrow. Or perhaps I'll go to Mag Hobson's house tomorrow.

Hating having to be in the position of awaiting someone else's actions while he himself was powerless to act, he settled down to his vigil.

She didn't come.

But, late in the day, Ninian did. Taking Josse completely by surprise, the boy suddenly burst out of the undergrowth that covered the sandstone ledge, jumping nimbly down and racing up to grasp hold of Josse's hand.

'You came back!' he cried joyfully. 'I'm so glad to see you! Shall we make a fire? Do you want to stay in my camp again?'

'No, Ninian, but thank you for the offer.' Josse bent down, taking both the boy's hands in his. Trying to think of a way to ask what he desperately needed to ask without alarming the child, he said, with an attempt at a casual tone, 'Er – did your mother say it was all right to come to play out here today? I mean, it's very cold and—'

'Oh, she doesn't know I'm out,' the boy replied with innocent pride. 'I waited till *she*'d gone out, you see, then I sneaked out after her.' A frown creased his smooth, high forehead. 'She says I've got to stay inside the house but I *hate* it, there's nothing to do and when she's gone out, there isn't even her to talk to. Anyway,' he glanced round him with a proprietorial air, 'I had to come to check on my camp.'

Josse said carefully, 'Do you know where your mother is, Ninian?'

'Yes, she's gone to Mag's house. She said she has to fetch something. In fact,' he was frowning again, 'she said some*one*, but I'm sure she meant some*thing* because we don't know anybody here except Mag, and Mag died.'

'I know,' Josse said gently.

The boy's bright blue eyes were fixed on him. 'I think she was very *old* and that's why she died,' he confided.

'Yes, Ninian, she was quite old,' Josse agreed.

'Much older than my mother,' Ninian said. '*And* you,' he added as an afterthought. 'Only old people die. Don't they?'

'Usually people are more likely to die when they get old, certainly,' Josse said. Poor child, he thought, what a life he's had recently. No wonder he seeks reassurance.

'My father died,' the boy was saying. '*He* was much older than you. About as old as Mag, I'd say. He fell off his horse,' he added.

Josse didn't think the child sounded particularly upset at describing his father's demise. 'That must have been awful,' he said.

'No, it wasn't awful at all.' Ninian was poking around in the entrance to his camp, tidying a stray branch of the thorn bush. 'He didn't like me and my mother much and when he was dead it meant he didn't beat us anymore. Mother said I didn't need to pretend to be sad if I wasn't really, so I'm not.'

'No reason why you should,' Josse said.

'The priest said my father was in heaven,' Ninian said in a whisper, as if afraid some representative of the church might be listening, 'but Mother and I think he's probably in hell. My mother says she hopes so, anyway.'

'And what about you?' Josse asked gently.

'Well, I don't really *want* him to be in hell,' the child replied carefully, 'although I think he's undoubtedly in purgatory. I hope he'll get to heaven in the end. In a few hundred years, perhaps, if he's good and if lots of masses and that get said.' He had finished with his branch, securing it to his satisfaction. 'There! Shall we go inside?'

'Ninian,' Josse said, thinking hard how best to phrase what he wanted to say, 'I think your mother might have gone to Mag's house to find me.'

'Really? Isn't she silly? You're here!'

'Aye, but she didn't know that.' He hesitated. 'Do you think it would be all right for you to take me to the house?'

'Mag's house?'

'No, your house. The house where you're staying, where your mother took me when it was too cold for me to stay out here in your camp.'

The boy chewed his lip. 'I don't know if I'm allowed,' he said. 'Mother made me promise not to tell anybody.'

'I understand about that,' Josse said, hating himself. 'But it's not as if I haven't been there before, is it?' He hoped Ninian didn't know about the blindfold. 'It's not as if the house's whereabouts are a secret from me.'

'Then why do you need me to take you?' the boy asked intelligently.

'Er – well, we've met up with each other now,' Josse improvised. 'Why don't we go back together?'

'She'll be cross,' Ninian said resignedly. 'I'll be sent to bed early, with bread and water for my supper.'

'I'll say it was all my fault, that I persuaded you,' Josse offered. 'I wouldn't ask, Ninian, only it's important I speak to your mother. As I say, I'm almost certain she's gone to Mag's house to look for me.'

Ninian stared at him for a long moment. What *was* it about those blue eyes? Josse wondered absently, about the boy's—

'Very well.' Ninian had made up his mind. 'My mother likes you, she said so. And *I* like you too,' he added.

'I like both of you,' Josse said. 'Wait while I fetch Horace, then we'll be off.'

'Can I ride him?' Ninian called out as Josse brought Horace down the sloping side of the little vale.

'Aye. Hold on tight, though.'

The last thing he wanted, he reflected as, with Ninian directing him, he led Horace off through the forest, was to arrive back at the secret house not only having persuaded Ninian to break his word to his mother, but with the child damaged from a fall from a large horse into the bargain.

Joanna was already back at the manor house when Josse and Ninian got there.

Having tended to Horace together, Josse and the child went on into the house, to find her pacing to and fro in front of the fire.

Ninian had predicted she would be cross. In fact, she was furious. Josse, who knew full well that her anger was born of anxiety – he didn't like to imagine what she must have felt on arriving home to find the child gone – let her rave for a while, then, with a protective arm around the boy, said mildly, 'He's safe, Joanna. Isn't that all that matters?'

Instantly she rounded on him. 'And just what do you think *you're* doing here?' she demanded. 'Nobody comes here without being blindfolded! Not even you!'

Even in her fury, there was a brief glint of something else in her eyes as she stared at him. Something that suggested she remembered their last farewell as clearly as he did. He tried to ignore the blood beginning to pound through his body; now wasn't the moment.

If there was ever going to be a moment.

'I thought you were going to let me help you!' he protested.

'Whatever made you think that?' she shouted. 'Perhaps I might have been, before this! But now that I've seen how you wormed your way in, how you've played on my son's youth to make him tell you where the house is, how you've – you've—'

He waited, but she didn't seem to be able to think of anything else. 'You're not to be trusted!' she finished.

Ninian wriggled out from beneath Josse's arm, still round his shoulders, and rushed to his mother. 'You mustn't say that!' he yelled at her, as furious as she was; he seemed, Josse reflected, to have inherited Joanna's temper. Thumping at her stomach with both fists, Ninian cried, 'I don't want to be just with *you* anymore, I want *him!*'

'Ninian, we—' Joanna began.

But Josse interrupted her. Stepping forward, he grasped Ninian firmly by the upper arms and said quietly, 'Ninian, a man *never* hits a woman.'

Ninian rounded on him, trying to break the grip of Josse's strong hands and, when that failed, attempting a sly kick in the crotch. But Josse, who had several nephews, was used to small boys. Easily evading the child's foot, he said, 'And an honest fighter doesn't do *that*, either.'

The small face was scarlet with rage, making the eyes even more blue in comparison. With a voice full of authority, Ninian said, 'Let go of me.'

After a moment, Josse did so. With unexpected dignity, Ninian straightened his tunic. Then, turning first to his mother and then to Josse, he said, 'I apologise.'

Josse bowed and said, 'Accepted.' Joanna, less easily mollified, merely sniffed.

'I expect you're going to send me to bed,' Ninian remarked.

A smile twitched at the corners of Joanna's mouth but she managed to suppress it. 'Indeed I am,' she said. 'I wish to speak privately to Sir Josse.'

Ninian sighed. 'Very well.'

Joanna took her son's hand. 'Come with me to the kitchen and we'll put a tray of supper together for you,' she said. 'You can eat it in bed.'

Ninian turned to Josse. 'I wish you good night,' he said politely.

'Good night, Ninian.'

The child paused. Glancing to see if his mother could hear – she had gone on ahead along the passage that, presumably, led to the kitchen – he said, 'I'm *still* glad I brought you, even if she's not.' And he gave Josse a beaming smile.

'I think she might be, just a little bit,' Josse said softly back. 'It's just that sometimes people have a funny way of showing that they're pleased.'

Ninian laughed happily. 'Especially ladies,' he said. 'See you tomorrow!'

Especially ladies, Josse thought as the boy's footsteps receded up the passage. Now how, he wondered, did the child know that?

It was some time before Joanna returned to the hall. Josse had made up the fire and the brilliant flames took the sombre darkness from all but the far corners of the room. Sitting on a leather-seated chair in front of the hearth, it was a luxury to feel warm.

'Sorry I was so long,' Joanna said, coming to sit on the floor by the fire; there was a loose pile of fur rugs and a few thin cushions to take the chill off the flagstones. 'I was talking to Ninian. I had to make him see that he really must *not* tell people where this house is.'

'Am I "people"?'

She glanced up at him. 'How is a child of seven to know the difference?'

'But—' Josse began. And then stopped. She had, he realised, just played right into his hands.

'Joanna,' he said instead, 'supposing it had been Denys de Courtenay who found Ninian's camp today instead of me. What do you think would have happened?'

'Ninian would never have brought *him* here!'

'Does he know who Denys is? Have they met?' She shook her head. 'And have you told the boy about Denys?'

'No! He – what Denys wants is – No.'

'And does Denys know of Ninian's existence?'

She gave him a very strange look. 'Oh, yes. Indeed he does.'

'Then, Joanna,' Josse went on relentlessly, 'just think about it. Denys knows you to be somewhere in this vicinity. He knows about Mag, he has tried and failed to make her tell him where this house is. In his hunt he comes across Ninian's camp – it would be difficult, I grant you, the boy has hidden it well. But Denys might have seen the boy on his way to or from the vale. Somebody else might have seen Ninian, and sold the information to Denys for the price of a couple of drinks.'

She was looking pale. 'I've been so careful!' she whispered.

'Of course you have! But, no matter how careful you are, you can't cover every possibility.'

'I can! I *have* done!'

'Joanna, Denys *tortured* Mag!' Josse said urgently, keeping his voice down – with difficulty – so that Ninian would not overhear. 'Supposing she had given way and told him what he wanted to know?'

'She wouldn't!' Joanna said scornfully. 'She would have given her life for us, she knows what is involved and . . .'

'She would have given her life,' Josse repeated softly. 'She *did* give it, Joanna.' He got off his chair and went to kneel in front of her. Again, her nearness prompted his body to a response but he made himself ignore it. 'And just think what might have happened if Denys had found Ninian out in the forest today. Might he not have used similar tactics to make your son tell him what he wanted to know?'

She gave a sort of gasp and her pale face went even whiter. She whispered, 'No! Oh, don't!'

'I don't say this to wound you,' he said softly. 'But you have to realise what Denys is capable of, what he might do in order to find you. And – What is it?'

For, amazingly, she had begun to smile. A very faint smile, but, without doubt, her expression had lightened. And a little colour was returning to her cheeks.

'I have let your passion persuade me,' she observed, sitting back on her heels and edging away from him slightly. The brief sparkle in her dark eyes suggested she knew very well what she was saying and had employed the words deliberately. 'Which was foolish of me, sir knight.'

'I don't understand,' he said. 'I have persuaded you? Of what?'

She twisted her legs from beneath her and, pulling out a fold of the soft fur rug and covering herself with it, folded her arms on top of her raised knees.

'Oh, I don't blame you,' she said, 'I see full well that you are telling me what you think could well happen. And, were it any other man and any other child, I would agree. I, too, would think that Denys would use Ninian as he used Mag, to get to this house.' She gave a great shudder. 'To get to me.' The dark eyes met Josse's again. 'And Denys, I assure you, would not hesitate to beat a child in order to get what he wanted.'

'I need no assurance of that,' Josse said quietly.

'No, I'm sure you don't.' She was still watching him. He met her eyes, not looking away.

'You speak in riddles,' he said. 'Just when I think I have grasped the whole story, you say something that surprises me, and I am forced to realise that I haven't yet begun to comprehend.' He leaned towards her. 'Won't you confide in me?' he asked. 'Lady, you need help, even you must admit that. And here I am offering you mine. Will you not put your trust in me?'

There was a long pause. Then she said, 'Yes. I will.'

Chapter Ten

'It is a long story,' she said, still looking up at him.

'I have nothing else to do but listen,' Josse replied.

'It – I shall have to tell you many things that I would rather not.'

'What things? There is no need to distress yourself, Joanna. No need, for my sake, to speak of matters that pain you.'

'But there *is* need,' she insisted, 'if you are to understand.' She lowered her eyes. 'The things I would prefer not to have to tell you relate to myself, sir knight. To my own past. And I am reluctant because it is to *you* that I must tell them.'

'I don't see why you—' He stopped. Yes, perhaps he did see after all. 'Oh.'

She laughed softly. 'Oh, indeed. I thought for a moment I was going to have to explain still further. I am reluctant, Josse, because of what I feel for you, because of what I sense you might feel for me. I am not proud of my past.'

'Which of us is?' he countered. 'We have all done things, lady, which we would rather forget.'

'Forget,' she murmured. 'Yes.' She seemed to go into a reverie and, from her face, he judged it was not a happy one. Then, lifting her chin and staring into the fire, she said, 'Ah, well, my decision is made. For better or worse, I have a tale to tell you, if you are prepared to hear it.'

Settling back in his chair, Josse said, 'I'm listening.'

★　　★　　★

Taking a very obviously steadying breath, she began.

'My father died just before my sixteenth birthday, in the summer of 1184. He picked up one of those wretched summer fevers – it was during a hot, sticky spell of weather and many people fell sick – and he was dead within a week. My mother took it badly. Well, I'm afraid to admit my mother took everything badly – she was never a strong woman, or so they say, and when my elder brother died in infancy, it undermined what little fortitude she once had. Father dying so unexpectedly and inconsiderately certainly did make problems for Mother, and there really wasn't anybody she could turn to. Her own family consisted of an elderly and addled aunt who never knew if it was Christmas or Midsummer Day, and my father's only sister was dead. Father's side of the de Courtenay family was very much the minor branch – his uncle Hugh was the ambitious one, and he and his wife Matilda and their four surviving adult children all moved regularly and easily in court circles.'

'One of those children being Denys de Courtenay?' Josse asked.

'Indeed.' She gave him an admiring glance. 'You *are* paying attention.'

'I'm hanging on your every word,' Josse agreed.

'Yes, Denys was my father's uncle Hugh's youngest child. Hugh and Matilda had a spread-out family – I once calculated that Matilda must have spent more than twenty years bearing children. Denys came along quite a long time after his siblings – although he was cousin to my father, he's actually only nine years older than me.'

'And so your mother went to this more worldly branch of the family for help?'

Joanna smiled. 'Oh, no. My mother wouldn't have had the courage to do that. No. It so happened that word of my father's untimely death reached court – we were, after all, related to people who moved in those circles and you know how gossip goes around.'

'Aye, I do.'

'Way back in her youth, my mother had once met the

Queen. Henry's queen, I mean, the lady Eleanor. The two of them spent some time together – although my mother would never have said so, I think she was briefly a lady-in-waiting.'

'Queen Eleanor is a fine woman,' Josse interrupted.

'You and she are acquainted?' He nodded. 'I'm impressed, sir knight. As you say, a fine woman, and one ever willing to help a friend fallen on hard times. I don't know if you will recall, but that autumn – I speak still of the year 1184, the year my father died – the King sent for Queen Eleanor, and they had a partial healing of the rift between them. Everyone said it was because Henry wanted to stop the endless squabbling and plotting among his sons and, since Queen Eleanor encouraged them in scheming against their father, then it was sensible to involve her in the peacemaking.'

'I do remember,' Josse said. 'The Queen, they do say, was overjoyed to be out and about again, after her years of confinement.'

'Do they?' Joanna smiled. 'I dare say they say right. The Queen, anyway, didn't like to think of my mother shutting herself up within her own four walls, away from the world and everything in it, so she suggested to the King that my mother's name be added to the list of summonses to be sent out for the royal Christmas festivities.'

'A rare honour,' Josse murmured.

'Indeed. And, naturally, my name went on the list, too.'

'You must have been thrilled,' Josse remarked. 'At that age, to be invited to a court Christmas.'

'I was. So much so that, when Mother began to vacillate and cry that she really couldn't face it and nobody should expect it of her, after her tragic loss, I knew I had to find a way to persuade her.' A faint smile crossed Joanna's face. 'After all, there I was with two new gowns, new slippers and a jewelled headdress, and they weren't going to get much use during a miserable Christmas spent alone with my grieving mother.'

'What did you do?'

'In fact, I didn't need to do anything. The senior de Courtenay family heard of our invitation and Denys was despatched to visit us to make absolutely sure we accepted it. I imagine that they remembered what Mother was like, and had a fair idea she might decide she wasn't up to it. They would be there, of course, but it could well reflect poorly on them if a relation did the unspeakable and rejected a royal summons.'

'You can appreciate their point,' Josse murmured.

'I know. And, at the time, I was overjoyed to have someone weigh in on my side. When I got home from a ride one afternoon and found Denys busy charming my mother, I thought he'd been sent from heaven in answer to my prayers.' Her face had gone expressionless; Josse wondered what was going through her head. 'He was sitting on a footstool before her, one of her hands in both of his, simply oozing charm. And I, fool that I was, fell for it.'

'You were only sixteen,' Josse said. 'And, I would guess, inexperienced in the ways of the world.'

'Totally,' Joanna agreed. 'Although many, if not most, young women of sixteen are at least betrothed, if not wed and running their own households, my own particular circumstances meant I was not like them. And, unworldly as I was, I thought everybody must flirt with their nieces – or their cousins, whatever we were – and I took my cue from Denys. He wasn't repellent, I'll say that for him.'

'So I understand.' Josse recalled Helewise's impression of the man. 'And, Joanna, you were of an age to be taken in by a handsome face.'

'Yes, perhaps. And he made me laugh. It was wonderful – I'd never had such fun as with Denys. He never seemed to take anything seriously. Of course, I realised later that *that* was an illusion, too. He took quite a lot of things very seriously indeed.'

'So you went to court for Christmas?' Josse prompted.

'Yes. The festive season was celebrated at Windsor that year, in the newly-rebuilt apartments. My, they were superb – I'd never seen such luxury. Gorgeous hangings, the most beautiful tapestries, and colours that I hadn't even known existed, furs all over the place to keep out the cold, and the people! Well, you probably know about court people already.'

'Not all of them,' Josse admitted.

She gave a tut of impatience. 'Yes, but you know the *sort* of people who go to court.'

'Aye.' And that, Josse thought, was precisely why he didn't attend court, unless he had to.

'Perhaps it's not always like that,' Joanna admitted, 'like it was that Christmas, I mean. I don't see how it could be, really – the country would be bankrupt if they feasted and fêted so grandly all the time.'

'You enjoyed it, then.'

'How could you not?' Joanna turned a radiant face to him. 'The brilliance of a thousand candles, huge fires, tables covered in rich cloth coloured like jewels and simply *bending* with the weight of food and drink! And, everywhere, these sophisticated, laughing, joking, beautifully-dressed people, singing, dancing, watching the entertainments, joining in – oh, Josse, I'd never experienced anything like it in my life!'

'And your mother?'

'Oh, my mother! She came nervously down to dinner the first night, sat in a corner whispering to her nearest neighbour, then retired to bed as early as she decently could. And, having set her own timid pattern the first evening, that was what she continued to do for the rest of the celebrations. My mother! Huh!'

'Wasn't that a good thing, for you? Not to have her watchful eyes on you while you were having fun?'

Joanna glanced at him. 'How perceptive,' she murmured. 'Yes, naturally. At the time, I thought it was the best thing that could happen. Especially as, with Mother out of the way, Denys stepped in, promising he'd make quite sure I wasn't – what was his word? ah, yes! – *neglected*.' She gave an abrupt, bitter laugh.

'And he kept his promise?'

'He did.' Stony-faced, she poked savagely at the fire. 'When, on the second night, the tables were cleared and the dancing began, he made sure he whirled me right round where everyone could see me. I had on the more vivid of my new dresses – it was bright blue – and Denys said I looked beautiful, good enough to eat, I seem to recall, and lovelier by far than the jaded court women. And, like a fool, I lapped it all up.'

'You would indeed have been lovelier than the rest,' Josse said softly. 'Your youth and your innocence would make sure of that. Youth and freshness soon fade, in court circles.'

'Do they so?' She cocked her head up to look at him. 'I can well imagine why. Josse, *is* it always like that? Are there always the flirtations, the intrigues, the drunkenness that leads to people pawing at each other, in full view of everybody?'

'Ah.' Josse could understand her dismay. A country girl, an innocent, must have found the goings-on at a Plantagenet Christmas a great surprise. 'It's not to be taken too seriously, you know, Joanna. People drink too much, as you say, and sometimes a dalliance goes a little too far. But usually there's no harm done.'

'Is there not?' she said softly.

'A sore head in the morning, an awkward moment when you come face to face with the man or woman to whom you promised undying love the night before, or—'

'I hope,' she said coolly, 'that you do not speak from personal experience.'

'I?' He laughed shortly. 'No, Joanna. I do not.'

She nodded. 'Thank you for that.'

'So there you were, all eyes on you as you laughed and danced with your uncle Denys, and—'

'That was why he did it, of course,' she interrupted. 'He made me dance where everyone could see me on purpose.'

'What do you mean?'

She stared at him, her dark eyes glittering with emotion. 'I might have been a prize heiffer at a market!' she cried. 'Look at her face! Her hair! Her young budding breasts – do you know, that rat Denys made me lower the line of my bodice! He told me it was the fashion to show as much flesh as possible, and, fool that I was, I believed him! Went along with him! Danced there, in King Henry's great hall, with half my chest exposed!'

'Don't be so hard on yourself, Joanna.' Josse put out a hand and briefly touched her shoulder; she was rigid with tension.

'You were young, you didn't know. Most young girls entering court life have an older woman to help them, you know. To advise on what is right and what is wrong. And all you had, poor love, was Denys.'

'Who had his own secret plan,' she agreed angrily. She took a deep, shuddering breath. 'It got later and later,' she said, speaking faster now, 'and people – couples – began to disappear. There was a lot of laughter about the King and some woman called Bellebelle – I didn't know which of the women around the King she was, there were always quite a few – and somebody said that he was missing a woman called Alais, who had long been his bed-warmer, and that this Bellebelle did as good a job as someone called Rosamund.'

'That would have been Rosamund Clifford,' Josse said, 'only she's dead now, and the other would be Alais of France. King Philip's sister.' Joanna didn't seem any the wiser. 'King Henry arranged for Richard to be betrothed to the King of France's sister,' he explained, 'but—'

'But King Henry seduced her first and then King Richard refused to marry her,' Joanna finished. 'Yes, I know about that. I remember Denys talking about it. I didn't realise that the Alais they spoke of at court was the same woman.' Her eyes widened. 'There was scant respect in the gossip about her, considering she was a princess of France.'

'Perhaps her behaviour was not of a kind to earn repect,' Josse suggested.

To his surprise, Joanna laughed. 'How very pious, Sir Josse! A princess should not allow her reputation to be tarnished, is that it?'

'Indeed it is.' Josse felt the need to defend his remark. 'If those in positions of power do not set a good, moral example, then there is little hope of ordinary folk living decent lives.'

There was a short silence. Just as he was beginning to think he had offended her, she spoke. 'You're right, of course.' She sighed. 'Perhaps you *should* attend court, Josse. They could do with your influence.'

'King Henry is dead and buried,' he reminded her gently. 'I

doubt if his son and heir carries on his father's traditions.'

'No, perhaps not.' She sighed again. 'Oh, Josse, in view of what you have just said, you make this far harder than it need have been!'

'I'm sorry. I did not intend to sit in judgement of – of anything that happened in your past.'

'No.' As if gathering herself, she paused, then went on, 'The company were retiring, as I said. I was more than a little drunk and beginning to think I'd like to lie down. It was late, and I had been dancing for hours. Denys had his arms round me – he was helping me to stand, if the truth be known – and I said, Denys, I wish to go to bed now.'

She had gone pale, Josse noticed. Reliving that night was taking a lot out of her.

'He said, go to bed you shall, young Joanna! and he took my hand and ran with me towards one of the stairs leading to the upper apartments. I said, not that way! Mother's and my rooms are the other way, down the passage and out across the court-yard! but he kept laughing, saying that my night was just beginning, and when I pleaded with him to let me go, he laughed all the more and said didn't I realise? I'd done what all girls dream of, I'd made people notice me! So I said, that was all very well, and there was tomorrow, and the next day, and countless more to enjoy, couldn't I go to my own room now? And, again, he said no.'

She drew her knees up under her chin, hugging them close. It looked, Josse thought, a touchingly defensive gesture.

'He took me along a dimly-lit corridor – I had the impression that there were a lot of people about, behind half-closed doors, and I could hear mutterings, whisperings, suppressed laughter and cries. Of course, I know *now* what was going on.' A brief, hard laugh. 'Denys tapped softly at one of the doors and somebody opened it. We went in. It was a big chamber, with a fire blazing and a few candles and, by one wall, a huge bed. It was rumpled, as if it had been slept in, with the covers half on the floor. In it was a man, well-built, strong-looking, with reddish hair going grey.'

'Did you recognise him?' Josse asked.

She shrugged. 'I didn't. By the magnificence of his bed-chamber, I thought he was some lord or other – there were so many at court that Christmas, I got confused over which was which. He was sitting propped up on pillows, and there were two other men perched on the end of the bed. Denys said, Here's my little cousin! and the man in the bed said, Ah, the Queen of the Dance! Come here, little maid. Denys pushed me forward, till I was standing right up against the bed – it didn't smell very nice, sort of fusty, as if people had sweated in it and hadn't changed the sheets – and the man in the bed reached out a hand and touched my – touched me on the top of my thighs. He said, You *are* a maid, are you not? Denys said, Aye, she is, and all the men laughed.'

Josse put out his hand and laid it on her arm. She didn't seem to notice.

'Then – then Denys started to take his clothes off, and they gave me warm wine to drink, and I began to feel even more fuddled, and the other men said, we shall *all* take off our clothes, and the man in the bed said, come in and join me before you get chilled, little maid.' She bowed her head. 'I didn't want to get undressed, but they were laughing and joking and saying every-one was doing it, it was part of the fun and getting into bed together helped you all keep out the cold. Before I knew it, my lovely blue dress lay in a heap on the floor, and my under-garments too – and I was naked.'

Her voice dropped, as if she could hardly bear to speak of her shame. 'I was the only one with no clothes at all, although I only noticed it when I was standing there with the men all admiring me. They said I was pretty, that I was fresh and innocent, a plum for the picking. I remember that in particular, that was when the man in the bed put his hands on my breasts and squeezed them. Then the other men picked me up, put me into the bed and, with Denys pressing up to me from behind, I was pushed hard against the man in the bed.'

She fell silent. Josse said gently, 'Joanna, there is no need to tell me this. I can guess what happened next and I can see that it was in no way your fault.'

She repeated softly, 'My fault.' Then: 'No, Josse, perhaps not.' After another pause, she said, 'Denys was – touching me, where I hadn't ever been touched before. I – for a moment I thought he would – But he didn't. The man in the bed began to kiss me and then *he* was touching me, and I knew in a flash that it was he who'd seen me dancing, he whom Denys had spoken about, and that they'd brought me here for him. I started to struggle, because although, God help me, I was prepared for Denys – I knew him, I thought I quite liked him, and he wasn't unattractive – I didn't want the man in the bed. But *he* wanted me. Oh, he seemed to think it was all a laugh, and when I tried to wrest myself out of his grasp, he thought I was joining in the fun, just pretending not to be as eager for him as he was for me.' She suddenly closed her eyes, squeezing them tight shut. 'He said to the other men, We've got a little wriggling fish here, you'll have to help me get her on my hook! and then the men took hold of my hands and laid me on my back, and Denys took hold of my ankles and forced my legs apart, and the man got on top of me and took me.'

Josse, horrified, watched as two slow tears emerged from Joanna's closed eyes and made trails down her cheeks.

'Joanna, I—' he began.

'He sent for me every night over Christmas,' she whispered. 'At first the others were there too – sometimes the same men, sometimes different ones. And, each night, they were drunk, they were laughing, they acted as if it was all part of the jollity.' Crying openly now, she sobbed, 'And I did, too! Oh, Josse, *that's* my sin! It *was* my fault, because I went along with it, pretended it was great fun, all a laugh, and exactly what I'd expected, what I'd come to court for!'

'You were sixteen,' Josse reminded her.

'As I reminded you just now, many women are married and have families at sixteen!'

'Perhaps,' he acknowledged, 'but you had led a sheltered life, you knew nothing!'

'I soon learned,' she said grimly. 'My new lord and master made sure of that.'

'What happened at the end of Christmas?' Josse asked.

She shrugged. 'Everybody went home with their own husbands and wives and got on with their ordinary lives.'

'Including your seducer?'

'Including him. But then, in February, I discovered I was pregnant.'

'And your lord, having gone back to *his* wife, would not help you?'

'I didn't bother to tell him.' She flashed angry eyes at Josse. 'I'd had enough of *him* to last a lifetime.'

'What did you do?'

'My mother virtually expired on the spot when I told her, so I knew there would be no good ideas issuing from *there*. The only person I could think of was Denys – he'd been there, he knew what had happened, and he was the one person who wasn't going to throw up his hands in horror at my condition.'

'So you sent word to him?'

'Yes. He came to see me – Mother would have none of it, she'd taken to her bed weeping and wailing, and didn't even descend to greet him. I told Denys I was with child and he gave a sort of whistle. It was strange – well, with hindsight it wasn't, although it seemed so at the time – but I had the impression that he was not at all displeased.'

'What did he suggest?'

'He said we must protect my good name and that meant we had to find me a husband. He said with a laugh that I mustn't go hoping the baby's father would marry me, there was no chance of *that* and I'd better get used to the idea, and I said I wouldn't marry *him* if he were the last man left alive and whole.'

'Did Denys have any other husbands in mind?'

'Yes. Again, I had the feeling that this wasn't as much a shock to him as I'd expected. He said to let him ponder the matter for a few days, and that he'd return as soon as he could, when he'd spoken to some people. I waited – there wasn't really anything else I could do – and, a week later, Denys came back and said he had betrothed me to somebody called Thorald de Lehon, that we would be married as soon as it could be arranged, and that I would then go with my new husband to live in his manor in Brittany.'

'Brittany,' Josse repeated.

'Yes.' She met his glance. 'I thought, as I suspect you are thinking, that Brittany was a goodly way away from England and therefore from English court gossip.'

'Did you think you were being hustled away and out of sight, into some rural backwater where everybody would forget all about you?'

'I did. Even more when we got to Lehon, I assure you. There's an Abbey, quite grand, with a holy community who devote themselves exclusively to their prayers. There's a mill and a river, there are acres and acres of low-lying fields, there's a nice town nearby, only I was never permitted to visit it unless Thorald accompanied me. And he was a virtual recluse – he only went outside to go hunting, and he didn't allow me to hunt. Then Ninian was born.'

'Did Thorald believe the boy to be his?'

She raised her shoulders. 'I have no idea. We never spoke of it. We barely spoke at all. Thorald treated Ninian roughly, but then he treated me roughly too, so that in itself didn't imply a particular grudge against Ninian.'

Josse remembered Ninian speaking of beatings: *when he was dead it meant he didn't beat us anymore.* 'You had a bad time,' he said, trying not to let his huge sympathy show lest it undermined her.

'I probably deserved it,' she said. 'Thorald said I did. He kept saying women were full of sin and must repent, and he made sure I went regularly to confession.' She grinned briefly. 'Those holy men at the Abbey must have loved me. When I ran out of real sins – and that did take quite a while, it was a long Christmas season containing many nights of lust – I started making things up.'

'You shouldn't have done that,' Josse said gently. 'The Church should be given respect, and—'

'The Church has done nothing for me!' she countered. 'It gave me no support in my trials, no comfort when first I went to confess my sins! D'you know what the priest said I must do? Honour my husband and be his obedient wife, and in that way prove that I had it in me to live a *right* life! Oh, Josse, don't go lecturing me about *respect*! I'll tell you what that priest's inter- ference meant – it meant I had to endure *six years* of being bedded whenever he felt like it by a foul-smelling, unwashed man older than my own father, who, while I gritted my teeth and prayed for him to finish, would dig his fingers into my flesh and tell me that my sufferings were ordained and sanctioned by God in order to rid my soul of its stains!'

'He lied to you, Joanna,' Josse protested. 'He was twisted, warped, and he used your own guilt as a way of making you comply. Don't blame the whole Church for one evil old man!'

'He happened to be the evil old man I'd been handed to in marriage!' she shouted. 'And why shouldn't I blame the Church? I'm quite sure Thorald was in league with the priest – they spent long enough closeted away together! Why, I wouldn't put it past Thorald to have outlined exactly what new perversion he wanted of me, so that the priest could include it in my penance!'

She was on her feet now, hands on her hips, leaning over Josse with an expression like thunder. He read in her face and body her humiliation, her hurt pride, her misery, her helpless subservience. To a woman like her, what a burden it all must have been.

'And then,' she resumed, calmer now, 'Thorald died. Went out hunting, put his horse at a brook, and shot off head-first when his horse stumbled.' She looked at Josse, looked away again. 'They do say the horse was lame. A sore foot, where a stone had lodged beneath the shoe.'

'And then you fled to England,' Josse finished for her.

'Before any of my horrible in-laws could arrive and conjure up any other sort of imprisonment for me. Yes. I fled, all right.'

'Why here?'

'You *know* why,' Joanna said, exasperated. 'Because Mag Hobson lived here.'

'Why not return to your mother?'

'My mother died, for one thing. And for another, if she *had* been still alive, wouldn't that be a sure way of allowing Denys to find me again? It'd be the first place he'd have looked. And surely you can see that I'd hardly have welcomed *that*.'

'He is your relative, though,' Josse persisted. 'Family duty would ordain that he offer you help, and—'

'*NO!*' Joanna shouted. 'Josse, *he* was the one who got me into such a mess! He—' She stopped short. After a brief pause, she said more calmly, 'He was the last person I wanted to see.'

Josse had the distinct feeling she had been going to say something else but had changed her mind. He waited in case she spoke again, but she didn't.

'You came to Mag Hobson,' he said slowly, 'and she brought you here, to this house.'

'Yes. It belonged to my mother's great-uncle and his wife. They were nice – I used to be brought to stay with them when I was a child.'

'When you met Mag, who worked for them?'

'Yes. I spent hours with her – she used to let me help her, and she taught me a great deal. My great-uncle and aunt thought the world of her and, when they died, she went on looking after their house. She always thought that, one day, someone would come along and claim it, and she said it was her duty to the old couple to keep things neat and tidy.' She paused. 'I truly loved her, you know. She was a wonderful woman. And I believe she loved me, too.'

'I think she must have done,' Josse agreed. 'Hiding you here was a good solution. Nobody knew about this house, and the chances of anybody – of Denys finding it by pure accident were slim.'

'He must have been waiting for her when she went back to her shack after coming here to see Ninian and me,' Joanna said slowly. 'Any number of people could have told him where to find Mag Hobson – he'd only have had to ask. I wanted her to stay here, with us, where it was safe, but she said no, she didn't like to leave her place unattended. Unloved, was what she said.' Joanna smiled faintly. 'I wish she had stayed, though. We knew Denys was in the vicinity – we'd . . . Never mind. But, even then, she wouldn't stay with us.' Joanna's eyes had filled with tears. 'So she went home,' she whispered through them, 'and he found her. Found her, beat her, broke her fingers, and *still* she didn't tell him where we were.' She swallowed. 'Then he pushed her in the water and drowned her.'

She stood shaking, crying as if her heart had broken. Josse, unable to stand the pitiful sight, stood up and took her in his arms.

This time, there was no passionate reaction from her, and he hadn't expected there would be. She leaned agaist him like a weary child, her pride and her courage spent, her defences finally breached.

With one hand he smoothed her hair, as he had done before. He held her, murmuring quietly, but she couldn't have heard. Not that it mattered, since he was talking nonsense. He went on holding her, giving her the warmth and support of his physical presence, while she cried out all her pain, her guilt and her sorrow.

And, eventually, she stopped.

Chapter Eleven

'That was quite a tale,' Josse said, gently disentangling himself from Joanna.

She was busy wiping her eyes and her face with the end of her sleeve. 'Yes.' She managed a rainbow smile. 'I'm sorry to have been such a child, crying like that. Only it's really the first time I've spoken of it.'

'Is it? You didn't confide in Mag?'

The smile was more confident now. 'There was no need. Mag knew.'

'I hadn't realised she had gone on being involved in your life. While you were married, I mean.'

'She wasn't.'

'Then how did she know?'

The smile was positively mischievous now, as if Joanna were enjoying the teasing. 'Had you known her, you wouldn't need to ask. She just *knew*. She had a way of studying you, perhaps holding your hand, and she'd ask one or two apparently irrelevant questions, then she'd say, Ah, yes. I know what *you* need, my girl. And she did. Whether it was one of her infusions for some small ill when I was young, or whether it was the need for a safe, loving refuge when I was all but defeated by my own problems, she provided it. And she always made you feel whole again.'

There was a silence, as if they were both honouring Mag Hobson's memory. Then Josse said, 'I wish I had known her.'

Joanna looked at him. 'You'd have liked her. She'd have liked you, too, what's more, and that would have been quite an honour. She didn't hold with men as a rule.'

'She didn't?'

'No. Can you blame her? She wanted to be an independent woman, living honestly on the small amounts she made from her cures and her comforts. Not that she ever charged much, only what people could afford. If they couldn't afford anything, she treated them for nothing. You saw how she lived, you can see she wasn't wealthy!'

'Aye, I can.'

'But that wasn't good enough for God's Holy Church. Oh, no. All her life, Mag had to cope with meddlesome priests and clerics, poking their long noses in, demanding to know what she was up to, how she brought about her cures, what she thought she was doing making her potions, and all but accusing her of consorting with devils.' Joanna was rapidly working herself up again. 'Just because she was different, just because she saw God in terms other than those laid down by those blasted priests, they shunned her, cast her out, turned her into someone who had to hide herself away, so that people who genuinely *needed* her help had to sneak out to see her in the middle of the night!' She paused for breath, turning blazing eyes on Josse. 'Surely you can understand why she disliked male company!'

'Not all men are priests,' Josse said reasonably.

'Oh, I know, but sheriffs and lordlings and puffed-up knights were almost as bad. It's the way of the world, Josse. Men take against women who demonstrate that they can do well enough on their own. Without some husband telling them what they may or may not do. It hurts their pride, I suppose.'

Josse was thinking. 'I believe you may be right,' he said.

She grinned. 'I *know* I am. Did you ever marry, Josse?'

'No.'

'Why not?'

'Perhaps because I reckoned I'd do well enough without some *wife* ordering my days for me.'

Her brows went down in a scowl as her mouth opened to

make some retort, but then her face cleared and she began to laugh. 'Sir knight, I believe you are making fun of me.'

'A little,' he admitted. 'It's good to hear you laugh.'

'It's good to want to,' she murmured.

They stood facing one another, an arm's length apart. He thought, I could embrace her now, kiss her sweet face and, in all likelihood, awake that passion in her again. Which would be joyous, for both of us, and would perhaps give her comfort of a sort she has never before received.

Or I could do as my conscience tells me I should and, for all that it is late, set out for Hawkenlye. The gates will be barred for the night, but I can beg a bed from the monks in the vale. I've done it often enough before.

Joanna, he saw, was trembling slightly. She wet her lips with her tongue, then began, 'Josse, I—'

Making up his mind, he said swiftly, 'I know, Joanna. It's late and I ought to be gone.' He made a brief bow. 'I'm going back to Hawkenlye Abbey. If you approve, I intend to ask Abbess Helewise if she will help us by hiding you and Ninian. Just for a few days, while we decide what to do.'

Whatever she had expected him to say – and he had a pretty good idea what that might have been – it obviously wasn't that. With a frown, she said, 'An Abbey! You propose taking me to an Abbey, when you know very well what I think about God and his church?'

'I – Hawkenlye is under the rule of a woman,' he said gently. 'A woman who wishes as fervently as your Mag did to live a life not ruled by a husband. Who—'

'I thought nuns were meant to be married to Jesus,' Joanna said scornfully, as if the very idea were risible.

'Perhaps. I can't speak for Abbess Helewise. But, in any case, it must be different from an earthly marriage.' He frowned; he was feeling well out of his depth. 'Mustn't it?'

'What's so wonderful about Hawkenlye Abbey?' Joanna demanded. 'Why do you want us to hide there? Why is it better than here?'

'A hundred nuns, fifteen monks and several very muscluar

and sturdy lay-brothers, for a start. Brother Saul, now, he's a good fellow. Devoted to the Abbess, too. He'd knock a man down if she told him to. A man, let's say, intent on taking away a young relative who didn't really *want* to be taken away . . .'

She was nodding, holding up a hand to stop him. 'Yes, very well. I accept, but for Ninian's sake, not for mine. I – well, never mind. When will you come back?'

He was backing towards the door. Her continued nearness was affecting him, undermining his self-control. Especially when she kept fixing those wide, dark eyes on him. 'Tomorrow. As early as I can. By noon, anyway. God willing.'

'Amen,' she echoed automatically. 'Very well.' She followed him to the door, and he hurried to open it and get himself on the other side.

She must have noticed. 'Don't worry, sir knight, I'm not coming to hurl myself into your arms. I'm going to bolt and bar the door, as soon as you're through it.'

With her taunting laughter ringing in his ears, he fetched Horace from the barn and, as stealthily as he could, made his way back to the Abbey.

Helewise had been expecting Josse for some time when, halfway through the next morning, finally he knocked on the door of her room. Brother Saul had informed her at Prime of Josse's late-night return to the vale, and she had added thanks for that to her morning prayers.

She hoped fervently that the completion of this dreadful business might be in sight. It was deeply worrying, knowing that Denys de Courtenay was at large, that someone of his ruthless nature was out there, hunting for a young and defenceless woman. He had killed once, after all. Helewise found she was constantly half expecting to hear that he had done so again.

'Sir Josse, welcome,' she said, as Josse came in and sat down. 'May I offer you some wine?'

'Aye, that you may.' She poured the steaming, spicy drink from the jug she had ordered from Sister Basilia – she had been fairly certain Josse would visit her sooner or later – and watched as he warmed his hands on the mug.

'Ah, that's good.' He put the empty mug on to the floor.

'Now, tell me what has been happening,' she said, trying not to let her impatience show. 'Did you find Joanna and her boy?'

'I did. I waited at Ninian's camp. Eventually he came and I persuaded him to take me to his mother. They are still in the old manor house where Mag Hobson installed them. Comfortable enough, but, Abbess, I fear for them, alone out there.'

'Is it very well-hidden?'

'Aye, that it is. Which is a blessing because it lessens the chances of Denys finding them. But, if ever he does, then it will rapidly become a curse.'

'Nobody to call on for help,' she said, nodding. 'Yes, I see what you mean.' She hesitated as a thought struck her. 'Sir Josse, are we right in assuming Denys *is* still searching for her? It is now – let me see – three days since he was here. Would he not have returned to check on us again were he still in pursuit?'

'You forget Mag Hobson,' Josse said.

'No, no, I do not.' How could I? she thought. That poor woman, that terrible death. 'But you said yourself she could have been lying there for several days. Denys de Courtenay might have given up the chase and be away on the other side of the land by now.'

'No, Abbess, I don't think so. I – Joanna told me something of her past last night. And I've been thinking, all the way back here last night and again this morning, and I believe I've worked out why he's trying to find her.'

'Which is?' she prompted.

'Abbess, remember how he said she was his niece, whereas in fact they are cousins?'

'Yes.'

'And you said it made a difference because they could marry as second cousins, given that they were granted the necessary dispensation, but never as uncle and niece?'

'Yes, of course.'

'Well, what if he'd been pretending to be her uncle to allay suspicion?'

'Of what?' Was she being particularly dense this morning, or was Josse being unusually long-winded? She frowned, concentrating hard.

'That he's actually planning to make her marry him!'

Helewise felt a distinct sense of anticlimax. 'I believe, Sir Josse, that you are going to have to explain. Why should he want to do that?'

'She's both a widow and an orphan,' he said, leaning forward eagerly. 'Her father died some time ago, her mother more recently, she has no siblings and there are no other kin to speak of. Now she's a widow, too, of a man who had estates in Brittany. Joanna spoke of family of *his*, but, even so, a widow surely is not likely to be ignored in a man's Will? All in all, Joanna must be worth a tidy sum now.' He sat back again, folding his arms across his broad chest. 'What do you think?'

What she thought was that there was a very obvious hole in his reasoning. 'Sir Josse,' she said gently, 'Denys de Courtenay employs strange wooing tactics if he thinks to win his lady's favour by brutally killing one of her few friends.'

'Ah, I've thought of that!' Josse said. 'As I said, Joanna's told me quite a lot about herself, and, without breaking any confidences, I can tell you that I believe he may think to coerce her into marriage by threatening to reveal certain things in her past.'

'Things?' Helewise echoed faintly. Her imagination was racing.

'Aye. Unfortunate things, it has to be admitted, but none of them her fault, Abbess!'

Ah, Josse, Helewise thought, but you *would* say that, being smitten as you are with the lady. 'Indeed?'

'No! She was young, an innocent, with nobody to chaperone her and—' Clearly realising he'd already said too much, Josse very firmly shut his mouth.

Tactfully she changed the subject, moving them away from the fascinating but forbidden ground of Joanna's lurid past. 'I would do anything I could to prevent a woman being coerced into marriage,' she said. 'It is an estate which, chosen of one's own free will, can be rewarding and very happy. But to be forced into union with a man one despised . . .'

'She's had to suffer that once already,' Josse agreed. 'It would be dreadful to contemplate it happening to her again.'

Especially dreadful for you, dear Josse, Helewise thought. 'What do you propose?' she asked. 'How may I help?'

'You guess that I need your help?'

'I don't think you'd be here otherwise.' You would, she added silently, be with Joanna de Courtenay, fighting off cousins, uncles, dragons, sea monsters, hobgoblins and any other creatures that threatened her.

Josse leaned towards her, resting his forearms on her table. 'Abbess, may I bring them here? Joanna and Ninian? There are a hundred hiding places, and there are people here who would defend her, if need be, and—'

'I'm not sure we can rely on my nuns,' Helewise said gently. 'Some of them could be useful – Sister Martha, I imagine, might wield a pitchfork to good effect – but as for the others, I think not.'

He raised his eyes to the ceiling in despair. 'Abbess, don't be ridiculous. Oh. Sorry.' He gave her a weak grin. 'I meant that, with so many people around, Denys can hardly arrive, turn the place upside down till he finds Joanna, then fling her across his saddle and make off with her.'

'Safety in numbers,' she agreed. 'Yes, I realise that. *I* am sorry, Sir Josse. I was teasing.'

'Well, don't,' he grunted.

'And,' she went on, 'if Denys de Courtenay should return with reinforcements, which I pray he does not—'

Josse's head shot up in alarm. 'Reinforcements!'

'– then we can call on Brother Saul and his companions. They won't let you down.'

'Aye,' Josse muttered. He was looking doubtful. 'Abbess, you are worrying me. I admit I hadn't envisaged an abduction by force, but, now that you have done so, I begin to see it is quite possible.' His frown deepened. 'Do we – do *I* – have the right to put your Abbey, and your nuns and monks, in jeopardy?'

'They would not stand by and see a young woman taken against her will,' Helewise said stoutly. 'Nor, indeed, would I.'

'Thank you, Abbess. But all the same . . .'

'May I make a suggestion?' she ventured, when he didn't go on.

'Aye, I'd be grateful.'

His honest, concerned eyes met hers, and she berated herself for having thought his urge to protect Joanna was prompted purely by self-interest. He would, she now decided, be working as hard on the young woman's behalf were she elderly and plain. It was a matter of gallantry.

'Although he did not admit it when he spoke to me,' she began, 'Denys de Courtenay knows Joanna to be accompanied by a child, a young boy. Ninian. Is that correct?'

'Oh, aye. He knows about her child all right.'

'Then he will be looking for not a woman alone, but a woman with a boy. Yes?'

'Aye.'

'Well then, why not split them up?'

'Joanna would never have it!'

'Hear me out! What I suggest is this. Return now to the secret manor house, fetch Ninian here to us – oh, don't worry, we would make absolutely certain that he was safe – and then go back to Joanna and—'

'I can't leave her alone there!'

'No, no, I'm not proposing that you should. But, Sir Josse, you have a house. Some distance from here and very comfortable, I dare say?'

'Aye, but—'

'And is it in the least possible, do you think, that Denys de Courtenay would find her there, when he is not even aware of her connection with you?'

'Less possible than that he'll somehow discover the location of the old people's manor house,' Josse agreed. There was a long silence; she sensed he was thinking it through, planning, perhaps, how he would put the idea to her. To Joanna.

The only slight drawback, Helewise thought, was that this

arrangement meant she herself would not meet Joanna de Courtenay. Which, she had to admit, was something she quite wanted to do.

Josse stood up suddenly. 'It's a sound plan,' he said decisively. 'I'll go and see if she agrees.' With a grin and a sketchy bow, he was gone.

Helewise sat as her table for some time more, thinking very hard. Thinking how best, in an Abbey full of nuns, to conceal a seven-year-old boy . . .

By the time he returned a few hours later, she was ready. Warned by Sister Ursel of their approach, she went outside into the frosty afternoon to greet Josse and his young companion.

'Abbess Helewise, this is Ninian de Lehon,' Josse said, slipping down from his horse and gesturing for the boy to do the same. 'Ninian, this is Abbess Helewise.'

He came up to her, made a reasonably elegant bow and said, 'I am honored to meet you.' Straightening, he looked up at her with frank curiosity.

Looking back, she studied him. Quite tall for his age, and sturdily built – he could have passed for more than his seven years. Longish dark hair, an open, friendly face. And those brilliant blue eyes. Yes. He would do.

'And I am delighted to meet *you*, too,' she replied.

'Don't stare, Ninian,' Josse muttered.

'Sorry.' Ninian glanced at Josse, then his eyes returned to Helewise. 'It's just that I don't know any nuns. Lots of monks – there were any number of them, where I used to live. They always looked very serious, and they prayed most of the time. And they were terribly strict. I didn't really like them very much.' A shadow crossed the young face.

In a moment of intuition, Helewise thought: you say you didn't like them. Were, perhaps, afraid of them. So that, when Josse told you he was bringing you here to our Abbey, maybe you thought we would be like your monks. 'We're not all that serious here,' she said gently. 'We pray quite a lot of the time –

it's what monks and nuns do – but we don't insist that people go about with long faces when they *aren't* praying.'

'Don't you?' The boy didn't look convinced.

'No. I'll tell you what, Ninian.' She bent down to his level. 'Because I'm always quite busy, I thought, when Sir Josse said he was bringing you here, that it would be nice if I asked one of the younger sisters who isn't quite so busy if she'd look after you. What do you think?'

'Younger?' Ninian repeated. 'Lots younger?'

'Oh, years and years,' Helewise assured him. 'In fact she's one of our youngest nuns, and she's only been a proper one for a few months.' She glanced up at Josse, who, she thought, had probably guessed which nun she referred to. 'Her name's Sister Caliste – shall we go and find her?'

'All right.'

Standing up, Helewise wondered if the boy would take her hand. Tentatively, she reached out. And, instantly, felt his small fingers wriggle into her palm.

'Sister Caliste usually works with Sister Euphemia, who is our infirmarer,' Helewise said as they walked off, 'which means the person who looks after the sick people who come here. Only today she – Sister Caliste – is busy doing the mending. She's in a snug little room down here –' she led the way along the path round the infirmary and approaching a small door in its end wall, opened it – 'with all sorts of things that she's got to sew. She'll be very glad of your company, Ninian.'

Reaching past the boy, Helewise pushed the door further open. Inside, Sister Caliste jumped up, spilling a load of sheeting on to the floor, and, making a graceful obeisance, said, 'Abbess Helewise! Good afternoon!'

'Sister Caliste – oh, sit down, child! You're standing on your mending – this is Ninian, whom I told you about. May he sit with you while you work?'

Sister Caliste's response, Helewise thought, was perfect. 'Oh, Ninian, how glad I am to see you!' she exclaimed. 'I've just sewn a hem that's at least ten leagues long and I've now got to begin on another, and I'm so bored I could scream!'

What a fine actress, Helewise thought. She happened to know – because Caliste had confessed it to her – that there was little the girl liked more than an occasional afternoon by herself in the tiny sewing room, thinking her own thoughts, peacefully stitching away.

'Come on, sit here –' Caliste was clearing a space on the floor – 'and tell me what's happening in the wide world out there. Has there been a lot of snow yet this winter? Have you been sledging? Have the birds all flown off yet?'

'I saw a hare today,' the boy said, making himself comfortable, apparently instantly at home in Caliste's company. 'He was still brown, though, and I thought they went white in winter, so—'

Helewise withdrew and quietly closed the door.

Returning to Josse, she found him chatting with Sister Martha, who had come out to take his horse and Ninian's pony.

'No need, thank you, Sister Martha,' Josse was saying, 'since I must be off again straight away. And I'll take Minstrel here with me. Just in case.'

Just in case, Helewise added silently, Denys comes looking . . .

'Thank you, Sister,' she said, and Sister Martha, assuming herself dismissed, returned with a bow to her stables.

'Is the lad all right?' Josse asked.

'Yes. He's fine. A nice boy.'

'Aye, that he is.' Josse gave her an admiring look. 'A stroke of genius, Abbess dear, to put him in Caliste's care. She does well?'

Helewise, remembering the affection which Josse had clearly felt for the young nun during her time of troubles the previous summer, nodded. 'Oh, yes. As I believe I've said to you before, she makes a fine nun. Happy, cheerful, loving, and, according to Sister Euphemia, a born nurse. Gentle, you know. And with an air of trusting confidence that the Lord will do his best for her patients, which she communicates readily to them.'

'You had your doubts over permitting her to take her final vows,' he reminded her, 'she being so young.'

'I did. But neither she, nor I, nor indeed any of the community here, have had any cause to regret her admission.'

'Aye, well, she'll do a worthy job just now, if she can take that lad's mind off worrying about his mother.' Josse put his foot in the stirrup and swung up into the saddle. 'And, speaking of Joanna, I must be on my way.'

'Of course.'

'Farewell, Abbess, and thank you. I don't know when I'll be back, but it will be soon, I promise.'

'Goodbye,' she said, raising a hand in blessing. 'God go with you.'

His 'Amen' reached her faintly as, kicking Horace into a smart trot, he hurried out through the Abbey gates and off down the track.

Chapter Twelve

Josse knew that there were several things he could be doing that would make more sense than riding as hard as he could to the secret manor.

He could return to Mag Hobson's house, for instance, and see if there were any signs that Denys de Courtenay had been back there, hunting for Joanna. He could ride down to Tonbridge, spend an hour or so in the inn, catch up on the latest talk. What were the townspeople saying about the poisoning in the inn? Was anybody under suspicion? Had anybody there seen little Tilly's handsome man again?

Yes. That would be an area he ought to explore . . .

But Joanna was on her own. In an isolated, empty house where nobody would hear her cry for help. And in his head he carried a picture of her face, when she had stood in the doorway earlier and watched him ride away with Ninian.

The quick lift of the chin and the smile hadn't fooled him for a moment, because he'd seen how she had looked when she thought he wasn't watching her. And he'd rarely seen a more forlorn expression in his life.

He reached the hidden manor house soon after nightfall.

He spent longer than he need have done seeing to Horace and to Ninian's pony. For some reason, he was nervous about entering the house. He kept having a strange fluttering sensation in his belly, as if a small bird were caught there, flapping its wings, frantic to escape.

The palms of his hands were sweaty, and, unfastening the buckles on Horace's harness, he noticed that his fingers weren't quite steady.

Fool, he told himself. You ought to be beyond feeling like a love-smitten youth.

Nobody gets beyond that, another part of his mind said sagely. When you're beyond those feelings, you're probably ready for your grave.

He made sure the water trough was full, then slapped Horace's rump and bade him good night. Then, fastening the barn securely, he straightened his tunic and strode across the courtyard to the house.

She was sitting in her usual position, on the rugs, furs and cushions in front of the fire. Her long, dark hair hung loose over her shoulders, half-shielding her face, and right down her back. She was smoothing it with her hands, holding up thick hanks in front of the heat from the hearth.

Hearing him come in, she said, 'I've washed my hair.'

'Aye.' He bolted and barred the door. 'Joanna, the door was open. I could have been anybody.'

'You could,' she agreed, 'but I knew you were you. I heard you ride into the yard. Well, I heard somebody ride in, and I looked out and saw it was you.'

'Oh.'

'You've been a long time,' she said softly. 'I was beginning to wonder if you were going to bed down out there with your horse for the night.'

The combination of her low voice and the words she spoke were rousing him. Was she doing it on purpose? he wondered. Trying to keep some control, he said, 'Ninian was made very welcome at the Abbey. Abbess Helewise has put him in the care of a young nun whom I know – she's a good girl, kindly and loving, and she's not very much older than he is.'

Joanna had closed her eyes. 'Thank you,' she said. Then, looking at him, 'Please do not imagine that, just because it wasn't the first thing I asked about, it was not the first thing on my mind.'

'I don't imagine that.' He came over to her, kneeling on the floor beside her. 'I understand full well what you feel for your son. You have demonstrated it, if it needed demonstrating, by your willingness to have him removed from you, for his own safety. Removed from the danger that *you* are in, from your cousin.'

'But—' Joanna began.

He watched her. As had happened before, he had the feeling she was about to say something important. But the sensation was far stronger now.

'But what?' Her eyes on his held a strange expression, almost pleading. 'Joanna, what is it? Can you not tell me?'

For a moment, she did not respond. Then, very slowly, she shook her head. 'It's nothing. I was just thinking about Ninian.' She shifted her position a little, making room for him in the direct heat from the fire. 'Come, warm yourself – it's a cold night, and you have had a long ride.'

She was, he realised, determined to change the subject. 'Not that long,' he said, settling beside her. 'My, you've got a good blaze going!'

'I have a lot of hair to dry.'

Presently she said, 'Are you hungry? I have food prepared. Not much, but I could bring it in here, and we could eat in front of the fire.'

The thought of food made him feel slightly queasy. 'Thank you, but I'm not hungry, in fact, I feel rather—' He stopped. No, best not to admit to his faint nausea. 'I don't want anything to eat. What about you?'

'I ate earlier.' Now why, he wondered, am I so certain she didn't? 'But I could prepare some wine. Yes?'

'Aye, that would be welcome.'

He watched her get up, in a smooth, lithe movement that was all in her strong legs; she did not use her arms to lever herself and the effect was particularly graceful. She padded barefoot across the flagstones – she had, he noticed, very small, narrow feet – and returned with a jug and several little packets on a tray.

'What are you doing?' he asked, watching as, kneeling before the fire, she took varying amounts from each packet and sprinkled them into the wine jug. 'What are you putting into the wine?'

'It's Mag Hobson's secret recipe,' she said, smiling, 'to warm you from the heart outwards on a cold night.' She paused to stir the contents of the jug, glancing up at him. 'Don't worry, all the ingredients are wholly beneficial.'

'I hadn't imagined they wouldn't be.'

She dipped a finger in the wine, tasted it, and added some more from one of the packets. Then she opened a small jar and put a great dollop of something golden into the jug.

'Honey,' she said, in answer to his raised eyebrows.

Then she extracted a poker from where it had been pushed into the flames, and stuck the end, glowing pale-yellow with the heat, into the wine.

There was a hiss, and a cloud of steam rose from the jug. The aroma floated out over them – spicy, sweet, with a sort of bitter tang underneath the surface smells . . .

'Nice?' she asked.

'The smell is wonderful,' he said.

She poured some into a mug. 'Try the taste. Careful – it'll be hot!'

He sipped. Delicious! Sipped again, and, as the extreme heat faded, took a mouthful.

Something to warm you from the heart outwards. Aye, it did that all right. He could feel the warmth and had the pleasant sensation that the wine's sweet smoothness was flowing right through his body, relaxing him, soothing him. Stretching out his legs, he lay back on the cushions.

It seemed quite the natural thing to do when she stretched out beside him. He moved over to make room for her and put out an arm. Accepting his unspoken invitation, she came nearer, lying against him, her head on his shoulder.

He stroked her hair. 'It's almost dry now,' he remarked.
'Mm.'

His eyelids felt slightly heavy. Letting his eyes close for a moment, he thought he could see a vision of golden clouds, and he felt strangely that he might be flying . . .

He opened his eyes again.

He turned his head slightly so that he could look at her. She was staring into the flames, her expression unreadable.

'What are you thinking about?' he asked. 'If it's Ninian, I do assure you he'll be quite all right.'

She raised herself on one elbow and looked down at him. 'I wasn't thinking about Ninian. Not at that moment.'

He waited. He was sure she would tell him what she *was* thinking about. In her own good time.

She did.

'Josse,' she began, still staring at him, 'I – out in the woods, we—'

She did not seem to know how to go on. So he did it for her. 'We kissed?' he asked softly. 'Like this?' Reaching out with both hands, gently he held her face and brought it down to his. Then, tenderly, he kissed her lips. She gave a sort of sigh, then kissed him back, exploring his lips with her tongue as he had done to her, in that first explosive embrace beside Mag Hobson's house.

'Like that?' she asked some time later.

'Oh, Joanna,' he murmured, 'aye. Like that.'

The kiss on the lips developed and soon they were loosening one another's clothing, exploring neck, chest, breast. Her mouth on his flesh felt soft, moist, thrilling, and his desire for her was escalating so rapidly that he was having difficulty controlling it.

But something was on the edge of his mind, something he knew he must pay attention to . . . something she had just said . . .

He made himself detach from the sensations she was engendering in him and think.

Think!

Aye. He remembered. Aye, that was it.

Very gently, so that she would not think it a rebuff, he pushed her away. 'Joanna, wait.'

The dark eyes intent on his, she said, 'Wait? What do you mean?'

Cradling her to him, resuming his stroking of her sheen of hair, he said, 'Just now, when we began to kiss, you said, like that? As if you didn't know.'

'Was it not right?' Her voice was full of anxiety. 'You *said* it was, when I asked, you said, aye, like that.'

'Sweeting, there was nothing wrong with the kiss! Quite the opposite – can you not tell?'

She whispered, 'No.'

'But you have been married? You have born a child?' Oh, but there was no delicate way of saying this! 'Joanna, you do know about love between a man and a woman. Don't you?'

She rolled over on to her back, and instantly that side of his body missed the warmth of her, the highly-charged feel of her firm flesh against him. 'Do I know about love?' she repeated. Her voice had taken on a hard quality. 'I know about sex, if that's what you mean. I know about being raped, and about being made to do my wifely duty, which really amounts to exactly the same thing. Do I know about *love?* No, sir knight, I do not.'

He raised himself up and leaned over her, fingers on her cheek, delicately feeling its soft texture. 'Sex is not love,' he said. 'One person taking his pleasure, with no concern for what his woman wants or feels, is nothing but selfishness. It is not how it should be, my love.'

Her eyes were shining in the firelight. 'I knew it couldn't be,' she whispered. 'I was always sure, even during those first times at Windsor, when I conceived Ninian, even through all the years I was married. Something within me kept telling me, one day you'll know. And Mag—' She broke off.

'Mag? She enlightened you?'

Joanna gave a soft laugh. 'She said I mustn't let the Great Mother's gift go unused, that a selfish man and a sadistic man were only two out of the entire male population, and weren't to be taken as representative of the whole sex.' She laughed again, more strongly. 'She did add, I might tell you, that they probably represented the majority.' She reached up her hand, touching her fingertips to his lips. Her hands, he noticed absently, smelt of cinnamon and honey.

'I am not a sadist,' he murmured, 'and I hope I'm not selfish.'

She smiled. 'I don't believe you are either. I think, as I thought in the woods by Mag's house, that you were the one she spoke of.'

'Mag spoke of me?' Despite all the other sensations racing through his body, he felt the slight atavistic chill up the spine that comes from a brush with the powers beyond.

'Don't worry, she meant you no harm.' Joanna's voice was a caress. 'She did not mention your name – I don't think she knew it. She just told me, when I was raging against men, marriage, and sexual subservience, that, one day, somebody would show me there was another way. And, when I was scornful, she said, wait and see, my girl. I read it in you, and in this place. One day, you'll understand.'

'And then you came across me, right there in Mag's clearing,' he said wonderingly, 'and we both felt that fierce attraction, and I kissed you—'

'*I* kissed *you*,' she corrected him. Lifting herself up towards him, she did so again.

And, as if Mag Hobson's prediction had just been shouted again, out loud, as if the old woman's benediction hovered over them, the full passion that had been hinted at that time in the woods came roaring back. Moaning, he wrapped his arms around her, pulling her fiercely to him, crushing her breasts to his chest, feeling the firm thighs against his legs.

She was reaching for the cords that laced up her gown, pulling at them impatiently. Helping her, he felt the cord tangle into a knot; he tugged hard, and the cord broke. She laughed huskily and, lifting herself, swept her gown and her loosely-fastened undergarments away in one wide gesture.

Kneeling up, swiftly undoing his tunic, pulling his shirt over his head and removing his hose and breeches, he stared at her, lying naked on the rugs and furs. The firelight lit up the curves of breasts, hip bones, the muscles on her thighs. She was strong, aye, he could see that – fleetingly, as from another world, he recalled her saying that she had recently developed muscles she hadn't known she had – but yet she retained her woman's shape. Narrow waist, full breasts, belly curving down to that dark, inviting place . . .

She, too, was studying him. Staring, steadily, at his erect penis, reaching out, touching.

He said, 'I will not hurt you, I swear.'

'I know,' she said. 'I feel – for the first time, I know what it is to *want*.' She put her hands on his shoulders, pulling him down towards her. 'Please,' she murmured, 'please . . . I don't know what – don't know how—'

He lowered himself down on top of her, gently, supporting himself so as not to crush her. Putting one arm behind her head, his face nuzzling against hers as he dropped little kisses on her cheeks, her nose, finally, lingeringly, her mouth, he let his other hand move slowly and steadily right down her body. Caressing her neck, the deep hollows above her collarbones, her breast, her nipple, her waist, her belly.

'It's all right, Joanna my sweet,' he said. 'I know how.'

They lay exhaused on their bed of rugs and furs. Josse, drowsy, slipping in and out of sweet dreams, felt the sweat begin to cool on his naked body. Lifting his head, he looked around him, and found the end of one of the furs. Pulling it towards him, he draped it over himself and Joanna.

Joanna.

She lay cradled on his chest, breathing deeply, and he thought she was asleep. Oh, but she had every right to sleep, after that great explosion of energy! Great saints, he'd never known anything like it – it had been as if seven years of dammed-up sexual response had been released in one vast, shattering orgasm.

Her first.

And, penetrating her deeply, he had felt every spasm of it with her, holding her as she cried with the joy and the ecstacy of it, sobbing and laughing at the same time as, finally, she knew what it was her body had been saving up for her.

His own ejaculation had been almost as earth-shattering; it was a long time since he had bedded a woman, but, more than that, he didn't think he had ever been aroused to the extent she had aroused him. That combination of innocence and natural, untapped, eager sexuality had raised him to heights he hadn't known himself capable of . . .

Amazingly, he found himself becoming firm again. So soon? Ah, but she's asleep, I mustn't disturb her.

Think about something else. Think about . . . Joanna.

No! Think about the frost outside, the icy ponds and puddles, the dark, the chill wind . . .

He felt her move, stretching out her legs then twining them in his, one thigh thrusting in between his, and she reached down under the covers and enclosed his penis in her hand, gently at first, then, as she felt him stiffen, with plainer intent.

'Do you think,' she said, rolling over on to him and kissing him, 'we might do that again?'

And, kissing her back, wanting to laugh and, oddly, half wanting to cry, he said, 'I don't see any reason why not.'

Chapter Thirteen

He was awake before her.

In the pale early light, he studied her face. Asleep, she looked younger; her habitual expression of wariness put strain in her features, giving her a false maturity. But now . . .

How old would she be? he wondered. Her son was seven, and Joanna said she had been sixteen when he was conceived, so that made her twenty-three. At that moment, she didn't look it. She looked about eighteen.

She was sleeping with her head on his shoulder, his arm around her. Leaning against him as she was, he could feel the soft warmth of her breasts. He was very tempted to caress them, gently to wake her, arouse her—

No. Let her sleep. Poor lass, this was probably the first night in a long time that she'd allowed herself to relax into deep, healing sleep. With him there – he hoped he wasn't flattering himself – at last she could let her vigilance slip a little and take the proper rest she must so sorely have needed.

To take his mind and his body off thoughts of making love to her, he looked around the bedchamber. He had noticed almost nothing about it last night save for the wide wooden-framed bed, with its thick woollen hangings and its pile of covers. Now, easing himself up a little so as to be able to view the whole room, he studied the rest of it.

It must surely have been the old people's chamber – Joanna's mother's great-uncle and his wife – he decided, for it had an air of long use about it. Not that it was dirty – far from it. Joanna must be maintaining Mag Hobson's exacting standards, Josse thought, for, throughout the house, there was an air of freshness, so that the visitor received the impression that the rushes on the floor had been newly replaced, the dark corners swept clean of dusty cobwebs, the bedclothes taken outside into the sunshine, hung on a line and given a good beating.

He was dozing now, drifting in and out of light sleep, and in a half-waking, half-sleeping vision, he thought he saw Mag, as she must have been in life, a sturdy and vigorous woman, ever on the move, sharp eyes ever observant to the smallest detail. Here she was now, in Josse's dream, coming up the narrow stair into the bedchamber with a besom in her hand, saying, 'Joanna! Come along, my girl, no time to lie idle! Just you stir yourself, now, and get this room swept out, you don't want your company thinking you can't keep a clean house, do you?'

He saw her stand over the bed, and there was a sudden softening of her stern features as she looked down at Joanna lying in his arms. 'Aye, that's right,' she said gently. 'You sleep, child. Sleep, and, when you wake, let him bear a little of your burden.'

With a start, Josse opened his eyes. The dream had been so vivid that he was quite surprised to find that he and Joanna were the only occupants of the room.

She finally awoke around mid-morning. Josse had slipped out of bed, collected his clothes and tiptoed out of the chamber and down the stair into the hall below, finding his way to the kitchen to build up the fire and heat water for a sketchy wash. Dressed, he returned to the bedroom to find her awake, lying propped up on an elbow and blinking in the soft sunshine coming through the narrow window.

'You let me sleep!' she greeted him, a faint note of accusation in her tone.

'Aye. You needed your rest.'

She smiled at him, a wide, happy grin. 'I did indeed. You rode me hard, sir knight, and fair wore me out.'

He came to sit on the edge of the bed, taking her outstretched hands and turning them over to drop a kiss in each palm. She smelt arousingly of sex . . .

Turning his mind from thoughts of their lovemaking — which took a great deal of effort — he said, 'I wasn't referring to that. I meant that, for once, you had no need to sleep with one ear cocked for danger.' No. That sounded self-congratulatory. 'That is, there were two of us to listen for untoward sounds, and—'

She was laughing, and he found himself joining in, despite the fact that he was pretty sure she was laughing at him.

'Ah, yes,' she said teasingly, 'I can just picture it. There we are, deep in the throes of our passionate embraces, and suddenly you say, "Hark! What was that, my lady? A rattle of the barn door? A warning whinny from one of the horses?"'

'Oh, very well,' he acknowledged. He gave her a rueful look. 'I only meant to help you.'

'Oh, Josse, I know that!' She sat up and flung her arms round him, the violent gesture throwing off the bedcovers so that her upper body was naked. Nuzzling her face up to his cheek, she murmured, 'Are you coming back to bed?'

'Joanna, we should be thinking about—'

But she had slid her hand up his thigh to his crotch, and the teasing fingertips were already fluttering up and down his erection. Whatever they ought to have been thinking about flew right out of his mind as, ripping off his clothes, he slid into bed and gave himself up to the delight of Joanna.

Soon after noon, they were up, dressed, and downstairs in the kitchen, where Joanna was preparing food.

Josse was thinking about the Abbess Helewise's suggestion that he take Joanna to his own house, and hide her away at New Winnowlands until whatever danger Denys de Courtenay represented to her was past. He was musing over how best to put the idea to her when she said, 'You've gone quiet, Josse. What is it?'

He looked up at her. Having decided that, for someone like her, the best approach was probably the direct one, he said, 'I have a house, Joanna. Not far from here – a short morning's ride, perhaps, certainly no more – and I have a staff of two. My manservant, Will, and his woman, Ella. Both discreet, trustworthy people, and each most capable at their own skills. My house has been newly renovated and it is comfortable. If you would accept, I can think of no safer place for you. For one thing, you would not be alone – even when I am from home, Will and Ella are always there. For another, nobody would ever think of looking for you in my house, because they don't know that you know me. Whereas it is more likely known that you had a connection with Mag Hobson, and, in addition, with this house. I fear that it is only a matter of time before the deduction is made that you are here. If you agree, then New Winnowlands is at your disposal, for as long as you want or need a refuge.'

She had heard him out without interrupting. The silence continued after he had stopped speaking, and he was just beginning to think that he must have offended her when she said, 'Josse, I thank you. You have thought this out well.' A slight frown crossed her face, as though she were weighing up the advantages of accepting his offer. Preparing himself for an enquiry or two – she might want to know what sort of accommodation he could offer her, for instance, or whether the house was warm and draught-free, that sort of thing – but, when she finally spoke, her question was quite surprising.

'A short morning's ride away, you said?'

'Aye.' He could not immediately see the relevance.

'And – your house – New Winnowlands – is easy to find? It's not so deep in some rural backwater that nobody knows it is there?'

What on earth was she driving at? Unable to work it out, he answered as honestly as he could. 'New Winnowlands is, as I said, a modest ride from here. It stands quite close to a reasonably well-used road, and we are visited by the occasional passer-by – in fact, as I recall, we had a tinker push his barrow into the courtyard not a fortnight ago. But, Joanna, what would it matter that we are not hidden away at the back of beyond, when nobody knows you are there?'

'But somebody determined could find it if they really wanted to?'

He was puzzled by her insistence. 'Aye, of course, but—'

She came over to him, putting her hands on his shoulders, silencing him with a kiss. When the kiss was finished, she said, 'I accept, and with deep gratitude. Please, Josse, take me to your house.'

He helped her fasten her pack on to the back of Ninian's pony – she did not seem to want to take much with her, but perhaps she did not possess many belongings – and, in the early afternoon, they set out.

He rode ahead, leading the pony, and she followed behind. He looked back at her once or twice as they left the secret manor – she had been very particular over leaving it neat and tidy, and over securing it thoroughly – and, each time, he saw that she was craning round in the saddle, eyes fixed to the house as if trying to impress every detail in her memory.

'We'll be back,' he said when, the house now hidden from view, she kicked her mare into a trot and came alongside him. 'When this time of troubles is over, you can return, if you wish to.'

'I shall,' she said quietly. 'It – this house and the little dwelling in the woods are where I can sense Mag most strongly.'

Her recalled his dream of the morning. 'Aye,' he said. 'That I can understand.'

There was so much he wanted to know, so many questions that kept rising insistently into his head. Tentatively he said, 'When you were young, did you—'

But she interrupted him. As if she hadn't even registered the beginning of his own question, she asked one of her own. 'Do you know what they did with Mag's body?'

He recalled Sheriff Pelham's words: *we'd better see about taking this here into town for disposal.* Was there a kind way of telling Joanna that? 'Er – the Sheriff's men took her back to Tonbridge. She would have been buried there, I think. That was what the Sheriff appeared to have in mind.' He wondered if, like him, she was imagining some hurried interment in an unmarked grave. 'We can enquire, if you wish. We can—'

But she was shaking her head. 'No, it doesn't matter.' Belatedly she added, 'Thank you.'

Again, he was puzzled. So much about her puzzled him! 'Joanna, I'm sure it could be arranged for the body to be moved.' He had no idea how these things were done, but, in his experience, it was usually the case that almost anything was possible if you were prepared to grease a few palms. 'If that's what you were thinking.'

She turned her head to look at him. Her eyes were wide, unfocused, as if she were seeing something a long way off. 'No, Josse. You are kind to be making these suggestions, but, as I said, it doesn't matter. Where Mag's body is buried is of no concern to me.'

It sounded a strangely heartless thing to say, and he didn't believe Joanna to be heartless. Certainly, not where Mag Hobson was concerned. 'Then why did you ask?' he ventured.

'Oh—' She seemed to have to think about it. 'I just wanted to make sure that she *had* been buried.'

'As opposed to what?' he asked, half laughing.

But she had ridden ahead of him and didn't appear to have heard.

New Winnowlands looked every bit as clean and well cared for as the house they had just left. Making a mental note to thank Will and Ella, Josse led the way in through the gates, across the yard and into the stables, where Will, having heard them ride in, came hurrying to help.

Josse, working on the principle that what a man doesn't know he can't tell anybody else, said, 'Will, this lady is a friend of mine. She is visiting the area, and is to stay here for a while. Would you please ask Ella to prepare accommodation for her?'

Will had been staring at Joanna with undisguised curiosity. 'That I shall,' he said. 'Just let me see these three horses comfortable, then I'll speak to Ella straight away.'

Josse took Joanna up the steps and into the house, aware, as surely she must be too, of Will's keen interest. What on earth would he say to Ella? Josse could well imagine something on the lines of, the Master's found himself a woman, and a fair looker at that. He's ordered a chamber prepared for her, but, judging by the way they look at one another, it's my opinion that she'll not be using it. You might as well save yourself the trouble, Ella.

Ah, well. There was nothing he could do about it. Showing Joanna to a seat by the fire, he risked a quick look at her. She was smiling slightly, as if the situation amused her. She didn't seem in the least offended nor awkward.

'Your arrival is bound to cause a bit of a stir,' he said quietly; Ella might well be within earshot, she moved so softly about the place that you really never knew where she was. 'It's not often I bring a beautiful young woman to my house.'

'I'm glad to hear it, sir knight,' she replied. 'I should not like to think that you make a habit of entertaining young women.'

'Aye. No.'

She was settling herself, clearly making herself at home. 'I like your house,' she remarked. 'Newly renovated, did you say?'

Thankfully they seemed to have lit upon a topic of conversation that was perfectly fit for the possibly listening ears of Ella. One that, moreover, he could elaborate on without feeling the hot blush of embarrassment which never seemed far away when he was close to Joanna. 'Aye, there was a deal of work necessary when I first came to live here. It had been built as the dower house to the main manor, up the road a mile or so, but was in a sorry state. Nobody had lived here for years, so there was a long list of problems to address. For a start, we had to . . .'

He had been droning on for some time, listing all the work he had had to put in hand to make his house habitable, when he noticed that she seemed to be suppressing laughter. 'What's the matter?' he asked.

'Oh, Josse, nothing's the matter.' She straightened her expression. 'There is little I enjoy more than a long sermon on the repair of masonry and the replacement of interior woodwork.'

'You did ask,' he said, stung.

'I did,' she agreed. Getting up, she came across to him. 'Do your servants live in the house?' she asked softly.

'Well, not exactly. They have a small cottage, a lean-to, really, on the end of the row of outbuildings. It suits them to live a short step away from me, or so I assume, since it was Will himself who requested the place, and—'

'A simple "no" would have done,' she whispered, placing her finger to his lips. 'Would have done very well, in fact, a lot better than "yes".'

He had a good idea what she was thinking. 'You prefer that we are alone here, at night?' he whispered back, excited by the very thought of the night. 'With no fear of servants' gossip to ruin your reputation?'

She smiled. 'My reputation was ruined seven years ago.' She slid her arms round his neck, pulling him down towards her so that she could kiss him. 'Now, I please myself what I do.'

'And it pleases you to be here? With me?' His voice was husky with growing desire.

'Oh, yes.' She kissed him again. 'It pleases me very much.'

'I'll look after you,' he said, lips to her ear. 'I swear to you, I'll help you, care for you—'

'I know,' she interrupted. 'I thank you for it.' He had the strong sense that, momentarily, she had withdrawn from him, as if something he had said or done had caught her up short.

He began to wonder what it could have been. But then she was pressing herself to him again, and, with his rapidly-accelerating heartbeat sending the blood pounding through his body, he didn't have the power to wonder any more.

Chapter Fourteen

The first sign of imminent trouble came after Sext.

Helewise, who had gone to check on Ninian on her way back to her room, had found him only a little embarrassed and annoyed at what she and Caliste had devised for him.

'Yes, I do understand how you must feel,' Helewise had said soothingly. 'And I know that, because you are sensible, *you* can understand why we are doing this. Yes?'

The boy had given a grudging nod.

'Good!' Helewise said briskly. 'Now, here's Sister Caliste, back from her devotions, so I shall leave you in her care.'

She was in the act of opening her door when she heard pounding footsteps.

'Abbess Helewise! Oh, Abbess! Stop!'

Helewise froze. Oh, dear God, no! I can't do this, I'm not prepared to—

Then she remembered her promise. Straightening her shoulders, offering a swift, silent prayer asking for the sense to act quickly and wisely, and the strength to carry out whatever might be demanded of her, she turned round.

And greeted the red-faced, panicking Sister Ursel with a calm, 'Sister? What is it?'

'Denys de Courtenay is approaching. He's just ridden into sight on the track up from Tonbridge. He's got three men with him, mean-looking ruffians they are. The gates are barred, as you ordered, Abbess, but what am I to do when they request admittance?'

Helewise paused. If what I plan is not right, oh, Lord, she prayed, then please send me a sign. Please, of thy mercy, do not let me commit a folly . . .

She emptied her mind.

Nothing.

Taking a steadying breath, she said to Sister Ursel, 'Go and open the gates, Sister. We must show Denys de Courtenay that we have nothing to hide.' She fixed her eyes to Sister Ursel's, trying to give her some of her own certainty, and was gratified to see a response. Sister Ursel squared her jaw, hitched up her robe and said, 'Right. I'll let the b – the wretches in.'

Helewise watched her hurry off, then followed her, at a more leisurely pace, out of the inner courtyard and towards the main gates.

There were three men at the gates – Sister Ursel must have miscounted – and they had dismounted. The two companions Denys de Courtenay had chosen were both big and ugly. The sort of men, Helewise imagined, likely to be found at the root of a tavern brawl. Not that she knew anything about tavern brawls. One had a scar from his ear to the side of his nose. The other seemed to be suffering from an unpleasant skin condition. Both were armed with staves, and bore knives thrust into their belts.

'. . . can't bring your weapons into the House of God,' Sister Ursel was saying, bravely standing her ground, hands on hips, not quite managing to fill the gap left between the partially-opened gates.

De Courtenay muttered something, and the men put their sticks and knives against the wall. 'You and all,' Sister Ursel commanded, waving a hand at the sword by de Courtenay's side.

With a faint smile, as if the whole scene privately amused him, he did as she said.

Helewise stepped forward, and de Courtenay noticed her.

'Ah,' he said, 'the very lady I have come to see.' With a wide smile that exposed his white, even teeth, he nodded to his men, who shuffled in through the gates and stood, in poses of varying degrees of aggression, just inside the walls. Then he strode up to Helewise, made her a brief bow – little more than a nod of the head – and said, 'A word, Abbess, if I may.'

Then he took her by the elbow and marched her off towards her room.

Her instinct was to shrug him off, but something told her to wait, to act in a thoroughly nun-like way, submissive, obedient. She bowed her head and suffered herself to be led away.

She opened the door of her room, and gestured for de Courtenay to precede her inside. Then, carefully closing the door behind him, she turned and said meekly, 'How may I be of service?'

He was staring round the room as if searching for something, and did not appear to notice her humble tone. Then, spinning round to face her, he said brusquely, 'You know a knight called Josse d'Acquin. Don't try to deny it, any number of good folk hereabouts have told me he is a frequent visitor to Hawkenlye Abbey, and, moreover, on excellent terms with its Abbess.'

'I should not dream of denying it,' she said calmly. 'Sir Josse is a good friend to Hawkenlye, and has given us his help and support on more than one occasion.'

'Hmph.' De Courtenay looked slightly put out, as if he had expected an argument. 'Well, is he here?'

'He is not.'

'Where is he?'

She hesitated. 'He spoke of a visit to Winchester.' That was no lie; Josse had described to her his mission to Queen Eleanor over the matter of his rent demand. 'I believe he may be there.'

That *was* a lie. But, Helewise told herself, in a very good cause.

'Winchester?'

She nodded. Sometimes the nun's well-known discipline of not speaking unnecessarily came in very useful.

De Courtenay strode to the door and flung it open. 'I'm going to fetch my men. I want to search the Abbey.'

She flew ahead of him and, repeating Sister Ursel's action at the gates, stood between him and the cloister outside. 'I do not permit that,' she said icily. She met his eyes unwaveringly. 'This is God's holy place, not some felon's hideaway. Visitors enter at my discretion, and, once inside, are expected to behave with reverence and decorum. Your companions, sir, do not look capable of either.'

'What you think of my men is irrelevant,' he retorted. 'Search I will!'

'What do you imagine you will find?' she cried. 'I have told you that Sir Josse is not here!'

His eyes narrowed. 'I asked you before if you had seen my kinswoman, Joanna de Lehon,' he said, menace in his tone.

'And I said no!' Helewise replied. 'I undertook to inform you if I had word of her!'

'But you haven't, have you?' He put his face close to hers.

'No, because she, too, is not here!'

He said, with a cold detachment that was worse than anger, 'I don't believe you.'

'You should,' she insisted. 'I speak the truth!'

He raised his hand and for an instant she thought he was going to push her out of the way. She put all the authority she could muster into her face – not difficult, since she was boiling with suppressed rage – and slowly he put his hand down again.

'I do need to look round your Abbey,' he repeated, softly now. 'Will you act as escort, Abbess, if I leave my men where they are and come with you alone?'

Stalemate. She could hardly refuse and it would surely arouse direct action from him if she did.

Wouldn't it be better to do as he asked? Then perhaps he would believe that they had nothing to hide, and leave them alone.

Perhaps.

Again, she waited for a sign that she was taking a wrong path. Again, none came.

Lowering her head – if she were going to take on once more the persona of humble nun, it was best he couldn't see her expression – she said, 'I am perfectly willing to show you the Abbey. If you would care to follow me, I shall introduce you to my community and show you something of our work here at Hawkenlye.'

After that, it was easy, for she had shown off the Abbey to interested visitors on many previous occasions.

It was relatively easy, at least; two major anxieties gnawed at her, and she had to exercise every bit of self-control she could muster to stop them from edging their way into her manner and her voice.

She began with the storage buildings and the stables.

'. . . these are the stables, where, as you see, Sister Martha keeps everything spotless.'

Sister Martha, who had obviously heard what was happening, stood with her pitchfork in her hand, looking as if she would just love an excuse to ram it into de Courtenay's belly.

De Courtenay glanced briefly into each of the four stalls. 'No horses?'

Sister Martha, having looked at her Abbess for approval, spoke. 'We keep a cob and a pony,' she said gruffly. 'Plain-looking animals, but sturdy. They're turned out today, in the sunshine.'

'Where?' he demanded.

Giving him the sort of look more usually directed at a pile of ordure, she led him outside, took him to the gates and pointed down the road. Helewise, watching from a distance, saw him give a brief nod.

If he had been expecting to see Josse's horse, or the sort of fine animals owned by a lady and her son, he was disappointed.

De Courtenay strode back to Helewise. 'Carry on,' he commanded.

Meekly she obeyed, leading him on towards the herb garden. 'In front of you you'll see where we grow our vegetables and our herbs,' she began, then proceeded to lecture him for some time on the various herbs and their uses. Half of it she made up as she went along. 'And up on your left –' she detached a hand from the opposite sleeve and waved it in the air – 'is the dormitory where all but the Virgin Sisters sleep.'

'I want to look.'

She hesitated, then nodded. Retracing her steps, she led him back to the entrance to the dormitory. She waited in the doorway while he strode the length of the long room and back again. Was it her imagination, or did his handsome face show a faint flush of embarrassment?

She led him back to the herb garden, walked past it, then stopped. She was beginning almost to enjoy herself. 'Ahead,' she said, lowering her voice dramatically, 'is the leper house.'

She felt him move involuntarily backwards – people always did that – and he muttered something under his breath.

'Do you wish to go inside?' she asked sweetly. 'I would not accompany you but, naturally, you are free to go in if you choose.'

'Wh – who lives in there?'

'Three of my sisters live there permanently. They have elected to give their lives to serve God in this way. The leper population fluctuates. At present, there are seven within.'

'Seven,' he repeated in a hushed whisper.

She did not, as she usually did at that point, make her little speech about the visitor being perfectly safe, in no more danger of contagion than when out in the world outside, since the lepers and their three attendant nuns lived quite apart from the community.

Let de Courtenay worry!

'Do you wish to enter?' She moved forward, going as if to open the little door in the wall; it was a gamble, and she was calling his bluff, because she knew full well the door was locked and barred from the inside, and had rarely been opened since the Abbey had been built.

'No!' he said. Then, more calmly, 'No. I would not wish to disturb the sick.'

'Very laudable,' she remarked. He shot her a quick look but her face was hidden by her coif.

She led him on past the leper house and stopped by the entrance to the Virgin Sisters' house. Opening the door, she said, 'This is where the Virgin Sisters sleep. You may go in and look, but please move quietly, some of the sisters have been in attendance on the sick throughout the night and are presently sleeping.'

She thought he would refuse the offer. But, after a pause, he went in. After a very few moments, he was out again. This time, there was no mistaking the flush on his lean cheeks.

She led him inside the Abbey Church, waiting just inside the great west door while he made his way all around the quiet, empty building. He found the door at the top of the stairs down into the crypt – of course he would, it was not concealed – and she waited a little longer while he went down, had a search and came back up again.

He rejoined her at the door. 'What next?'

'Next I will show you our home for aged nuns and monks,' she said, leading him past the end of the infirmary and on to the building forming the east side of the cloisters. 'Many of our brothers and sisters in God come to end their days here with us, when, after a life in God's service, they . . .'

She gave him the longest ever version of that part of her speech.

He wanted to go inside the aged monks' and nuns' home. Sister Emanuel, serene and distant as ever, appeared not to be put out in the least by a brusque stranger poking his nose into every cubicle. Helewise, trying but failing to conquer the unworthy impulse, was quietly delighted when de Courtenay chose quite the wrong moment to speak to Esyllt, Sister Emanuel's assistant; the radiant young woman, on being asked what she was doing, held out to de Courtenay a used urine bottle, full of dark-golden, steaming liquid.

'My own room you have already inspected,' she said, resuming the tour, 'and this is our Chapter House.' They both peered inside: it was empty. 'Next, the refectory and recreation rooms,' – again, empty – 'and finally, the reformatory.'

'Reformatory?' he asked, quickening his pace and hurrying forward.

'Yes.' She lengthened her stride to keep up with him. 'We offer help to women who have fallen into sinful ways.'

He stared at her. 'You mean whores?' There was infinite disdain in the way he said the word.

'I mean exactly what I said.' She kept her voice even. 'Only God knows what drives any of us to the actions we take. We are encouraged to hate the sin, not the sinner, and we take in those who repent of their ways and wish to make a new start in life.'

'Whores,' he muttered.

An angry retort rose to her lips, but she held it back. Why bother to argue with one such as he? He wasn't worth it.

He poked around the reformatory in a desultory way – she thought he might be beginning to believe that they really did have nothing to hide – then, emerging, said, 'What's that big building straight in front of us?'

'It is the infirmary.' Her voice, she was glad to notice, was calm. Unconcerned.

'I want to go inside.'

She hurried to follow as he strode towards the infirmary's main door. 'Of course,' she murmured.

He shot her a look. 'Many patients at present?'

She pretended to pause and count, although there was no need; she knew every patient by name, what was wrong with them, whether they were expected to recover, and, if so, how soon they were likely to be well enough to leave and release a bed for somebody else.

'We have about forty patients at the moment,' she said as they entered the infirmary. In fact there were thirty-seven.

He stopped dead, looking startled. And also slightly anxious. 'So many? What's wrong with them?'

'They suffer from a variety of maladies. Some have broken bones, some are having painful teeth removed, we have two women awaiting imminent childbirth, and one whose baby was born the day before yesterday. We also have many who have contracted the sweating sickness – they are in a separate ward –

and two youths suffering from the bloody flux.' She pretended to frown. 'One of our fever patients is causing particular anxiety. The sickness struck so suddenly – whilst he was attending a service at our Holy Water shrine, down in the Vale, and his descent into delirium occurred within the hour.' It was a slight exaggeration, and she was deliberately giving the impression that the man was more ill than he actually was. But it had the desired effect.

Denys de Courtenay now looked as if the infirmary was – after the leper house – the last place on earth he wanted to visit.

She edged past him, and, from within, said, 'Come along. We should keep our disturbance of the sick as brief as we can.'

Relentlessly she led him all round the infirmary. Sister Euphemia came bustling up to attend her visitors, and needed no encouragement from Helewise to expound on the symptoms of her patients.

While she was doing so, Helewise caught sight of Brother Saul, who had come in to bring a message to a man lying in a cot next to the door, a broken right thighbone strapped between splints. Murmuring an excuse, she glided over to him.

'Brother Saul!' she called.

He turned from the cot. 'Abbess Helewise?'

She beckoned him close, then, speaking softly, said, 'Saul, de Courtenay is asking for Sir Josse. I did wonder, might it be an idea to—'

'To forewarn him?' Saul, too, seemed blessedly informed of exactly what was going on. 'Of course, Abbess. My business here is done – I'll go straight away.'

'You will find him at home at New Winnowlands, or so I believe,' she said. 'But I'm afraid you'll have to round up the horse. Sister Martha's turned him out.'

Brother Saul grinned. 'She's just been to fetch him,' he said. 'I saw her bringing him in.'

'Oh, well done, Sister Martha!' Helewise breathed. 'God's speed, Saul.'

He bowed his head while she gave him a swift blessing, then hurried away.

Helewise returned to de Courtenay and Sister Euphemia, who had the young man by the sleeve and was making him look at an elderly woman whose face was covered with red pustules, some of which had burst to emit yellow matter. Euphemia seemed to be asking him if he'd ever seen anything like it before.

'Just a few more patients to see,' Helewise said – de Courtenay, she noticed, appeared very relieved at her interruption – 'so let's hurry on, shall we?'

They finished the tour of the infirmary's patients and went back outside. Helewise led him on without speaking; she was praying.

'And the last place to visit,' she said, after her silent and fervent *Amen*, 'is the little sewing room.' She opened the door and stood back to let him look inside.

Sister Caliste's black-veiled head was bent over her mending, and, beside her, a small white-veiled figure copied her actions.

'Sister Caliste is our youngest fully-professed nun,' Helewise said conversationally, 'and I often ask her to work with our novices, she being nearest to them in age. Here, she is mending torn bedding, and Sister Felice is learning the skill.'

She watched him watching the two nuns. Then, her own eyes moving to the sisters, suddenly her heart gave a great leap of alarm. She willed Caliste to look up, and, to her huge relief, she did. Helewise very deliberately folded her arms, tucking her hands in the opposite sleeves. With a faint nod, she indicated for Caliste to do the same. Caliste glanced at her companion, and her eyes widened briefly; she gave her a nudge, and the young novice put down her needlework and also folded away her hands.

De Courtenay stood staring down at the two bowed heads.

The moment lengthened till Helewise wanted to scream.

Then he said, 'Why have they stopped sewing?'

She said quietly, 'They are respecting the presence of a visitor. They will not resume until we leave.'

He spun round and strode out of the room. Waving his arm, he said, 'Oh, let them get on with it.'

Helewise felt for a moment that she might faint. But that would have been plain stupid, so she pulled herself together and set off after de Courtenay, who, with his angry disappointment evident in the way he was striding along, was heading for the gates.

As she walked, Helewise sent up a prayer of deep gratitude for Caliste's observant eyes and quick wits.

She reached the gates to find de Courtenay yelling for his men; they had grown tired of lounging against the Abbey walls poking fun at Sister Ursel, and had wandered off along the track, leading their horses and aiming punches at them when they tried to put their heads down to rake up mouthfuls of the thin winter grass.

'Get mounted!' de Courtenay bellowed. 'You there, bring me my horse!'

Sister Ursel came to stand beside Helewise. They watched de Courtenay's men inelegantly mounting up, and stared openly at de Courtenay himself, whose horse, still tempted by the delights of the vegetation beside the track, was reluctant to stand still for him.

'Oh, dear,' Helewise said with pretend concern, 'are you going to manage? Or should one of us come and hold his head for you?'

He shot her a thunderous look. One final effort got him into the saddle, and, putting harsh spurs to his horse's sides, he led his men off at a canter.

Sister Ursel muttered something: Helewise thought she heard one or two words not in common use among nuns.

'I shall pretend, Sister Ursel, that I didn't hear that,' she said.

'Thank you, Abbess.' Sister Ursel blew her cheeks out. 'Phew, I'm glad to see their dust. Lord, but what a rotten bunch!'

'They are, and their leader the rottenest.'

'Aye, aye.' Sister Ursel grinned briefly. 'Just as well for you, Abbess dear, that looks can't kill. That last stare he gave you would have had you breathing your last.'

'Quite,' agreed Helewise. 'Now, Sister Ursel, would you

please refasten the gates? I must go and speak to Sister Euphemia.'

And, she thought, refraining from saying so aloud, convey to that wonderful, quick-thinking Sister Caliste my heartfelt thanks . . .

Death by the Blade

Chapter Fifteen

Leaving the Abbey church after Compline, Helewise was wracked with anxiety over Brother Saul.

He still had not returned from his mission to New Winnowlands.

There was probably nothing to worry about, she kept trying to reassure herself. After all, Saul hadn't set off until gone noon and, even making the best speed – not very fast, on that old cob – he would have been hard put to it to get to New Winnowlands and back to Hawkenlye by nightfall. And that was assuming he'd been able instantly to locate Josse, to give him the message that Denys de Courtenay was looking for him. Even then, Josse surely wouldn't have let Saul set out again straight away – he'd have taken him inside, let him warm himself by the fire, given him something heartening to drink, possibly prevailed upon him to stay for a bite to eat. To rest there for the night.

Oh, yes. It all sounded most plausible.

Why, then, could the Abbess not rid herself of the dreadful fear that something terrible had happened?

Helewise sat alone in her room while the rest of the community set about turning in for the night. When at last all was quiet, the Abbey gates barred and bolted and the lanterns extinguished, she made her way back inside the church. The soft glow of the sanctuary lamp seemed to welcome her, and, kneeling down before the altar, she sensed a strong hand reaching down to her.

She began on her formal prayers. But, interrupting her concentration, she kept seeing the face of Brother Saul. Most reliable, most likeable, most trusted of friends, she was very afraid that she had sent him into danger.

Unable to think of anything but him, her prayers turned into a simple repetition of the same phrase: 'Oh, dear Lord, of thy mercy, please look after Brother Saul.'

Josse and Joanna had spent a delightful day. Or, at least, it had been delightful for Josse, although, judging by the preoccupied expression which he sometimes caught sight of on Joanna's face, at times her problems and anxieties must have intruded on her happiness.

Only to be expected, he told himself, trying not to allow dismay to ruin the day. Naturally she'll worry about Ninian, about the whole sorry mess she's in, and it's no reflection on the joy we've found together if, occasionally, her thoughts revert to her problems.

The bright sky of morning had clouded over as the hours went on, and, as the short February daylight came to a premature end, Josse watched Joanna, seated by the fire, staring into the flames. She had, he reflected, an air of expectancy. Any small sound made her start up, stare at the door. As if she were waiting for something . . .

To turn his mind from fretting about her, he thought back over everything they had done together since waking, in his bed, soon after first light. She had scorned his suggestion that she return to the small guest chamber which Ella had prepared for her: '*I* am not ashamed to have lain here with you,' she said grandly, sitting up in bed and waving an arrogant arm, 'and I don't care a fig for what your servants mutter about me.' She had given him a look through narrowed eyelids. 'If you, however, wish to be secretive about what you and I have become to one another, then naturally I will do as you ask, and set about making the bed assigned to me look as if I have been sleeping chastely in it all night.'

'I didn't *ask*,' he pointed out mildly. 'It was only a suggestion.'

She leaned over him, pinning him down with a hand either side of his head, her face hovering inches above his. 'I'll go if you really want,' she said softly. 'I was only teasing. After all, you'll be the one who goes on—' Abruptly she stopped.

'Goes on what?'

'Nothing.'

He wrapped his arms around her, hugging her close. 'Stay,' he said, nuzzling into her thick, soft hair. 'I don't care what Ella tells Will. I don't care what they think. Stay.'

She had lowered the length of her body down on to his, and he could feel her breasts, her belly, the firm thigh muscles. 'If they thought you *hadn't* bedded me,' she murmured right into his ear – her warm breath sent great shivers of excitement up and down his spine – 'they might mutter about your manhood.' As she said *manhood*, her hand slid down across his stomach and into his groin, making him throb so that he gasped aloud. She chuckled. 'Ah, he's saying good morning!' A pause. 'My, he's eager!' She put her mouth to his, kissing him at length. 'Just let Ella ask *me* about your manhood,' she whispered, 'I'll soon reassure her . . .'

They had gone out after breakfast. Will had saddled Horace and Joanna's mare, and they had ridden around the New Winnowlands estate. Not that it took very long: Josse's manor was modest. Drawing rein on a low rise, he had pointed out the road leading to the house of his nearest neighbour.

'He's a decent fellow,' he said, 'we enjoy an occasional visit when I'm in residence here.' He watched her. 'Would you like to call on him?'

'No,' she said instantly. Then, as if fearing she'd offended him, 'Josse, under any other circumstances I'd love to meet your friends. But just at the moment, I feel that the fewer people who know I'm here, the better.'

'Of course.' He could have kicked himself for his dullness.

But, riding out with her, watching her free, flowing movements, hearing her talk, hearing her laugh, just for a moment he'd forgotten.

Ella had prepared a fine midday meal, and, after that, Josse and Joanna had settled in front of the fire. He sat in his chair, and she curled up on the floor at his feet. He had wanted to ask her more about herself, but, forestalling him, she said, 'Now, I've told you enough about me. Please, Josse, what about you? Acquin – where is that?'

So he had told her. Told her everything there was to tell about himself, really, since there was nothing he wanted to keep secret. Not from her.

And, as they sat cosy and warm inside, gradually the day wound to a close.

Josse had just sat down again after putting more logs on the fire when there came the sound of voices from the courtyard. Will's voice and another, one that was shouting something . . . Something about a man, attacked, lying beside the track out there, frozen half to death, poor soul . . .

Josse leapt up. Taking Joanna by the shoulders for a hurried instant, he said, with all the command he could muster, 'Stay here. Bolt the door behind me, don't open it again till you hear me tell you to.'

'But—'

He gave her a little shake. '*Stay here!*'

After a moment, she gave a meek nod.

He raced outside, jumping down the steps and running across the yard to the gates. Will, looking highly relieved to see him, said, 'This here fellow tells me there's a man injured, out in the road. I was on the point of going to have a look, only—'

'Quite.' Josse gave him a warning look; no need to elaborate in front of a stranger, to reveal that Josse had given Will orders not to open the gates to anybody, all the while Joanna was with them. 'Thank you, Will, you did right.'

Will, with a nod, stepped back, and Josse went up to the

gate. 'Someone lying injured?' he said to the man outside, a rough-looking fellow dressed in a sacking cloak, the end of which he had draped over his head, presumably in an attempt to shelter his face and ears from the keen wind.

The man edged closer and put one hand on the gate. 'Aye, that he does! Been struck on the head, I reckon, there's blood trickling down his face.'

Josse was torn. What should he do? Go out and tend to this poor soul, attacked on the road? Or do as his instinct strongly told him to, and ignore this as an elaborate bid to get him to open up and go out?

Once I am outside, he thought, Joanna will be alone within.

But supposing there really *was* an injured traveller out on the road! It was quite possible the man had merely taken a tumble from his horse, it might just be Josse's heightened sense of danger that was making a threatening situation out of something perfectly innocent.

'Any sign of a horse?' he asked. 'Could the man have had a fall?'

'Oh.' The peasant at the gate appeared to think about it. 'Could have, I reckon. Could have crumped his head as he fell, aye.'

Josse made up his mind. He said to the peasant, 'A moment.' Then, turning, he beckoned to Will and, when he was close enough to speak to without the man at the gates overhearing, he said, 'Come with me.'

He led the way up the steps, rapped on the door and said, 'Joanna, open up.' She did so instantly; she must have been standing right by the door.

Once inside, Josse strapped on his sword and stuck his dagger in his belt. As an afterthought, he collected a heavy bolt of wood from the stack by the fire; it was a clumsy weapon, but would serve as a club in an emergency.

Joanna was beside him. 'What's going on?' she demanded. 'Tell me! Where are you going?'

He turned to her. 'There's a rough-looking fellow at the gate, who claims he's found an injured man on the road. It's possible he's been thrown from his horse. He's hurt his head, so I'm told. I'm going out to have a look.'

She was shaking her head. 'You mustn't,' she said urgently. 'It's a trap, Josse. They – he – Denys is behind this, I'm sure.'

He stared into her eyes. It was strange, but, while he read in them a thrilled response to this sudden danger, he read no fear. No alarm.

'What do you suggest?' he asked softly.

'I don't – I'm not—' She looked down, frowning. Then, meeting his eyes again, she said, 'No. I do see, you have to investigate.'

'Oh.' He would almost rather she had pleaded with him a little longer.

She gave him a quick, hard hug. 'Be careful,' she said.

'I shall.' He pushed her away gently, staring down at her. 'Hide yourself,' he urged. 'Get Will to help you, and get into some secret corner where nobody can find you.'

Her eyes widened. 'What for?'

He said, exasperated, 'In case this *is* a trap and I'm overcome! If that happens, Joanna my sweet, then they'll be in here, quick as you please, and looking for you.'

Again, there was that odd lack of fear. Nodding her agreement, she let Will hurry her out of the hall. It was, Josse thought, almost as if she'd had all this worked out beforehand . . .

But then he was outside again and the man at the gate was waiting.

Josse opened the gate, slipped out and said, 'Come along, then. Show me your injured man.'

'Aye, aye,' the man said eagerly, 'he's along here . . . just you follow me, sir . . . past this open stretch of track, then in under here, where the trees make a shadowy overhang. Maybe you're right, now, sir, and his horse spooked at sommat in the darkness, throwing him off, like. There!' Stopping, he pointed ahead.

Josse stared into the gloom beneath the trees. He could make out the edge of the track, and, beside it, a narrow grass verge which sloped down into a ditch. There were deeper patches of shadow behind the ditch, where the undergrowth encroached.

On the lip of the ditch was a long shape. A man's body, dressed in dark clothing. And, at one end, the pale blur of a face.

Josse ran forward.

He did not see the trap until hands descended on him, grasping him by the upper arms, smothering movement, effectively preventing him from reaching for his sword or his dagger. The makeshift club was knocked out of his hand and fell to the ground with a thud.

There were two of them, the man who had come up to the gates and another, who must have been hiding in the shadows. As Josse wrestled with them, managing to throw one of them off him and, with a swift kick to the head, put him out of action, a third man leapt up out of the ditch to take the downed man's place.

And, his eyes now adjusted to the darkness, Josse could see clearly what lay on the lip of the ditch.

Brother Saul.

His black habit was wound tightly round his legs, secured with a length of twine, and his hands were tied behind him. The man who had been crouching behind him – in his dark cloak, invisible in the darkness – had had a hand over Saul's mouth, preventing him from shouting a warning. Now that there was no more need for silence, the man removed his hand, straightened up, jumped nimbly across the ditch and stood before Josse.

And Denys de Courtenay said, 'Josse d'Acquin, we meet at last!'

Josse ignored him – even as the attack had begun, he had known who must be behind it – and called anxiously, 'Brother Saul! Are you hurt?'

'I'm all right,' Saul called back. 'Sir Josse, I'm so sorry – we thought to warn you, to tell you that de Courtenay was searching for you, but instead of helping, I led him straight to you!'

Denys de Courtenay laughed. 'You did that all right, Saul!' he said cheerfully. 'Your Abbess Helewise thought she was being so clever, slipping away to give you your orders! But she's not as clever as she thinks, because it didn't occur to her that I'd have guessed she'd do exactly that, and have a man in hiding outside the Abbey to follow her messenger.'

Brother Saul gave a violent wriggle but the cords binding him held fast. 'You are an evil man!' he cried to de Courtenay.

'Evil?' De Courtenay seemed to think about it. 'No. I don't believe I'm *evil*. Scheming, perhaps, but what man is not?'

'You—' Saul began. But de Courtenay turned his back and, nodding to his men to bring Josse, walked off in the direction of the New Winnowlands gates.

'You can't leave him there!' Josse protested. 'It's freezing out here and he's injured!' Was that true? Or was the injury an invention?

'He's warmly wrapped in that monk's habit of his,' de Courtenay said casually. 'And the chill will do his head good. Swellings usually go down when you put something cold on them.'

'You heartless bastard,' Josse said.

'Heartless, perhaps. Bastard, nay. My parents had been wed twenty years and more by the time my mother bore me.'

Josse barely heard. With a great heave, he shrugged off the lighter-built man holding his right arm, twisting the man's wrist viciously, and, before the man had a chance to grasp him again, he lunged forward and grabbed de Courtenay by the shoulder. 'What do you want of me?' he demanded. 'What is your purpose in trailing Brother Saul to my house? How *dare* you assault me in this manner!' His anger rising to boiling point, he spun round, caught the man on his left-hand side a great blow beneath the chin with his right fist, and, with a singing, jubilant satisfaction, watched as he slumped to the ground.

'Oh, dear,' de Courtenay said. 'Two down, and one disabled.' He glanced at the third man, nursing a wrist bent at an unnatural angle and moaning softly. 'Not that I am greatly surprised, they are hardly what one would call an efficient and disciplined fighting force. Still, needs must, eh?'

'If you live in the gutter, you are forced to use what little the gutter can provide,' Josse said sententiously.

'How true, how true.' De Courtenay was smiling again.

'Now, Sir Josse, I do believe you asked me a question a moment ago. Two questions, in fact. You seem to have reduced me to an army of one, so why not invite me into your house and hear what I have to say?'

Amazed, Josse repeated, 'Invite you into my house? Why in God's holy name should I want to do that?'

With a suddenness that was vaguely alarming, de Courtenay came up close, face full of some unknown emotion. The casual, light-hearted air was totally gone; he looked, Josse thought, like a man possessed. 'Because I have a matter to put to you, one of the gravest import!' he hissed. Waving round him at his fallen companions, he said, 'Oh, I admit I have made a poor start – you must excuse the brutishness of my initial approach, but it was the best I could think of.' He gave a faint laugh. 'Fancy me thinking they'd be any use! I'd have done far better to present myself at your door and politely asked for a few moments of your time.' He shot Josse a glance. 'Except that you wouldn't have listened. Would you?'

Josse said, 'Probably not.'

'Well.' De Courtenay's eyes still held that fire. 'What do you say, Sir Josse? Will you hear me out?'

Joanna is hidden, Josse thought rapidly, and anyway, Will is there. That makes two of us, against de Courtenay; I'll make quite certain his ruffians can't follow him in. And I'll be receiving him on my own home ground, which adds another advantage.

A further point occurred to him. Relaxing his grip on de Courtenay's shoulder – with a wince, de Courtenay instantly began to massage it with the opposite hand – Josse said, 'You may come into my house – alone – on one condition.'

'Which is?'

'That you release Brother Saul from his bonds and help me bear him inside, where we may attend to him.'

De Courtenay sighed. 'I might have guessed. Very well.'

Josse watched as he returned to the figure in the shadows. Soon afterwards, he emerged again, supporting the stooped figure of Brother Saul. There was a murmur from one of the men on the ground; de Courtenay, answering, said, 'Oh, do as you like. No, I've no further use for you. You can go to hell, for all I care.'

There was another murmur – something about being paid – and de Courtenay shouted, 'You've had all you're getting from me! And *that's* being more than generous, considering how little use you've been!'

He was still shaking his head and muttering under his breath when he reached Josse. 'What has become of the honest serving man?' he asked as Josse put Brother Saul's arm round his shoulders and helped de Courtenay bear him along to the gates.

Treating the question as rhetorical, Josse didn't bother to answer.

They got Saul inside – he had a deep cut on the front of his head, and they wrung from him the confession that he was feeling a little sick – and carried him along to the kitchen. Ella volunteered to take care of him, and Josse laid him gently down on a hastily-prepared pile of mats.

'I am sorry for your pain,' he said gently, studying the pale face.

'No, no, Sir Josse! It is I who am sorry, for my failure.'

'It was no fault of yours, Saul. Now, rest. Let Ella see to your wound, then sleep.'

Even as Josse turned away, Saul was gratefully closing his eyes.

Josse returned to the hall. De Courtenay was standing just inside the door, as if, having got Josse to admit him, he did not want to presume any further on his host's hospitality until invited. Let him stand by the door a while longer, Josse thought grimly. He's right in the draught just there. That'll cool his passion for him.

There was no sign of either Joanna or Will, Josse noticed with vast relief. He went up to the hearth, and, holding his hands to the lively flames, he said, his back to de Courtenay, 'Well?'

He heard the cautious footsteps coming nearer. 'Er – may I too, warm myself?' de Courtenay asked politely.

'I don't know about that.' Josse turned to study him. 'You were happy enough to leave poor Brother Saul outside in the frosty night.'

'Oh, Sir Josse, don't be petty!' Incredibly, de Courtenay sounded as if he were suppressing laughter. Was this all such a game to him, then? Josse wondered. But what of that brief, intense moment outside? What of *that* man, the one who, despite the easy charm and the humorous manner, seemed to have some fixed and determined purpose which, against all expectations, drove him on regardless of the obstacles put in his way?

I hate to admit it, Josse thought, but I'm intrigued.

He pulled his chair up close to the fire, gestured to the piled rugs and furs on the opposite side of the hearth and, trying to ignore images of Joanna sitting there not very long ago, he said, 'Sit down.' De Courtenay settled himself, with a considerable grace.

Josse studied him. De Courtenay, noticing the scrutiny, smiled. 'Do I pass muster?'

Josse ignored that. After a moment, he said, 'You seem to have gone to some trouble to get to me. The least I can do, I suppose, is to hear what you have to say.'

The smile extended. De Courtenay said, 'Ah, a wise decision, if I may say so,'

'Go on, then. Tell me what you want of me.'

And, with a brief closing of his eyes as if summoning concentration, de Courtenay began to speak.

Chapter Sixteen

'I have the distinct feeling,' de Courtenay began, 'that much of what I would start by telling you will be a repetition of what you already know.'

'How so?' Josse asked.

'Because I imagine you and your friend the Abbess Helewise have few secrets from one another, so that everything I told her at our first meeting, she will in turn have told you. Am I right?'

Josse thought quickly. There seemed no point in denying it. 'Aye. I know that you are a relation of Joanna de Courtenay, now Joanna de Lehon, and that, following the death of her husband, she is alone in the world and, according to you, grief-stricken and without a protector. As a good kinsman should, you are searching for her and you have come to this region because Joanna has an old friend who lives here. You believe she might have come to see that friend.'

'Ah, yes,' de Courtenay sighed. 'All of that is, alas, all too true.'

'And you have received no news of Joanna?'

'I have not.' Another sigh.

'What of her woman friend? Did you manage to locate her?'

'Again, no.' De Courtenay's handsome face creased into a worried frown. Josse, observing that there was not the trace of a sign that the man had just told a lie, reminded himself that he was dealing with a very skilled opponent. A very calculating and devious one. And – as the only recently-healed wound on Josse's head testified – a potentially violent one.

'You yourself have friends here,' he said. 'The Clares of Tonbridge.'

De Courtenay's head shot up. 'The Clares friends of mine? No, Sir Josse, now there you are mistaken.'

Putting that denial aside as probably another lie, Josse said, 'Obviously so. However, you did, I believe, visit Tonbridge.'

Would he deny that, too?

There was a brief pause. Then, as if de Courtenay had worked out that his presence in Tonbridge would be impossible to refute, since too may people might well swear they'd seen him there, he said, 'I did indeed. I took supper at a tavern. Quite a pleasant inn – a fine mug of ale, and a fresh slice of pie. Rabbit, I seem to recall. Or was it chicken? No matter. Served by a scrawny, dim-witted girl with a drip on the end of her nose.' He grimaced in distaste.

Poor little Tilly, Josse thought. So much for trying to win your handsome stranger's favour by swapping the last of the old pie for the first of the new.

'But, naturally, nobody there could give me any information about my cousin,' de Courtenay was saying. 'Not that I expected it – Joanna is a lady, not the sort of person one would find frequenting a bawdy tavern.'

A lady. Against his will, Josse had a memory of Joanna in bed. Making love to him, laughing at some vulgar remark of his, just like any tavern wench.

Deliberately shutting off the image, he said, 'So you went to Hawkenlye Abbey, in case she'd sought refuge there.'

De Courtenay gave him a sharp look. 'I did. Not once but twice, and the second time the gracious Abbess allowed me to have a good look around.'

'No sign of your cousin?'

'No.' De Courtenay's eyes seemed to bore into Josse. 'No. No sign of her.'

Uncomfortable under the continuing scrutiny, Josse was prompted to speak more bluntly than he intended. 'Why are you so keen to find her?' he demanded. 'The duty of a kinsman is all very well, but searching Abbeys and –' he had been about to say, and tormenting old women, but stopped himself – 'and waylaying innocent men like Brother Saul is surely going too far. I think, de Courtenay, you had better explain yourself.'

De Courtenay was lying back on one elbow, long slim legs crossed, studying the toes of his boots. 'Explain,' he murmured. He shot a glance at Josse. 'Yes. I, too, think I had better explain.' Sitting up suddenly, he said, 'You assume, Sir Josse, that it is Joanna for whom I am searching so diligently. Why?'

Taken aback, Josse said, 'Because she is both an orphan and a widow, and likely to be wealthy. And, since you are not, as you say, her uncle, but her cousin, there is no reason why you should not try to acquire your dispensation and marry her.'

The surprise on de Courtenay's face had to be genuine. He echoed faintly, '*Marry* her?' and then, to Josse's consternation, burst out laughing.

'Do you deny that you have been posing as her uncle?' Josse demanded, puzzled and irritated by the laughter.

'No, no, I don't deny it.' A fresh chuckle burst from de Courtenay. 'I never can get these complicated strands of family ties straight. I've always *felt* like Joanna's uncle, that's for sure.' He was looking intently at Josse, no longer laughing. 'But, uncle or cousin, you must believe me, Sir Josse, when I assure you I have no thought to marry her. Once, maybe, when she was virginal and unsullied, I might have, although even then I had – No.'

There was a silence. Josse, fighting to control his rage – when she was virgin and unsullied, indeed! And who was responsible for the ending of *that* innocent state? – wanted very much to slam his fist into de Courtenay's pensive face.

Eventually, mastering himself, he said, 'So what *do* you want with her?'

De Courtenay looked up. 'I have not, Sir Josse, been entirely frank with you,' he said. 'I have spoken all along as if Joanna were alone, whereas in fact that is not true.'

'Indeed?' Josse said coldly.

'Indeed. She has a son, a boy of seven years. I do not know

his name – I have never met him – but I do know of his existence.'

Of course you do, Josse wanted to say. It was Joanna's pregnancy with that very child which led to you arranging for her the hell on earth that was her marriage to Thorald de Lehon.

He managed to keep the accusation back. 'What of it?' he said instead.

De Courtenay seemed to be thinking. 'Joanna was married to a man named Thorald de Lehon,' he said, 'but the child was not his.' He looked up at Josse, his face expressionless. 'The boy was conceived at court, in Windsor, during the Christmas festivities of the year 1184.'

'Ah, Christmas at court,' Josse said, putting on a smile as if happily reminiscing. 'Fun and games under the Lord of Misrule, eh?'

'Quite so,' de Courtenay agreed. 'You'll recall, Sir Josse, how it is? How we all tend to forget ourselves in the celebrations, when we've been dancing all evening and have had more to drink than is wise?'

'Oh, aye.'

'Especially –' de Courtenay was leaning closer now, watching Josse for any nuance of reaction – 'when there is such a clear lead given from the top.'

'From the top?' Josse tried to work out what de Courtenay was implying. Then, remembering Joanna speaking of the old King and his numerous mistresses, he nodded. 'Aye. King Henry, they do say, enjoyed the company of many women. Rosamund Clifford, the princess Alais, and—'

'And?' de Courtenay prompted.

Josse shrugged. 'Any number of other passing fancies, I dare say.' He was beginning to have a dreadful suspicion. 'And, where the King leads, his sons will follow,' he murmured, horrified at his own tentative conclusion yet, at the same time, appreciating how very possible it was.

'His sons?' de Courtenay said.

Josse was picturing Ninian's brilliant blue eyes. Why on earth had he not realised sooner? Not Joanna's eyes, not inherited from his mother.

Blue eyes, the like of which Josse had been so sure he'd seen once before.

In the face of the boy's father.

'I speak,' he said softly, 'of King Richard.'

De Courtenay stared at him. 'Do you?'

'Aye.'

De Courtenay leaned back on his elbow again. 'Are you often at court, Sir Josse?'

'Infrequently.'

'Yet they speak of you as a King's man.'

'I have had the honour to serve King Richard and I await any further instruction he should care to give me.' Good God, but if Josse were right about this . . .

'But you do not attend your King at court,' de Courtenay was persisting.

'No. Not often.'

'Then,' the voice was low now, 'you will not know how our blessed King Richard used to comport himself during such festivities as the Christmas season. He was not a man to dance and to carouse, Sir Josse, not once he had put in the appearance which court etiquette demanded of him. Do you know what our beloved King was wont to do then, as soon as he could make himself scarce?'

Josse shook his head. He was intent on what de Courtenay was saying – how, indeed, could he not be! – but, at the same time, he was wondering, with a grim feeling of foreboding, why the man insisted on speaking of his King in the past tense.

'King Richard preferred to retire to his room with his men and play at mock battles,' de Courtenay said. 'I have it on the best authority that his favourite was a re-enactment of the battle of Jericho, and that he himself would blow the trumpet that brought down the city walls.'

Josse said firmly, 'I don't believe you.'

De Courtenay shrugged. 'Please yourself. It is of no import. But what you *must* rid yourself of, Sir Josse, is any idea of King

Richard summoning pretty young maidens to his bedchamber and seducing them. He was never, I do assure you, that sort of man.'

'I—' Josse couldn't think how to go on. De Courtenay's words had the ring of truth, that was the problem; what little Josse knew of King Richard made him believe his sovereign far more likely to prefer discussing ancient battle tactics to deflowering virgins.

But if not Richard, then who?

'I believe Prince John was at court that Christmas,' he began, hating himself for the questioning tone.

'Why do you speak of the sons,' de Courtenay murmured, 'when there was then so much life and vigour still in the father?'

It took a moment or two for it to sink in.

The father.

Henry Plantagenet, Richard's father, the man who had passed down to this son, too, those bright blue eyes. Strong and bull-headed ruler of England for thirty-five years, and, at a generous estimate, some fifty or more years old that Christmas when Joanna's son was conceived.

And she a child of sixteen!

Was it true? Was Henry of England truly the father of Joanna's son?

Josse leaned forward and took hold of de Courtenay by the shoulders. Tightening his fingers till they dug deep into the sinewy flesh – he could sense de Courtenay brace himself against the pain – Josse said, 'If I ever discover that you are lying to me, and that Joanna's son is *not* the child of Henry Plantagenet, then, so help me, I shall find you and kill you.'

De Courtenay met his eyes. You could not, Josse had to admit, fault his courage. 'It is the truth,' he said simply. 'Believe me, I led her to his bed. I was there when he took her.'

Josse almost killed him there and then. Digging in his fingers still further, eliciting a faint moan from de Courtenay, he said, 'She was a child, man! Your own kin! And you sacrificed her to an old man's lust!'

'He'd had his eye on her from the moment she arrived,' de

Courtenay panted. 'If it hadn't been me, then somebody else would have fetched her to him. Aaagh! And I thought – *aaaagh!*'

Josse slackened his grip a fraction. 'You thought you might as well gain the glory,' he finished. 'Attract a little of the royal benevolence for yourself. Eh?'

'Why not?' de Courtenay countered. 'And he was grateful – you had to give the old King that, he never forgot when you'd done him a favour.'

'And, not content with that, you then gave your beautiful niece to an old goat who used her like a whore throughout her marriage,' Josse breathed. 'Why Brittany, de Courtenay? Why send her so far afield?'

De Courtenay was looking at him strangely, an expression of calculation mixing with the pain in his face. 'You've spoken to her,' he said softly. 'Great God, but you know all about this from *her*! Don't you?'

Josse tightened his hands again and de Courtenay screamed in agony. 'You haven't answered my question,' he said. 'Why dispatch her to Brittany?'

De Courtenay's face was dead-white. 'Because I wanted everyone to forget about her,' he said, gritting his teeth. 'To forget she'd been at court, to forget, if they'd ever known it, that she'd slept with the King. To be ignorant – aaagh! – of the fact that she was pregnant when she wed de Lehon.'

Josse was nodding his understanding. 'So that nobody but you and she would know that the boy was King Henry's son. So that you could keep that precious piece of information secret. Yes?'

'Yes.'

Josse relaxed his grip. Instantly de Courtenay curled in on himself, nursing his shoulders with the opposite hands.

'And,' Josse went on, thinking out loud, 'now that Joanna is a widow, you think to persuade her to join you in whatever you are plotting and—'

'You don't see it, do you?' de Courtenay said, his voice husky. 'You don't understand why I want the child *now.*'

'Now that his father – his adoptive father – is dead. No, I can't say that I do.'

De Courtenay gave a sigh of exasperation. 'It has nothing to do with de Lehon,' he said. 'Forget about him, everyone else has, he was a terrible old man. Think more widely, sir knight. Think, if you are able, of court circles.'

Court. The old King dead, King Richard away in Outremer, Prince John putting it about that he might not come back and dropping heavy hints that he would make a better King than his absent brother. But, despite his progressions around the land, failing to win popular support.

'Who,' de Courtenay prompted, 'stands to be King if Richard does not return?'

'Prince John believes it should be him, but—'

'But Richard instructed that Arthur of Brittany be confirmed as his heir. Yet who in England wants to be ruled by a four-year-old baby, with a Breton mother into the bargain?'

'Well, I—'

De Courtenay was kneeling up in front of Josse now, face alight. 'Don't you see what a pearl we have, Sir Josse, very nearly within our grasp? If I can only find him, what a prize! Eh?'

'You mean Ninian,' Josse whispered.

'Ninian? Is that what she calls him? Well, we can soon change that – William, perhaps, or Geoffrey, and we'll tack on a FitzHenry, heaven knows the lad's entitled to it. Then we'll present him. Look, we'll say, King Henry's true son, of the blood royal, conceived at Windsor, with witnesses to prove it!'

'Prove it?' Panicked, Josse lit on the one thing that was at all approachable. 'How so?'

'There were more than just the King, Joanna and I in that bed,' de Courtenay murmured. 'And I already have assured myself of their support. In return for what I have sworn to pay them, they will attest to the dates and identify Joanna. The child's date of birth is on record. Anybody who can do simple addition can work out the rest for himself.'

'And there's the eyes,' Josse muttered. 'I *knew* I recognised those brilliant blue eyes.'

'Ah, all to the good!' de Courtenay cried. 'A family resemblance was almost too much to hope for.'

Joanna, oh, Joanna, Josse was thinking, this was why you were on the run. Not escaping from de Courtenay for your own sake, as I thought, but for Ninian's. Because you could not stand by and see your precious child made a pawn in a desperate power game. A pawn who, if de Courtenay were to miss his footing for an instant, would be swiftly and silently disposed of. Never to be heard of or seen again.

That's why she let me bring her here! he realised in a flash. Why she agreed to the plan to lodge Ninian at Hawkenlye, while she laid a false trail elsewhere! That was why, of course, she asked those strange questions. Was New Winnowlands far off the beaten track? Could somebody find it if they were determined? I, poor fool that I was, believed it was because she feared for her own safety, feared that de Courtenay would find her. In fact, it was quite the opposite.

She *wanted* de Courtenay to find her.

Because, all the while he was pursuing her, it meant that Ninian was safe.

Feeling sick, he realised that she had used him. Oh, aye, she had her reasons – he had never doubted the power of mother-love – but, remembering those passionate nights with her, he felt as if she had just spat on him.

He raised his head and saw that de Courtenay was watching him, with what looked remarkably like compassion.

'She can be very charming,' he said. 'It runs in the family. She quite won the old King's heart that Christmas. He couldn't take his eyes off her, he'd have given her anything she asked. Only she was too proud.'

'She—' Josse's voice broke. He began again. 'She would never agree to her son being put forward, being paraded openly as Henry's son.'

'No, I fear you are right,' de Courtenay admitted. 'But then it is not crucial to have her agreement. If I can only find the boy, tell him who he is and spirit him away to where I have friends and supporters waiting, then Joanna swiftly becomes irrelevant.'

'You—' Josse started. Then he made himself stop. Better,

surely, to let de Courtenay continue. At least then Josse would know what he was planning to do.

'Join us!' de Courtenay said eagerly. 'What a future we could have, Sir Josse! You could say, quite reasonably, that as a loyal follower of King Richard, you were keen to do what was best for the realm he left behind, and what better, from Richard's point of view, than a new start? God knows, he detested all the kin he knew about, why not crown one he'd never met? It could scarce be worse!'

'Aye, aye,' Josse said, 'you may be right. And we could win popular support, think you?'

'Of course!' de Courtenay said confidently. 'The people are so fickle, so shallow of thought, they'll believe anything if it's presented to them plausibly enough. And, in all conscience, they won't take readily to either John or Arthur of Brittany.'

'No, no, I can see that.' Josse was thinking hard. 'So, we take the boy off to London or to Winchester, proclaim his parenthood, get your witnesses to swear that it's all true and then have him adopted as heir?'

'Yes!' De Courtenay was on his feet now, almost dancing. 'Why, man, he could be crowned King before we know it! And then we'll be sitting pretty. The power behind the throne, eh? What a prospect! What do you say?'

Josse, too, got up. Slowly, pretending to stretch, pretending still to be working it all out. But, as he straightened up, he reached down surreptitiously to ensure he still carried his dagger. His sword, he could see, was within reach, propped beside the fireplace.

'I think,' he said, keeping his tone calm, 'that it is an outstanding plan.'

'I *thought* you would!' de Courtenay said gleefully.

'Except you've forgotten something.' Josse tried to sound merely a little worried, as if the objection were only a small point.

'Oh, there are any number of details still to be worked out,' de Courtenay agreed. 'What has occurred to you?'

'What has occurred to me,' Josse said, pretending to reach for another log to throw on the fire, 'is this.' His hand flew past the stacked logs and landed on the hilt of his sword.

Swinging the blade up, aiming its awesome point straight at de Courtenay, he said coldly, 'You are premature, Denys. Clever, devious, but premature.'

He took in the surprise on de Courtenay's face, the very first look of doubt. He found that, despite everything, he was quite enjoying himself.

'What you have forgotten,' he said pleasantly, 'is that, as far as we know, King Richard is still alive.'

Chapter Seventeen

Even then, de Courtenay rallied and went on the attack again.

'You can't be sure of that!' he cried. 'And he's on Crusade! Even if a Saracen scimitar doesn't get him, the dysentry probably will!'

'You do not convince me,' Josse said coldly.

'And if he dies, then what?' De Courtenay took no notice of the interruption. 'Queen Berengaria means nothing to him, they say, he spends so little time with her that, if she's to become with child, it'll more likely be a second immaculate conception! And John has no children – his wife hasn't been seen anywhere near him since the day they said their marriage vows! I tell you, these ruling Plantagenets have no future! Oh, *think*, Sir Josse! Put up your sword and let's talk our plan through!'

'*Our* plan?' Josse shouted. 'No, de Courtenay! Do not *dare* to include me in this!'

'But—' The handsome face creased into a puzzled frown. 'Just now, you were – you seemed to—' His expression cleared. 'Ah, I see. You were amusing yourself at my expense, weren't you? Playing me on your line, like a fisherman with a leaping salmon.'

The smile was still there, as wide and as radiant as ever, but, in some all but imperceptible way, de Courtenay's face had altered.

For the first time, Josse had a tiny glimpse of what lay behind the charm and the affability. What, when he thought about it, he had always known must be there. For this man had tortured and killed Mag Hobson.

What he saw was infinite cunning. And a ruthless, limitless capacity for evil.

But it was there and gone so quickly that it could have been a trick of the light . . .

When in doubt, take the initiative.

Gripping his sword tightly, gaining a rush of confidence from the familiar feel of it in his hand, Josse said, 'We have nothing more to say to one another, de Courtenay. I think you should leave.'

'Leave,' de Courtenay repeated quite softly. 'Yes, yes, perhaps I should.' He gave an elegant shrug. 'Ah, well, I did my best. We should have made a formidable team, d'Acquin, you and I. But it was not to be.' He gave an exaggerated sigh. 'A pity.'

He began to turn away, walking slowly, with slumped shoulders, towards the door. Josse, only partly taken in, let his concentration lapse. His brain still trying to assess the implications of that momentarily-glimpsed, alien look that had so briefly crossed de Courtenay's face, he let the point of his sword drop.

Only by a little.

But it was enough.

Spinning round, his own sword drawn so swiftly that its movement was a silvery blur, de Courtenay was on to Josse.

And there was something else: a vitally important factor which, considering de Courtenay had always been a potential adversary, Josse ought to have noticed instantly.

He was left-handed.

The quick and automatic reactions that came from a lifetime as a fighting man came to Josse's rescue; his own sword was up again even as de Courtenay launched the first savage swing, and he made contact with the blade as it homed in towards his chest. But the attack came from Josse's right side, and de Courtenay's sword, held in his left hand, bounced off Josse's blade and, as it fell, sliced into Josse's upper arm.

It did not hurt, not straight away. But Josse knew he was injured, gravely so, by the gush of his own warm blood which he felt flood up from the wound, seeping through his sleeve and beginning to drip on to the floor.

And, more significantly, by the sudden loss of strength in his right arm.

Shifting his sword to his left hand, he rushed at de Courtenay, trying to find the space in the man's defence, trying to see how he swung, where he left himself vulnerable. He made contact, and a flower of bright blood appeared on de Courtenay's chin.

But it was a small wound – de Courtenay appeared barely to notice it.

Again, Josse lunged, but de Courtenay seemed to be thinking too quickly for him, so that, whatever Josse tried, whichever quarter he attacked from, his adversary was ready, parrying the heavy sword blows, his own weapon always there to defend him from Josse's fury.

But Josse was the attacker, that was for sure, and de Courtenay the defender; I must keep this up, Josse thought, fighting the worrying dizziness that was threatening to unbalance him. My only hope is if I keep him on the retreat.

For the alternative – for de Courtenay to gain the advantage and make Josse defend as he attacked – was not to be contemplated.

Josse did his best. But he was losing too much blood. And, although he was trained in the use of his non-dominant hand, he had never had to fight a man of de Courtenay's vicious determination under such a combination of handicaps.

Slowly, steadily, de Courtenay wore him down.

There was a moment of perfect balance, then, as their two swords unlocked, Josse experienced a split-second's blackness. He let his left arm fall.

When he was once more himself, it was to find de Courtenay forcing him backwards, sword whistling through the air, aiming for the junction between Josse's neck and his left shoulder. Gathering what strength and wits that remained to him, he tried to deflect the blow.

And, throwing himself off balance, fell to his knees.

He tried to fight the nausea and the faintness, tried to reach for his dagger – de Courtenay was above him now, he might be able to slide the smaller blade into his belly, or, if not that, then wound him sufficiently to arrest this onslaught . . .

He slumped forward, sword falling from his hand, his head drooping between his shoulders.

And waited for the end.

After a small eternity, he felt the edge of de Courtenay's sword kiss against his neck. Closing his eyes, he offered a swift prayer: forgive me, oh, Lord, my many sins, and . . .

Nothing happened. No whistle of a fast-descending blade, no sudden appalling agony as the blade bit.

He opened his eyes and tried to look up at de Courtenay.

He had drawn his dagger, and, with his sword shifted to his right hand, was trailing the dagger's point across the bare skin of Josse's neck and cheeks with his left.

'A more handy weapon,' he murmured, 'for what I have in mind. Not easy, is it, Josse, to slit off a man's ears and nose with a sword?'

Josse tried to elbow him away but the removal of one of his supporting arms made him fall to the floor.

'Oh, dear,' de Courtenay said with mock sympathy, 'the lion has turned into a kitten! Here, puss! Feel the tickle of my blade!' Josse winced as the dagger nicked a piece of flesh on his neck.

Then, as if he had abruptly tired of playing, de Courtenay bent low over Josse. He put down his sword and pressed his right hand to Josse's throat, constricting the windpipe, making Josse's already blurred sight fail altogether as the blackness encroached. The dagger pressing against Josse's cheek, de Courtenay hissed, 'Before I slit your throat, you will tell me where I may find her boy. Don't try to tell me you don't know, because I am fully aware that you do.' The dagger punctured the skin. 'And, each time you answer my question, where is he? with the answer, I don't know, I shall slice off one of your features.'

Josse, lying on his right side, tried to find his dagger with his left hand. There! No, no, no. There! No . . . yes.

His hand closed over the slim hilt.

'Now,' de Courtenay said, 'where is Joanna's child?'

'I . . . ' Josse closed his eyes and moaned, faking a rush of faintness; he didn't have to try hard to make the act convincing. 'De Courtenay wait, I—'

The dagger bit again. 'Where is the boy?' came the inexorable voice.

'You must let me think!' Josse cried, 'I'm so dizzy I can't get my wits to work!'

De Courtenay's hand on his throat tightened, and Josse lost consciousness for a few seconds. Opening his eyes again, he found de Courtenay's face directly above his, and the eyes were burning with a dreadful mixture of furious intent and sadistic pleasure.

'There!' he said. 'Now, breathe deep, Josse, while I permit it, then tell me what I want to know.'

Josse filled his lungs and, as he did so, drew his dagger from its sheath.

'That's better!' de Courtenay said conversationally. He began to tighten his grip on Josse's throat again. 'Now, this time, sir knight, you *will* tell me. Before I choke off your air, you will reveal what you have done with the boy. Or else, when you next regain your wits, you will find that you lack an ear.'

De Courtenay's dagger pressed against the back of Josse's left ear. At the same time, de Courtenay's other hand was slowly stopping him from breathing . . .

The world seemed to swoop and whirl around Josse's slumped body. The blackness before his eyes was shot through with brilliant, painful bursts of light. Opening his mouth, gasping for air, he said, 'The boy is – I've put him in the care of—'

With the last of his strength, he thrust upwards with his left hand. The dagger held firm, and he felt his fingers entangle with de Courtenay's tunic. Then there was a sudden weight on him, crushing him, sending shock-waves of white-hot pain through his wounded right arm, and he lost consciousness.

But not for long. The pain sliced through his faint, and, with a desperate heave, he thrust de Courtenay's body off him and breathed in deeply. Lying flat on his back, he drew several vast breaths. His throat burned like hellfire, and he could feel trickles of blood from various points on his face and neck.

But I'm alive, he thought wonderingly. I'm alive.

After a few moments, he managed to prop himself up. Edging carefully towards de Courtenay, he looked at the body.

The man was dead. No doubt about that.

He lay on his side, one arm flung behind him. His sword was half-underneath him, his dagger lay where it had fallen from his dead hand.

There was a large pool of blood beneath his chest. As Josse watched, one or two sluggish drips formed on the torn tunic and fell with a soft plop into the spreading puddle beneath him.

Sticking out from between de Courtenay's ribs was the handle of a dagger.

I got him! Josse thought wonderingly. By some sort of miracle, I found – was given – the accuracy and the strength to stab him to the heart.

For the cut had to have pierced the heart; no other part of the body suffering a wound could, in Josse's experience, produce so much blood so quickly.

He looked at the straight black handle of the blade.

Something was wrong with it . . .

He shook his head, trying to fight the befuddlement of his wits, trying to *think* . . .

Aye. That was it.

Josse's dagger had a narrow hilt, and it was not black.

And, besides, he still held his own dagger in his left hand.

Turning, raising his head with an effort as though he were lifting a tree, he saw her.

She stood a few paces back, as if horror kept her at bay.

He said, his voice so hoarse that the words were barely audible, 'Your knife.'

And she said, 'Yes.'

There was silence. Then he said, 'I once said to you that I wouldn't back your small blade against de Courtenay.' He looked down at the body, then back at Joanna. 'How wrong I was.'

Her face deathly pale, she whispered, 'I thought you were going to tell him where Ninian was.'

Josse managed a smile. 'No. I wasn't going to do that. I was trying to get him off his guard while I prepared to slide my own blade into him.'

She came towards him out of the shadows, kneeling down, taking his face in her hands, gentle fingers touching the marks on his face. 'He was about to mutilate you,' she whispered. 'Would not any man weaken, under such torture? And you were already so wounded.' Her voice broke on a sob.

He raised his hand and clasped her wrist. 'You command loyalty in your friends, Joanna,' he said. 'Which is no surprise. Mag Hobson didn't talk. And neither would I have done.'

She slumped against him, and he could feel her trembling. 'I'm sorry,' she muttered. 'So, so sorry.'

'That you killed him? he asked gently. 'Lady, there is no need, he was a man whose way of life must constantly have put him at risk. And—'

She had raised her head and was looking at him. 'No, Josse. All things considered, I don't believe I *am* sorry I killed him,' she said. 'I'm sorry about *you*.' She was trying to pull his sleeve away from the cut in his right arm, hands gentle but insistent, causing waves of agony to shoot right through him.

'Joanna, I—' he began.

Then he passed out.

Chapter Eighteen

He awoke to find himself lying quite comfortably on the floor in front of the fire. Joanna was sitting in his chair, looking quite composed, hands folded in her lap.

He turned his head a little, enough to look at the place where de Courtenay had fallen.

The body was no longer there.

Relaxing – had he dreamt the whole thing, after all? – he closed his eyes and did a quick tally of his wounds.

The great slice into his right arm felt hot, but numb. Whatever Joanna had done had dulled the pain and he thanked God for her skills. If you've got to earn yourself a deep wound, he thought vaguely, then what better time than when you have an apprentice wise woman under your roof?

The main pain came from his neck, where, it seemed, one of de Courtenay's dagger pricks had gone in more deeply. The wound was throbbing in time to his heartbeat. Throb . . . throb . . . throb . . .

From somewhere nearby, a voice said softly, 'Don't fight to stay awake, Josse. All is well. Sleep now, and you will heal the quicker.'

It made sense.

Relaxing, giving in to the drowsiness, he let himself drift off.

When next he awoke, it was almost totally dark. The hall was lit by a solitary candle, and someone – Joanna – had covered him warmly with a fur rug.

He was, he realised, terribly thirsty.

Opening parched lips – he experienced a dry, cracking sensation as he did so – he whispered, 'I need to drink.'

Instantly she was there, swooping down beside him, one hand behind his head to support him while, with the other hand, she held a cup to his lips.

'There – gently now! Not too much!'

The cool, refreshing water slid into his mouth. He swallowed, and she let him take another sip. Then she took the cup away.

'More!' he protested.

She was wiping his mouth with a cold, damp cloth, and he licked his lips to take in the moisture. 'No more for now,' she said. 'Soon, another couple of sips.'

He relaxed against the cushions under his head. 'Thank you.'

'How do you feel?'

'Sleepy.' Then: 'It's dark. Is it night?'

'Yes. Are you in pain?'

He did his inventory again. 'My neck hurts.'

'Where?'

He raised a hand that felt as heavy as a boulder and indicated. 'I see.'

He sensed her move away. Quite soon she came back, and he felt something cool press against the throbbing wound in his neck. It stung at first, but then that stopped. And so did the pain.

'You,' he murmured, 'are a goddess.'

'No!' she cried instantly. Then she muttered, 'Ah, but he's joking, not blaspheming.' She said, in her normal tone, 'It's just something Mag taught me.'

'An apprentice wise woman,' he murmured. 'Just what I thought.'

'What's that?' She sounded wary.

'Nothing, my love.' He shifted his weight slightly, making himself more comfortable. 'Just a thought I had earlier, when I woke up and realised my arm didn't hurt.'

'It is a deep wound,' she said sombrely. 'I've stitched it together, but we must watch carefully for any signs of infection.'

'Stitched it together.' He felt slightly sick again.

'Yes. Don't worry, Josse, Mag taught me well.'

'Aye, I'm sure.' He fought with the sickness which seemed determined to rise. To take his mind off thoughts of her handiwork, he asked, 'Where is de Courtenay? He was lying just there, and now he isn't.'

'Don't worry about that, either. He's taken care of,' she said soothingly.

'You didn't manage that, all on your own!' He'd noticed she was strong, but not that strong, surely! De Courtenay had been no weakling, no lightweight.

'No, no,' she was saying. 'Josse, I'm not the only one with loyal friends. Your Will, now, would, I warrant, do anything for you.'

'Will?'

'Yes. Will. He and I took de Courtenay outside – we wanted to act now, under cover of night – and Will is burying the body in a ditch.'

'Burying him?'

'He is dead. You realise that?'

'Of course! But—'

But what? But we must send for the Sheriff, report the murder, describe the circumstances, hope that, by so doing, we convince them that it was self-defence?

And supposing they don't agree? What then?

Then I, Josse thought – for no part of him could even contemplate letting Joanna take the blame – then I would go on trial for murder. And I might very well hang.

But to bury de Courtenay in a New Winnowlands ditch! Not even to bury the corpse himself, but to have Will do it!

Could his conscience ever rest easy again, bearing the stain of all that?

His conscience was, he quickly realised, going to have to do its best. The alternative was unthinkable.

He said, 'Joanna, would you fetch Will?'

'Of course.'

She came back quite quickly – presumably Will's ditch was not far distant – and Will, looming behind her, said, 'Sir? I hope I've done as you'd wish, but I've put him right at the bottom of that long trench I was digging down at the end of the orchard, where we was worrying about the tendency for that corner to flood. He's down deep, sir, won't nobody find him, leastways, not if they don't know where to look.'

Will's earnest face touched Josse deeply. He reached out his hand, and, after a small hesitation, Will put out his too and grasped it.

'Thank you, Will,' Josse said. 'It's more than I have any right to ask of you, but thank you.'

'You didn't ask.' Will grinned briefly. 'You wasn't in no state to ask aught of anybody, sir.' He glanced at Joanna. 'And I couldn't stand by and see the young lady here struggling all by herself with such a task, now, could I?'

'But, Will, if there should ever be investigations about him, if anybody should ask you directly what you knew . . .'

Will waited courteously to see if he were going to finish. When he didn't, Will said, 'If anybody should ask about a body, I should say, body? What body?'

'De Courtenay's body!' Josse said, beginning to feel fuddled again.

And Will, adopting a convincing expression of bovine dullness, said, 'Eh? Who? Never heard of him.'

'I won't forget this, Will,' Josse said.

Will was getting up. 'I know that, sir. Now, if you'll excuse me, I have a trench to finish backfilling.'

Alone again with Joanna, Josse said, 'Is it safe? Do you think he'll ever be found?'

She shrugged. 'Who can say? But I doubt it. For one thing, Will has, as he said, buried him deep. For another, what is there to connect Denys de Courtenay with you or New Winnow-lands? I think we can safely discount the peasant who came here to summon you into Denys's trap – it's not likely that a wretch like him would speak out against a knight. What would be the point? Anything he said would be instantly dismissed.'

'He wasn't the only one,' Josse murmured. 'De Courtenay had another two outside with him.'

Joanna shrugged. 'The same applies to them. Apart from them, who else but you and I know that Denys followed you here?'

'Brother Saul,' Josse murmured, 'and the Abbess Helewise.'

'Both of whom are your true and loving friends,' she countered quickly, 'and who, if you tell them the truth, will understand that this death is not on your conscience. That you fought bravely, but were overcome. That, holding out against threatened torture, your courage cannot be faulted.' She paused, took a deep breath and said, 'That another hand killed Denys de Courtenay.'

He said softly, 'Never admit that again. Not to me, not to anybody.'

She stared deep into his eyes. And, after a pause, whispered, 'No. I won't.'

'I will tell the Abbess,' he announced presently, 'that de Courtenay was stricken as we fought. That it was by pure mischance that he fell on to my blade—'

'– which just happened to pierce his heart,' she finished. There was a wry humour in her voice. 'Josse, you won't do that. Whatever explanation you choose to give, I should, if I might suggest, keep it brief.'

'But she'll want to know,' he protested. 'I'll have to tell her *something*!'

Joanna put her hand on his brow, smoothing out the frown. 'Dear Josse,' she murmured. 'You can't bear to think of lying to those you love, can you?'

'I—' He stopped. She was right, it was something he could not contemplate. Helewise's face sprang into his mind, frowning as she worried over some matter he had taken to lay at her feet, willingly putting all her intelligence and her experience at his disposal. Which, considering everything else constantly clamouring for her attention, was a gift indeed.

'She's——' he began. 'She's a woman who——'

But he was attempting to explain Helewise to Joanna. And that, he realised, was something he would find difficult, even were he not suffering from a grievous wound.

'It's all right,' Joanna said soothingly. 'I understand.'

And, light-headed as he was, possibly seeing with a greater clarity than when he was fully himself, he knew that she did.

It was only when he woke the next morning that he remembered Brother Saul was also under his roof. Also under the care of Joanna.

He said, as soon as she appeared with a drink and a light breakfast of a bowl of thin gruel, 'How is Brother Saul?'

She smiled. 'Brother Saul is quite well. So well, in fact, that he left us soon after first light and is even now riding back to Hawkenlye to put his Abbess's mind at rest.'

'What's he going to tell her?' Josse struggled to sit up.

'Don't worry!' She put out a restraining hand. 'He will tell her the truth, but the truth as he has been told it.'

'Which is?'

Her eyes widened into an expression of innocence. 'Don't you remember? Oh, dear, it must be because you're still not yourself! Listen well, then, and I will tell you. There was a fight, between you and Denys, and you drew your dagger to defend yourself, and he fell against it when he tripped.'

He held her eyes. 'That's the truth?'

'It is,' she said firmly.

'Can you live with that?' he whispered.

And, raising her chin, she replied, 'I can.'

It was two days before she would let him ride, and, even then, she told him crossly that he was daft even to *think* of it, and he ought to be abed still, building up his strength. By the time he was a third of the way to Hawkenlye, he was beginning to agree with her.

He had resisted her attempts to persuade him to let her go too. If he were going to have to lie to Abbess Helewise – which he knew he was – then it would be marginally better not to have a witness. Particularly if that witness were Joanna.

He made himself ignore his weakness. He urged Horace on, infected now with a sense of urgency. Even though he knew Brother Saul would have told the Abbess what had happened – the version he had been given, that was – still Josse longed to reassure her himself.

Clinging on as Horace increased his pace to a sprightly canter, Josse gritted his teeth and tried to work out what he was going to say.

Helewise had spent an awful few days.

Brother Saul's return mid-way through the morning two days ago had given her the blessed relief of knowing he was alive and well, and apparently none the worse for his ordeal.

'But you were attacked!' she had protested after listening to his tale. 'Saul, you must let Sister Euphemia attend to your hurts!'

'What hurts I received were mild,' he reassured her. 'And Joanna looked after me – she has a gentle hand and a sound knowledge of remedies.'

Helewise had observed, with interest, the distinct softening of Brother Saul's features as he spoke of Joanna.

'Well, it's wonderful to have you safely home, Saul,' she said, 'an answer to my prayers.'

His face clouded. 'Abbess, you may not be so glad when I relay to you the news I bring.'

He had then told her about Denys de Courtenay's attack on Josse, the fight between the two men and de Courtenay's death.

'And they buried him out there at New Winnowlands?' she repeated, astounded. 'But why—'

She made herself stop. Brother Saul was not the person to whom she should address *that* question.

Thanking him, telling him again how grateful she was for his safe return, she dismissed him. And began her long wait for the arrival of Josse.

He came into her room two days later. She could see at once that he had been hurt; his face was deathly pale and he held his right wrist supported in his left hand. There were small cuts on his throat, neck and left cheek.

'Sir Josse!' she cried. 'Oh, but you've been wounded!'

'I'm all right,' he said instantly and unconvincingly; he was, she could see, swaying on his feet. She rushed round from behind her table, took him by the left arm and guided him to her chair, carefully sitting him down and hovering anxiously over him.

'Do you feel faint?'

'I'm all *right!*'

She tutted under her breath, then went outside into the cloister and summoned a passing nun to go and find Sister Euphemia. 'Ask her, please, Sister Beata, to prepare a heartening draught, and bring it back with you for our visitor. Quick as you can, please!'

Then she returned to Josse.

'I'm honoured,' he said, looking up at her with a faint smile, 'to be allowed to sit in your seat.'

'I shall not make a habit of permitting it,' she replied, trying to match his attempt at levity. 'But today you look as if you need it.'

'Aye, I do.' He moved his arm a little, wincing as he did so.

'A relic of your fight with Denys de Courtenay?' she asked softly.

'Aye.'

'And he tripped and fell on to your dagger, and suffered a fatal wound, Brother Saul tells me.'

'Aye.'

She noticed that he did not meet her eye. She knew straight away that he was lying; the perplexing question was, why?

She walked slowly back to the door, opening it to see if there were any sign of Sister Beata. If Josse killed Denys de Courtenay during a fight in which Denys was the instigator, she reasoned to herself, then that was surely self-defence and no crime has been committed. And there are witnesses to swear that Denys was indeed the instigator of the fight.

Why, then, would Josse . . .

Her thoughts trailed to a stop.

Yes. Of course.

Sister Beata was hurrying across the cloister, bearing a stoppered flask and a mug. 'Sister Euphemia says he can have as much of this as he wants, it's quite mild, and that if you need her, say so, except that could it wait a while as she's just setting a broken wrist and can't come right away unless it's terribly urgent,' she said, all in one breath. Helewise had the impression that Sister Beata was repeating the infirmarer's exact words, and wanted to say them quickly before she forgot any of them.

She took the flask and mug from Sister Beata. 'Thank you, Sister. Please tell Sister Euphemia that, for the present, there is no need for her to come. I will let her know if the situation changes.'

Sister Beata, knowing herself to be dismissed, made a bow and walked slowly away.

Helewise gave Josse a long drink of the infirmarer's restorative. A little colour returned to his face. With a deep sigh, he put the mug down on the table.

He said, without any preliminaries, 'Ninian is the child of Henry of England.'

Helewise felt her mouth drop open. 'The late King?'

'Himself.'

'This was one of the unfortunate things you referred to, when you spoke of Joanna's past?' she asked gently.

'Er – aye.' He leaned towards her, his face intent. 'That rat of a cousin took her to court one Christmas, paraded her before the King and, when the King took a fancy to her, made quite certain he got her. De Courtenay himself led her to the King's bed, held her down while the King took her. He—'

'Sir Josse, I don't need to hear any more,' she interrupted, laying her hand briefly on his shoulder. 'I had surmised, from what little you told me before, that something of this nature had occurred. I had not, however, imagined a seducer of such exalted rank.' She paused, biting her lip as she thought deeply. 'And de Courtenay wanted to make a bid to put the boy on the throne?'

'He did.'

'Which Joanna, obviously, didn't want.'

'Why is that obvious?' Josse demanded. 'I'd been taking it for granted until just now, riding over here, when it suddenly occurred to me to ask just why she's so set against the idea.'

'Oh, Sir Josse, think!' Helewise was quite surprised he should ask that. 'What good impressions can Joanna de Courtenay possibly have of Plantagenet court life? Seduced and impregnated by the King of England, then, when she became an inconvenience, married off to some Breton knight to get her out of the way. Would any woman want to introduce her beloved only son into such a world? I know I should not, in her place.'

'But the power and the riches!' he protested. 'The world would lie at the boy's feet, were he King!'

'Only part of the world,' she pointed out. 'And it would by no means be a foregone conclusion that he would ever *be* King, since there are several other contenders for the throne, even assuming King Richard no longer sat upon it. And just imagine the danger to Ninian, once his identity had been revealed! Why, every other faction with its eyes on the throne would be after his blood! No, Sir Josse. The reason for Joanna's reluctance is perfectly obvious to *me*.'

'Hmm.' He was frowning, his face creased in lines of anxiety. And also, she thought, studying him closely, of sorrow.

'Sir Josse?' she asked. 'What is it?'

He raised his head and turned mournful eyes on her. 'She didn't tell me,' he said quietly.

'Didn't tell you what?'

'Who the lad's father was. She told me everything else – oh, I had all the sordid details – but not that.'

'Perhaps she didn't know?' It seemed unlikely and Helewise knew she was clutching at straws.

'She must have done. Anyway, if she didn't, it makes a nonsense of her elaborate plan to keep Ninian out of de Courtenay's reach. That was why she agreed to his coming here while I took her off to New Winnowlands – she was leading de Courtenay away from him.'

'Yes, that makes sense,' Helewise agreed.

'So why didn't she tell me?' he demanded. 'She didn't trust me, did she?'

Helewise's heart hurt to see the pain in his face. Oh, dear Lord, but she's got under his skin! she thought. 'Josse, I'm not sure that it's possible for anybody but another mother to understand the protective instinct which a woman has for her child,' she said, her hand once more resting on his shoulder. 'I know, from my own experience, that, once a baby is born, he becomes, to begin with, the whole world to his mother, and, although that intensity lessens as he grows up and steadily becomes more independent, you never lose it entirely. Indeed, it's quite common for husbands to resent the children they have fathered, because the act of childbirth changes a wife into a mother, and there is no going back.' She paused. We speak of Joanna, she reminded herself firmly, not of me.

'In a loveless marriage, Ninian would have been even more precious to Joanna,' she went on, 'and the bonds between them would have strengthened as he grew older. So that, when she sensed the threat from Denys de Courtenay, she would have done anything – whatever it took – to keep her child safe. Josse, my dear, do you not see that, even though she probably longed to reveal the secret of the boy's parenthood, she just didn't dare?'

'She didn't trust me,' he repeated stubbornly.

'She *couldn't* trust you,' Helewise corrected. 'It wasn't Joanna who would be in danger if the secret came out, but Ninian.'

He did not reply. Watching him closely, she saw him pass his hand across his face a couple of times. Then he said, 'Aye. Aye, you're right. And I'm being foolish. It's just that we've grown so close, Joanna and I, and—'

He stopped.

This time, the silence was rather longer.

Helewise moved away, and stood with her back to him on the other side of her table. After some time, hoping her voice would sound quite normal, she said, 'Which of them, Joanna or Mag Hobson, do you think put the poison in the pie meant for de Courtenay?'

He began to say something, but his voice broke. Clearing his throat, he started again. 'I think probably Mag Hobson. She certainly would have prepared the dose – she's skilled in plant lore and, until her death, had been teaching Joanna. Mag would have been far less conspicuous – there are always a few old men and women hanging around the kitchen courtyard at the inn in Tonbridge, Goody Anne is generous with leftovers. They were busy that day, we know that, and with Goody Anne, Tilly and the serving boy all occupied with tending to people's needs in the tap room, it can't have been difficult for Mag to slip into the kitchen when nobody was looking.'

'How did she know what Denys had ordered?' Helewise asked.

'I've thought about that. She must have followed him into the tap room – he'd never met her, not then, and so he wouldn't have known what she looked like – and listened while he told Tilly what he wanted to eat. Then she must have got round to the kitchen before Tilly did and slipped the poison in Denys's pie.'

'Would that be possible? For her to reach the kitchen before Tilly?'

'Aye. If you went out through the main door and slipped along the side passage, you could do it easily.'

'I see.'

He was shifting in the chair, apparently about to get up. 'I must go back home,' he said. 'I promised Joanna I'd speak to Ninian, see how he is, take any message he may have for her. Can I see him?'

'Of course. Doesn't she want to have him back with her?'

'No,' he said shortly. 'Not yet.'

Why? Helewise wondered. Now that the danger was past, why should mother and son not be reunited?

But, sensing Josse didn't want to talk about it, she merely said, 'I will take you to him. You can reassure his mother that he's quite all right. He seems happy, he likes Sister Caliste, and he's eating like a horse.'

Josse grinned, very briefly. 'Can't be too much wrong with him, then.'

They were halfway across to the infirmary when Helewise stopped him. I have to speak, she thought, I can't let there be an untruth between us.

'What is it?' he asked, glancing down at her detaining hand on his sleeve. 'Why have we stopped?'

She looked round to make sure they were alone. Then, summoning her courage and taking a deep breath, she said, 'Josse, I know that the story which Brother Saul brought back, the story you have just repeated to me, is not true.' She noticed he was glaring at her, heavy eyebrows drawn down over his angry brown eyes. Go on! she ordered herself. You must! 'I cannot believe that a man just *happens* to fall on a dagger point which pierces him to the heart,' she hurried on, 'it's too convenient. And had you killed him as you fought, it would be self-defence and no crime, either in God's eyes or under the law of the land. The only other person who could have killed him is Joanna.'

He had hold of her by the shoulders, and he could not have realised, she thought, how hard he was gripping her. She held his eyes steadily, and, after a moment, he loosened his hands.

He said nothing.

She took his silence as an acknowledgement that she was right.

She was tempted to assure him, to swear that the secret was quite safe with her.

But she didn't really think there was any need.

Chapter Nineteen

Josse rode back to New Winnowlands with a heavy heart.

As well as everything else, he now felt he was a failure. The one thing he had wanted to keep from Helewise, and she had guessed it as easily as if he'd painted it across his forehead.

Ah, but it was a grave business, the whole damned thing.

And, to cap it all, his arm hurt like the very devil.

She came out to meet him as he rode into the courtyard. She took one look at him, and said, 'I told you the ride was too much for you. You're a fool, you should have had a longer convalescence. Now you're in pain, and it's your own fault.'

He slipped off Horace's back, gratefully handing the reins to the waiting Will. Stomping off towards the steps, he said, 'I'm a fool, am I? Well, I dare say I am.'

She recoiled at his tone. But she said nothing just then, merely accompanied him inside the hall, where, as soon as he had thrown off his cloak and settled himself in his chair in front of the fire, she knelt before him and asked meekly, 'Josse, may I dress your wound? I have prepared some of the pain-easing draught, if you will take it?'

He did not know what to make of her. First she hectored him like a fishwife, now here she was asking permission to care for him, with all the timidity of some docile maidservant.

Suddenly heartily sick of the whole thing, he said, 'Do what you like. You usually do.'

She bowed her head, as if accepting his rebuke.

She gave him some of her draught, then helped him remove his tunic and undershirt. As he sat there, keeping as still as he could, gritting his teeth against the sharp agony, she unwrapped the dressings on his arm, bathed the wound, applied some cool salve and re-wrapped it.

When he was dressed once more, she settled at his feet and said, 'Why are you angry with me?'

Because it was the thing that was uppermost in his mind, he said instantly, without pausing to think, 'You didn't trust me. You didn't tell me who Ninian's father was.'

'Denys told you?'

'Aye, he did.'

She sighed. 'Josse, I wanted to tell you. You must believe that! I *burned* to tell you and every instinct was assuring me I could trust you. And I usually do what my instincts tell me.' She paused, a slight frown between her brows. 'But I kept seeing Ninian's face. He's so loving, so trusting, and I couldn't help but think that if I gave in and told you about me and the King, then somehow it would be wrong. Dangerous. Oh, Josse, *please* don't ask me to explain! I can't, other than to say that it seemed to come down to a choice between you and Ninian, and I chose him.'

'Only another mother could understand,' he murmured.

She looked up sharply. 'Yes. Exactly that. How did you know?'

'*I* didn't. It was something Abbess Helewise said, when I told her—' Abruptly he broke off. Oh, God! What had he said?

Joanna was on her feet, face contorted with fury. 'You *told* her? You told your precious Abbess who Ninian's father was? When you *knew* how desperate I was to keep that knowledge secret?'

He, too, was on his feet. Taking hold of her, gripping hard and wincing at the pain shooting through his arm, he shouted, 'Aye, I did! And do you know why? Because she and I have perfect trust between us, *perfect* trust! We share secrets far more deadly than yours, let me tell you, and we have the faith in each other to confide anything we choose! That's what close friends do, Joanna, in case you didn't know!'

She was shaking her head, and he was surprised to see tears in her eyes. 'I'm sorry, Josse!' she cried, 'I'm so sorry! I didn't mean to hurt you, not when you've risked so much and done so much for me!'

He slackened his grip. 'It's all right, Joanna.' He couldn't prevent the coldness in his voice.

'But it's *not* all right!' she protested. 'You're probably thinking I only slept with you to make you help me.'

It was exactly what he *was* thinking. He made no reply.

She was staring up at him. 'You have to believe me when I say that's not true,' she said quietly. 'I've had enough of sex for reasons of manipulation. I was raped, I was made to give myself to a husband I loathed and I wouldn't even have considered bedding you as a means to any end at all. Even the safety of my son.' She paused. 'I wanted you, Josse,' she went on softly. 'Mag told me that one day I'd know what lovemaking really was and when I first met you, I felt the spark ignite. You gave me such joy, Josse. Such deep, wonderful pleasure.' She reached out her hand and lightly touched his cheek. 'However it ends between us, never forget that.'

Her hand fell.

For a moment, they stood facing one another. Then he reached out to brush the tears from her cheeks, and, holding her face in his hands, bent to kiss her very gently on the lips.

'Very well,' he said.

A swift smile crossed her face, there and gone. 'Very well?'

'I forgive you for not trusting me. And I'm honoured to have been the one who showed you what love could be.'

'I—' she began. Then she shook her head.

'What?'

She met his eyes. 'You speak of love, but I have to tell you that I cannot stay. Which is awkward, since you haven't suggested I should.'

He took a deep breath. 'Joanna, to meet your honesty with plain speaking of my own, it hadn't occurred to me that you would stay. If you wish it, however, then I will marry you.' That didn't sound quite right. 'I mean, I would be honoured if you would become my wife.'

There. It was said. He waited while she prepared her answer, and it seemed that his entire life hung in the balance.

She had half turned from him. Now, turning back to face him, she said, 'Josse, my dearest love, I do not wish to marry. I have been married and, although I would not dream of speaking of you in the same breath as my late and unlamented husband, marriage is not a state which recommends itself to me. Not in the least.'

'But—'

She smiled at him now, wholeheartedly, her face full of humour. 'Sweetest, do not try to persuade me too hard, when I know full well that you are scarcely more keen to be married than I am.'

Was she right? He shook his head, not knowing how he felt.

'Marriage is no good for women,' she was saying. 'At least, that's what I think. I don't want to be at a man's beck and call, be his possession, bought and paid for, with no more say in my own destiny than one of his cows or his sheep.'

'But—'

'Oh, don't interrupt, Josse – I'm telling you how I see it, which is, as far as I'm concerned, all that matters. No. I prefer to make my own way, answer to none but myself.'

'And how do you propose to live?' he asked.

She threw her head back. 'I shall make out very well,' she declared. 'I have skills which are ever in demand.'

'The skills Mag taught you?'

'Yes. I know only a tiny part of all there is to know – it takes a lifetime, and Mag and I had so few months together. But there are others such as she. And I know where to find them. They will be willing to teach me, because of Mag.'

'I see.'

She smiled again. 'No, I don't think you do. But it doesn't matter.'

'And where will you live?'

Her face lit with sudden radiance. 'In the little manor house, when I'm not staying down in Mag's shack in the woods.'

'The *manor* house?'

'Yes. It's mine.'

'But it can't be, it belonged to . . .'

'To my mother's great-uncle and aunt, yes. They left it to my mother and, as my mother's only surviving child, now it has come to me.'

He said, for want of anything else, 'You can't live in a place like that all on your own!'

And she said simply, 'Yes I can.'

He turned away from her, returning to his chair to slump down, suddenly exhausted.

She followed him.

'Poor Josse,' she said, gently stroking the thick hair off his forehead, 'so much to put up with. I will fetch food and drink for us in a little while, I promise – Ella has prepared what she says is your favourite meal – but first, there is one more thing I must ask of you.'

He looked up at her, managing a half-smile. 'Why stop at one?'

She answered his smile. 'I know, I'm sorry. But this isn't for me, it's for Ninian.'

'Ask away.'

She crouched beside him. 'The life I outlined is perfect, for me. It is exactly what I want. But it's not right for him – I can't take the decision to remove him from the mainstream of life and turn him into a wise woman's son, condemned for ever to live on the fringes of life. Not when I know who he really is. Can I?'

'No,' he acknowledged. 'I do see what you mean.'

'Had Thorald lived,' she went on, 'which I thank God he didn't – since we're to trust each other with all our secrets, Josse, I ought to tell you that it was I who put the stone in his horse's shoe that morning, in the fervent hope that it would result in a fatal trip, which happily it did – where was I? Oh, yes. Had Thorald lived, then Ninian would have been sent as page to join some other knightly household, and, in time, he would have become a squire. What I'm asking—' She paused, and he saw tears in her eyes again. Blinking them back, she said, 'Will you arrange that for Ninian? Put him into a good house somewhere, make sure he grows up as he should?'

Josse reached out and took her hands. 'You will lose him,' he said gently. 'You do realise, don't you?'

She nodded, the tears falling unchecked down her face.

'Once he's a squire, the next step will be to win his spurs,' Josse went on. 'He'll be caught up in his own life, Joanna. A good life – and I ought to know – but one so different from yours that I doubt he'll be able to bridge the gap.'

'I know,' she sobbed. 'But it's what he was born to. It would be a great sin for me to rob him of it, just to keep him with me.' She raised her wet eyes to his. 'Wouldn't it?'

His heart breaking for her, slowly he nodded.

'Will you do it?' she persisted. 'Will you give me your word to do your best for him?'

Reaching down, he lifted her up until she was kneeling before him. Then he wrapped his arms round her, and, pulling her face down against the bare skin of his neck so that he felt the moisture of her tears, he said, 'Aye, Joanna. I promise.'

Later, when she was calm again, she did as she had said, and fetched the meal which Ella had prepared for them. But neither had much appetite.

She said anxiously, 'Is your arm paining you? Is that why you don't eat?'

'No, the arm's all right. I'm sorry, Joanna. The food is good, but I'm not hungry.'

She pushed a chicken leg around her plate, holding it delicately between finger and thumb. 'Neither am I.'

'We have come to grave decisions today, Joanna,' he said. 'Decisions which will affect both of us, for the rest of our lives.'

'Yes,' she murmured.

He watched her. Slowly, as if aware of his scrutiny, she raised her eyes and met his. Wordlessly he opened his arms, and she got up and hurried over to him. He sat her down on his lap, cradling her to him.

'That's nice,' she murmured, as he began to stroke her back. 'I had wondered if, having decided we are not to stay together, that might mean we could not bed one another again. But—'

He smiled. 'But what?'

'Do you have an opinion on the matter, Sir Josse?' The teasing note was back. It was a shadow of its former self, but it was there.

'I see no reason to suspend our relations,' he said gravely. 'We are, after all, both over the age of consent, and—'

'Some of us further over than others,' she put in.

'– and there seems, on the face of it, no reason to abandon something which gives us both such pleasure.' He held her face in his hands, meeting her eyes. 'Shall we retire to bed, Joanna my sweet?'

She said, 'Yes.'

But now, knowing he was to lose her, lovemaking was bitter-sweet. At one point, feeling tears on her face, he wanted to cry with her. Controlling himself, he hugged her close to him.

She said out of the darkness, 'When God gave us the infinite gift of tears, Josse, I don't think He said anything about their being used solely to bring comfort to women.'

And so he wept with her. It brought relief, of a sort.

In the early morning light, she got out of bed and dressed. He watched as she collected her few belongings together, stowing them into her pack. Her black-handled knife, he noticed, was once more in its sheath on her belt. Had it been she who removed it from Denys de Courtenay's body? He imagined it had. Somehow he couldn't see her allowing Will – allowing anybody – to touch her own personal weapon.

'You are going,' he said. It was not a question.

'I am.' She looked up. 'I shall go first to Hawkenlye Abbey. If you think your Abbess will see me, I shall tell her what is planned for Ninian. Then I shall see him. I must explain to him why we—' She stopped. Recovering herself, she said, 'He needs to hear, from me, why I have arranged his future as I have.'

Wanting so desperately to console her, he said, 'It need not be for ever, Joanna. He will always know where to find you, and he'll be able to come to see you sometimes. Perhaps.'

She smiled at him. 'Thank you for that, Josse. It is, as I know you intended it to be, a comfort. But I don't think either of us truly believes it.'

He lay back. Just at that moment, he felt utterly exhausted.

She was ready to leave. Crossing to the bed, she bent over him and kissed him hard on the mouth. Then she said, 'Will you be all right?'

'Aye.'

'I meant your arm,' she said gently. 'Will you get someone at the Abbey to look after it for you?'

'Aye,' he repeated.

She had crossed to the door, and was standing there looking back at him. 'It wouldn't have worked between us, you know,' she said.

'How can you be so sure?'

'Because you've already given your— ' She stopped. 'Never mind. I just know. Goodbye, Josse.'

She was already out of the door as he echoed, 'Goodbye.'

Chapter Twenty

'. . . and, with a last look over her shoulder, she was gone,' Helewise said.

Josse, she noticed, seemed to be more his old self. It was now almost a fortnight since Joanna de Lehon – once more calling herself Joanna de Courtenay – had arrived at Hawkenlye, asked to see the Abbess, announced what she intended to do and sought out her son to say goodbye.

It had taken Helewise that fortnight to get over the experience.

'She's a most forceful young woman, isn't she?' Helewise went on. 'She appears to know her own mind.'

'Aye, she does that, all right,' Josse agreed.

'And strong,' Helewise said. 'I had the powerful impression that she is a born survivor.'

Josse sighed. 'Aye.' Then, with an obvious effort: 'You spent some time in conversation with her, then, Abbess?'

'No, indeed not.' Their meeting, Helewise recollected, had been all too brief. 'It was apparent that Joanna was steeling herself to do what she must do. I did not think it either right or kind to detain her by chattering away to her.'

He said, 'How did she – how was she, having bid her adieu to her boy?'

Helewise had been trying not to think about that. Not very successfully. 'As you would expect, Sir Josse. But, in Ninian's presence, she maintained a cheerful expression. She even managed to laugh when he told her about being dressed up as a nun, when Denys de Courtenay came here searching for him. Of course, we all thought then that it was Joanna he wanted, but—'

'Dressed up as a nun?'

'To hide him,' she explained. 'Where better to hide a tree than in a wood? In robe and veil, Ninian looked much like all the others, once his grubby boy's hands were tucked out of sight. A little smaller, but then there are plenty of grown women of short stature.'

'Joanna must have been grateful for that. I don't think she knew de Courtenay had actually searched the Abbey.'

'Indeed he did, and very thoroughly.'

There was a short pause. Then Josse said, 'Abbess, will she be all right?'

Helewise composed her reply before uttering it. 'I believe she will,' she said eventually. 'It near broke her heart to say goodbye to her son, but, as we walked to the gate, we comforted ourselves with the thought that, had she and Ninian remained where they were in her Breton knight's house, the time would soon have arrived for Ninian to go away to another man's household anyway, to begin his knightly apprenticeship. The break was harder for Joanna – for the boy, too – because they have spent these past months and years in such mutual dependence. But there would have been a break. And, I imagine, they both knew it, and had privately been preparing for it. I—'

She had been about to say, I certainly did, when it was my turn. But we are not speaking of me, she reminded herself.

It was a reminder she was needing quite frequently, at present.

Josse gave her a smile. 'You comfort me, too,' he said. 'As always.'

She bowed her head, studying her hands folded in her lap. It was not easy to accept his generous words, when her conscience was pricking her. Perhaps she should . . . No. Euphemia could so easily have been mistaken.

'. . . out in the wildwood?' Josse was saying.

'I'm sorry, Sir Josse, what did you say?'

He looked at her curiously. 'You were not attending, Abbess!'

'No, I was thinking of Joanna. You were speaking of the wildwood?'

'Aye. I was wondering how you thought she would fare, living in Mag Hobson's old shack. She did tell you of her intention, to continue learning the old crafts?'

'She did. And I think she will do very well. Sir Josse, bearing in mind Joanna's character and her recent past, I truly believe her best chance of happiness – perhaps her only one – is to detach from the world she has known. It has treated her roughly, and she bears a heavy burden of resentment and anger. Living alone out there in the woods, with nature all around her, she will have a tough life, but I believe it will heal her. She needs, above everything, to be mistress of herself. I feel that she will find contentment. I pray that she will.'

'Amen to that,' Josse muttered. Then: 'You are easy with yourself, living with the knowledge that she is out there in the forest, consorting with Mag Hobson's old friends, learning all that they will pass on to her?'

Easy with myself? Helewise thought. No, I am not. For, despite her strength and her self-sufficiency, Joanna is a human being, needing love, as do we all. Needing God's help and blessing, as do we all. Yet there she will be, alone, turning her back on Our Lord, following the old ways . . .

But, then, it was Joanna's choice. And, as Helewise herself had just said, Joanna knew her own mind.

Something told her not to repeat these reservations to Josse. Making herself face him, forcing a bright smile, she said, 'I must be easy with myself, Josse. As must you be. For Joanna has made her decision, and we must live with it.'

He was getting to his feet, preparing to leave. He still moved his right arm stiffly; Helewise had seen the wound, when Sister Euphemia dressed it earlier, and, even in its largely healed state, the sight of the great slash had near made her pass out. He had been lucky not to lose the use of the arm; the cut had gone deep into the muscle.

It was Euphemia's opinion that only Joanna's neat stitches and cleansing, healing salves had saved the arm, let alone Josse's use of it.

Another legacy of Joanna de Courtenay, Helewise thought, walking with Josse to the stables. He will always bear that scar, to the end of his days. As will he also always carry his love for her.

She stood by Horace's side as Josse swung up into the saddle. Looking up, she met his eyes. There was so much she wanted to say, about love never being wasted, about what he had shared with Joanna being of precious value, even though it was over.

But we do not have that sort of talk between us, she told herself. So she just said, 'Farewell, Sir Josse. Come and see us again soon.'

He gave her a vague wave, and turned Horace's head towards the gates. 'Aye, I will,' he said. 'Farewell, Abbess Helewise.'

She watched until he had ridden away and out of sight.

Then, with a sigh, she returned to her duties.

Postscript

Joanna was approaching the beginning of her first autumn of living in Mag Hobson's shack. It was October, still mild, but she had reluctantly to admit that summer was over. The midday sun was no longer as powerful, the leaves were starting to turn and, in some cases, to drop, and once or twice she had been tempted to stoke up the fire in her hearth to warm her through the night.

Since quitting Hawkenlye Abbey – and the precious person it then had contained – back in February, she had spent virtually all her time in the hut in the clearing. She went up to the manor house now and then, to make sure all was well and that doors and gates were secure. But the house was too full of the presence of people she had loved and lost. Ninian. Mag. And Josse. She far preferred life in the shack.

There had been little need to clean it or tidy it, for Mag had cared for it well. But Joanna had felt a certain impulse to add something of her own personality to the small dwelling and its surroundings; she brought from the manor house a few care-fully-chosen items, each of which was important to her in some way.

She brought the willow basket which Ninian had made, under Mag's tuition. She also brought his long-discarded hobby horse; she had painted its face herself, an age ago, and had given the horsy features a look of Ninian. It was comforting, to have standing in the corner of her little shack an object which radiated her son's elemental self.

She also brought the furs and the rugs which had lain before the fire in the hall, on which she and Josse had first made love. If she buried her face in them and breathed in deeply, she could conjure up Josse's presence. That, too, was a comfort.

There had been little need to bring clothing, for she always wore the same garments, washing them when they needed it and, while they dried by the fire, spending the time naked, making her tender flesh become accustomed to the air, the rain, the sunshine, the frost and the snow. She possessed only a loose linen shift, a hooded cloak, a white head-cloth and a generously-sized, dark-coloured veil. And she habitually wore her heavy woollen robe, stuck into the belt of which she carried her black-handled knife.

Lora had shown her how to purify it.

'It needs no purification from the sin of slaying Denys,' Joanna had protested, 'because that was no sin.'

'Nay, nay, child!' Lora had cried, scolding and laughing at the same time. 'More an act of charity, as far as the rest of the world's concerned, I'd say. Like putting down a malformed calf. But it has been stained with his blood, and that's why you cleanse it. See? It's precious, is your knife. Take good care of it.'

They had performed the ceremony together, their two right hands holding the blade in the flame of a specially built, small fire out in the woods. Joanna had burned her fingers quite badly, and Lora had said that was all a part of the cleansing.

The shack now had hangings at its tiny window, and over the door. Mag had been hardier than Joanna was, and, although Joanna was working diligently at toughening herself, she still keenly felt the draughts which whistled and wheezed their way through the many gaps. Joanna also felt a residual need to wash herself, a hangover from her old life, and, while Mag had been content with the cold water of the stream that ran along nearby, Joanna preferred to heat water over her fire and wash inside the hut.

It made Lora laugh uproariously to see her go through what

Lora referred to as 'all that fussing and fretting', carrying and heating water when there was a perfectly good stream not twenty paces away.

But Joanna knew that Lora, wisest of teachers, equivalent to Mag herself, was well aware how hard Joanna was finding her new life. And how earnestly she was trying to adapt to it. If warming water and washing indoors helped, Lora's attitude seemed to say, then what of it?

Sitting outside her shack now, watching the last of the sunlight fade from the clearing, Joanna reflected on how much she had learned in the seven months she had been there.

I can look after myself, she thought wonderingly. Just about. I have vegetables growing in my little patch next to the herb garden. I know which woodland plants I can safely eat, and I am beginning – just beginning – to understand their medicinal uses. I keep chickens, and I know how to snare rabbits and tickle trout. When I have to, that is, for Lora has taught me that all of life is to be respected, and that we only take another creature's life when it is truly necessary.

But then Lora had also said it was wrong to hesitate, when other factors indicated that there was a real need in the diet for the meat of a fellow creature.

Joanna stretched, putting a hand to her belly. I'm well, she thought. Thanks to Lora, I think I've got the balance about right.

Lora had taught Joanna much else besides how to attend to her physical needs. Sometimes, looking back over the months of intensive instruction, Joanna's head reeled at all the new information she had acquired. Some of the secrets Lora had revealed to her had been, quite literally, breathtaking – Joanna had never even dreamed there were such things in the world.

And Lora, to Joanna's delight, had pronounced her an apt pupil. 'Carry on this way, my girl,' she had said recently, 'and, come Imbolc, I'll take you with me to the Great Festival. You'd be ready come Samain, I reckon, but, by the look of you, you and I will have other things on our minds round about then. Aye. Samain night, I reckon.'

Then she had gone, leaving, as she always did, with neither a farewell nor any indication of when she might be back. But she always came back. And that was all that mattered.

'Come Imbolc,' Joanna murmured aloud. 'The Great Festival.'

It was a thrilling thought. Imbolc would be next February, and everyone would get together to celebrate the very first stirrings of the new year's life, deep under the ground. They would give praise for the coming into milk of the ewes, Lora had said, rejoicing in the distinct swelling of the udders that betokened new life within. They would make a huge fire, and prepare small bunches of the first flowers – snowdrops, crocuses – to wear in their hair. It was only right and proper, Lora said, to dress up to celebrate the Goddess's return.

And, most important for Joanna, Imbolc would be when she would meet the others.

She was very anxious about that.

'Don't you fret,' Lora had said. 'Stands to reason you'll be nervous, and that's as it should be, being as you'll be presented to the great and the good of our world. But they won't turn you away. That I do promise you. You will come to them with honest heart and pure intent, and, besides, you were Mag's special girl, you were. And Mag's memory is honoured. Now you're my pupil, and I will speak for you.'

It was heady stuff. Sometimes, anticipation of the feast haunted Joanna's dreams.

Just as well, she thought cheerfully, that it's still four months away. Before it comes Samain.

When, as Lora says, we'll have other things on our minds . . .

She stroked her belly again, saying to herself the ritual prayer which she had been chanting, both silently and aloud, several times a day since Lora taught it to her. Lora had understood why she was so desperate, understood and, as was her wont when she supported a desire for something, had instantly offered her help.

Finishing her plea, Joanna thought suddenly of Ninian. Well, it was only natural, really, one thought leading to another. Getting up, she fetched the dark-coloured bowl she used as a scrying mirror, filled it with water and, crouching over it, emptied her mind as Lora had taught her.

Sometimes it worked, sometimes it didn't.

This evening, it did.

There he was, and, as he'd been the last time she had seen him, he was laughing. He was with that same red-haired lad again, and they were playing some silly game with sticks, trying to trip one another up by thrusting them between each other's ankles. Not that Ninian was always playful – once she had seen him on horseback, sitting so erect and elegant, and a voice had said, 'He has a princely bearing, that one.'

If only they knew!

Ninian looks happy, she thought now. Josse, bless him, has carried out the duty I placed on him more than well.

On one occasion, watching Ninian, she had seen Josse, and that had been almost as hard to bear as seeing Ninian for the first time had been.

She returned to herself – Lora was strict about limiting her far-seeing times, since it took a heavy toll on the strength which Joanna needed for other things – and carefully emptied, dried and put away her bowl, saying aloud the appropriate words of gratitude.

Returning to her seat outside the door of the hut, her thoughts returned to Josse.

Was he happy? She hoped so. It was true, what I said to him, she thought. We would not have been right for each other, and it's better this way, so that our time together remains a pure and wonderful memory, heartening us when we lie awake, far apart, on a dark night.

He would not have adapted to what I want. To what I am becoming. And, besides, as I very nearly said to him, he had already given his heart away before he and I met. Although I doubt if he knows it.

I understand, now that I have met her.

Her belly suddenly moved of its own volition, and, putting

her hand to the little bulge – an out-thrust knee, or elbow – she whispered, 'Be patient! I know it's a tight fit in there, but wait only a little longer, and you shall have all the room you want!'

A girl, she thought. You're a girl. I have prayed for that every day since I knew that life quickened within me, for I should have to treat another boy as I treated Ninian. But a girl, now. A girl is different. A girl I can raise to be wise woman after me.

She murmured her prayer once more.

But, in her heart, she knew there was no need. Josse's child within her *was* a girl. There was no doubting it. Lora had said so, and Joanna herself knew it, in her very bones.

I shall call her Margaret, she thought.

I shall love her, care for her, teach her.

Oh, it was such a prospect! Such a miracle, to have conceived, to have carried the baby through the months of pregnancy, to be assured, by Lora and by her own instinct, that both the child and she herself were healthy, well, thriving.

'A little girl to love,' she whispered wonderingly.

I won't ever be alone again.